Triple Threat

The Story of a 1920s Broadway Star

LEISHA DOUGLAS

Sibylline Press

Copyright © 2026 by Leisha Douglas
All Rights Reserved.

Published in the United States by Sibylline Press,
an imprint of All Things Book LLC, California.

Sibylline Press is dedicated to publishing the
brilliant work of women authors ages 50 and older.
www.sibyllinepress.com

Sibylline Digital First Edition
eBook ISBN: 9798897409556
Print ISBN: 9798897409563

Cover Design: Alicia Feltman
Book Production: Aaron Laughlin

Although this novel is based on historical facts and family history, all characters, most events, and incidents have been fictionalized. Therefore, none should be regarded as a literal depiction of any person, events, or incidents.

HUMAN AUTHORED: Any use of this publication to train artificial intelligence (AI) technologies to generate text is expressly prohibited.

Sibylline
Press

*I dedicate this book to my grandmother, Elizabeth Hines,
whose example of tenacity, talent, graciousness, and equanimity
I strive to emulate.*

1913–1915

CHAPTER 1
WHAT IS IN THE NAME?

326 Madison Avenue, New York City

August 1913

Elizabeth stood, arms crossed, in front of her wardrobe. "Gert, I will wear my blue dress to dinner tonight," she said, "the one that makes me look older." Gert bustled around the room, straightening up.

"Someone special coming?" she asked.

"No, but I'm going to make an announcement—actually two announcements, come to think of it." Elizabeth twirled around. Her lower lip firmed and her bluish eyes grayed. Gert recognized her charge's serious look.

"I'm tired of everyone calling me Liz or Lizzie. My name is Elizabeth, Elizabeth Hines." Gert regarded the slim, emphatic girl.

"I don't see a problem with asking to be called your birth name," she replied, wiping her hands down her apron.

"It's more than a birth name," Elizabeth said. "It's going to be my stage name, too."

"Oh, Elizabeth! I think your parents have something else in mind for your future."

"I know, I know. But why can't I be a lady and be in musical comedy?" Gert shrugged her ample shoulders.

"I have no problem with that idea," she said, "but then I wasn't brought up like you." She raised and extended her left arm as if to present the bedroom in one grand sweep—the plush, full-size bed curtained in beige damask, the hand-painted morning glory motif that trailed discreetly across the soft green walls, the handsome floor-to-ceiling maple armoire, the set of matching green velvet chairs, built-in cushioned window seats, and cherry bookshelf crammed with leather-bound sets of Mark Twain, the Brontes and Shakespeare.

"I want to bring laughter and happiness to as many people as possible," Elizabeth said, performing a little soft shoe and then bowing to Gert, who smiled at her charge's antics. "Not just one man. Besides, Gert, you aren't married and you like what you do."

"Isn't because I don't want to be married exactly." Gert paused. "Let's put it this way. I did almost everything a wife and mother does for four years after Mum passed and I'm not eager to do it again yet." She shook her head. "Maybe if I met the right guy—maybe then. Here, let me help you."

Elizabeth peered into the long mirror on her closet door. She tried to hook her favorite small freshwater pearl necklace around her neck. Her fingers trembled.

"I guess I'm more nervous than I thought," she said. "I don't want to upset Pop and Momma like Palmer does."

"I don't think that's possible," Gert replied as she fastened the necklace. She gently squeezed Elizabeth's shoulders and looked at her in the glass. Elizabeth's thick, wavy, blonde chignon offset her beautiful face. "Your brother is what my da would call 'Rógaire.' He's a rascal and the life of the party, too, it seems."

"Did he come home yet, Gert?"

"Don't think so. Some pressing engagement with his pals, I'll bet. Not that I am the betting sort." Gert folded back the bedcovers and plumped the pillows.

"That's good news," Elizabeth said. "I won't have to deal with his sarcasm, too. At least not tonight."

Gert put her hands on her gray, uniformed hips and turned to face Elizabeth.

"Listen, Miss E., between you and me, you're the real thing. You practice, study hard, and you have a gift. Palmer just plays at everything. Lucky for him, he's charming and funny so people overlook his other habits."

"Thank you, Gert. You're the best." Elizabeth refrained from throwing her arms around Gert's solid, warm body like she used to when she was younger. "Do I look okay? I mean, do I look convincing?"

"I don't know what convincing looks like, but let's say I'd take you seriously." Gert nodded. "Go do your convincing, Miss E."

In the dining room candles burned brightly in their silver candlesticks. A large glass swan, holding yellow tea rose blossoms in water on its back, seemed to float on the burnished tabletop.

"And then I told him that the mayor would support that idea," explained Pop. He was updating Momma on his day at the *Evening Mail* office.

"Don't you look nice!" Momma exclaimed as Elizabeth took her usual place opposite her mother. "Doesn't she, Elliot?"

"Yes indeed, Anna," he answered, but Frannie's arrival cut him short.

"What have we here, Frannie?" Momma asked. "It looks gorgeous."

"Well, missus, you wanted poultry tonight so I made a chicken pot pie with carrots, peas, and onions. Nice and nourishing." Frannie paused, admiring her crusty masterpiece, and set it on the table. "Would you like to do the honors, sir?" She handed Pop a large silver serving spoon and left the room.

As the delicious smell of Frannie's dinner wafted over the table, Elizabeth realized that, in addition to feeling nervous about her announcement, she was hungry. *Best for us to eat first*, she thought as Pop handed her a steaming plate.

After poached pears and vanilla custard for dessert, they all leaned back in their chairs.

"I have an announcement." Elizabeth began softly before amplifying her voice. "I want to be called by my full name, Elizabeth. Not Liz or Lizzie. I am fifteen, not a little girl anymore."

"Of course, dear, you are definitely a young lady," Momma affirmed. "You're taller than me now."

"That's not all." Elizabeth cleared her throat. "Since we already decided that my voice isn't quite right for opera, I want to be in musical theatre."

"Nice girls don't go on stage!" Pop Hines's voice reached Frannie and Gert at the kitchen table where the two ate, as they always did after serving the family.

"What's he going on about?" Frannie asked. "Isn't like him to get upset."

"It's about Miss E. and her acting." Gert smoothed off her aproned chest impatiently.

"Out here in the kitchen most of the day, I am the last one to find out anything important in this household."

"Frannie, I didn't know 'til tonight that Elizabeth was going to announce her intentions. Elizabeth doesn't tell me everything anymore. She's grown. A young lady now, you know. It's natural. I don't know about you but when I was her age, I didn't tell adults anything—just a few girlfriends. Not that I don't miss our chats before bedtime." Gert rose to clear off, purposefully clattering dishes to block out the Hines family conversation.

Elizabeth sat rigidly upright in her chair at the dinner table as Pop paced the length of the dining room. He stopped midway.

"School plays are one thing," he said, "but a career in the theater is another thing altogether."

"Oh, Lizzie," Momma began. Her brown eyes grew large with alarm. Elizabeth dug her fingernails into her thighs and gulped.

"Please, Momma, I want to be called Elizabeth from now on."

"Yes, I understand and that I can try to do but letting you become an actress? Actresses are—" she trailed off, looking at her distraught husband. Pop finished her sentence.

"Actresses tend not to be respected nor respectable," he said.

"But there are exceptions, Pop. Sarah Bernhardt, for one."

"You're talented, my dear," Pop countered, "but she is beautiful and a diva."

"Yes, but she got there by studying and working hard just like I already do and will continue to do." Next Elizabeth purposefully addressed her mother. "Momma, not too many years ago, you were fine with the idea of an opera singer in the family. You encouraged me to study French, German, and Italian so I could sing them easily."

"Look, L—, ah, Elizabeth." Pop stopped pacing and peered out the window. "We didn't make society's unspoken rules. For reasons I can only guess, actresses are generally not well regarded and often suffer the brunt of salacious gossip. Also, life in the theater world is often grueling and underpaid. Look at your brother. He's on the road more than he's home, and half the time, he still needs me to help him out financially."

"I don't drink or gamble, Pop," Elizabeth said. Never before had she dared to reveal to her father that she knew about the ongoing stress with Palmer.

"Besides, he prefers vaudeville and burlesque. I don't want to be just a dancer or a singer. I want to act as well."

"I admire your gumption, young lady, but our job is to protect you as best we can. Right, Anna?"

"Of course," Momma said. "Besides, your education is mainly aimed to make you an interesting, desirable companion for a worthy husband when the time comes."

"Oh, Momma." Elizabeth crumpled her linen napkin and threw it on the table. "Why not an actress *and* a wife?" She pushed back her chair, stood up, and drew herself into her full stature.

"I am going upstairs unless you object," Elizabeth said.

"No, dear," Momma replied. Elizabeth wheeled around and left the room, stifling tears of frustration until she reached the safety of her bedroom. Her footfalls resounded so loudly on the stairs that Frannie and Gert looked at each other.

"Not like her to get angry," Frannie said.

"I had a feeling they weren't going to be pleased," Gert replied. She placed her palms down on the white marble countertop as if steadying herself. "Miss E. doesn't give up easy, though, once she's set her mind on something." Frannie gave a small knowing laugh.

"Ain't that the truth!" she said. "Remember the time she decided to learn to make meringue because it reminded her of eating clouds? Now that was a marathon. How many egg whites did she and I beat that day? Good thing Mrs. Hines doesn't make the egg order for the grocer. She would have scolded me and Liz."

"*Elizabeth* from now on," Gert said, winking. "It's her preference now. That's the name that she'll have when she's a star. Mark my words."

CHAPTER 2
TANGO DREAMS

The stocky, gruff Mr. Hemmer leaned back in his office chair, listening to Elizabeth's request.

"You'll not find a proper boyfriend learning the tango," he said.

At the time she wanted to respond, "I am interested in musical theater, not boyfriends." Since she didn't know him, she kept quiet and prayed he'd agree. He stretched back in his chair, hands behind his leonine head, and contemplated the weather-stained windows for several minutes.

"Ja," he said "After school, four p.m. Mondays and Thursdays. After a month, I'll evaluate whether it's worth my time and yours. Verstehst du?"

"Jawohl." Elizabeth quickly replied. "Danke, Herr Hemmer."

A slight smile washed over his craggy face. "It appears you understand German, Fraulein Hines."

"Some. My mother, who is a concert pianist and teacher, encouraged me so I could sing Lieder and opera. Also, I sing in the choir at Saint Bartholomew's, which my father directs. He sometimes asks us to sing Bach cantatas."

"A musical family, I see." He arranged the stacks of papers on his desk. "And you want to learn the tango, the dance of the people."

Several days later, Elizabeth stood awkwardly, facing Mr. Hemmer in the middle of his office. The floor-to-ceiling bookshelves on both sides of the room were crammed with books and yellowed stacks resembling librettos or playbooks. She couldn't quite tell. The two burgundy armchairs had been pushed into the corners, allowing for a triangular space in which to move freely. The dark floorboards were scored from usage. Heavy threadbare drapes were pulled back to let in meager light from the alley. The room had a tired look to it.

"Above technique and steps, communication between partners is foremost," Mr. Hemmer explained. In shirt sleeves and vest, his suit jacket removed, he leaned against the desk front, arms crossed. "And I don't mean talking while dancing, which is actually considered rude."

What does he mean and where is he going? Elizabeth wondered if she'd made a mistake asking Brearley's new dance teacher to help her. She felt conflicted since she kept the lessons a secret from Gert as well as her parents.

"If one is dancing in a crowd, there are some rules which we will cover later. Let's begin with a metronome so your feet learn the 2/4 beat. You're probably used to the waltz."

He reached to the bookcase behind the desk and set the metronome to tick.

"A primary aspect of communication is learning to listen. The tango is nonverbal listening. As tango partners, we listen with our bodies. Therefore the embrace is key. Chest contact, heads close, with a relaxed upper body. The invitation to tango is also nonverbal, through eye contact. If the man looks at you and you nod affirmatively, you have accepted a dance."

He straightened up, cocked his head as if querying her. Elizabeth hesitated, then nodded. He approached her, extending his open left hand. When her hand met his, his right arm encircled her, drawing her in until their chests met.

"Your feet on the inside of mine at all times. In other words, I walk on the outside of your legs." *So formal yet so intimate.* She realized that she had never danced as physically close to anyone as this. She swallowed and eyed his top button, not daring to look up at his face.

"Let's walk in 2/4 rhythm." He guided her backwards, maintaining their closeness. Although her legs complied, her upper body clenched. She longed to push him back an arm's length. As they circled the room, she sensed a strange split between desire to surrender to and resist his firm hold.

"You will get winded quickly if you don't breathe," Mr. Hemmer said. She wanted to say, *Let go of me! Then I'll breathe*, but she didn't. "And if you don't breathe, you won't be able to relax."

Despite her discomfort, Elizabeth willed herself to let go. She knew well how to balance the physical and emotional and move toward mastery. Her years of ballet, piano, and voice training came to the fore as they circled the room.

"Remember what I said about eye contact and communication," Mr. Hemmer said. "Lift your head, girl. This is a dance of affirmation, not defeat. Life's music is yours."

They swayed and glided to the tireless metronome tick. With each circle, Elizabeth felt her whole body synchronize and melt into his lead and the rhythm. One black eyebrow quizzically lifted over his blue eyes.

"That's it, Elizabeth. Your body is getting rhythm. Feel the difference?" She nodded. He twirled her out at arm's length as a finale. "Next lesson, we add some music." He walked her to the door.

Life's music is yours. His words resounded as Gert and Elizabeth walked home, dodging puddles and mud splattered by the occasional carriage. The sleek streets gleamed. Elizabeth inhaled deeply, taking in the stale odors of smoke, gas, and trash washed away by the steady rain. She felt like skipping but censored her impulse.

"You look happy, Miss E. I thought you were studying." Gert huffed as she kept pace with Elizabeth's long-legged stride.

"Oh, yes indeed, I was," Elizabeth replied, relieved not to tell a complete lie. A trolley clanged down the street, making further conversation impossible until they turned the corner. The doorman, Fred, grinned as they entered the small cobblestone courtyard.

"Lovely isn't it, ladies? In Ireland, we'd call this a soft day."

"Rainy is what we'd call it," Gert retorted. Elizabeth smiled. Gert always opposed Fred's attempts to engage them. Though he and Gert had met when Elizabeth was three and the Hines family moved into 326 Madison, the two of them still verbally sparred. Fred flung open the door and bowed as they entered the marble-tiled lobby. The gold sconces on the wall gave off warm light.

"Such charmers, them Irish men." Gert shook her head. "You beware, Miss Elizabeth. They spout poetry and tell stories but eventually they break hearts."

"Don't worry, Gert. Boys don't interest me much. I'd rather dance, sing, read books, and learn." *They must all remind her of some rogue from her past,* Elizabeth thought, smiling to herself.

"You keep it that way," Gert whispered. She grinned as they entered the quiet apartment. The pale silk bamboo-like paper and opaque tile floor were a welcome respite from the foul weather.

A fumbled rendering of a Chopin étude issued from the drawing room; someone was taking a piano lesson. Elizabeth quietly ascended the stairs to her bedroom, relieved her mother was occupied and wouldn't notice her daughter's somewhat late return.

When Elizabeth awoke the next morning, she luxuriated in the bed's lavender sheets and warmth. Dream images of twirling red skirts and handsome olive-skinned men in tight black pants lingered. The furnace's clanks and hisses sounded percussive, musical. Something had shifted yesterday and, although she was unsure what, she knew the change was for the better. Her frustration over her parents' objections to her proposed future had decreased significantly. Even the prospect of two hours of arithmetic, followed by Latin, didn't feel as onerous as it usually did on Wednesday.

"Top of the morning, Miss E." Gert called out as she knocked lightly on her door.

"I'll be right out," Elizabeth replied, swinging out of bed, wondering what this day might bring.

CHAPTER 3
THE REVELATION

Mr. Hemmer carefully lifted the phonograph needle off the copy of Villoldo's "El Choclo," a song he and Elizabeth frequently tangoed to.

"The headmistress asked me to put together a school talent revue, a song and dance spring celebration," he said. "I'd like you to dance a number with me. I was thinking of a Cohan number."

"I . . . I . . . thank you," Elizabeth stammered. "When?" Her mind accelerated, tripping over possibilities. She'd managed to keep up her tango lessons without her parents' knowledge. She hadn't told anyone. Her school friends thought she studied piano after school, branching out from her mother's tutelage.

"It will be sometime mid-May. We have at least six weeks to prepare. I have a few ideas about a number. We can talk about them next time we meet."

"Yes sirree." She tried to sound enthusiastic despite her trepidation.

"Don't worry. We won't tango for this audience."

"Oh, I hope not. They—" She scrambled to find inoffensive words. "—wouldn't appreciate it." Her hands were clammy, her face hot. Mr. Hemmer pulled on his suit jacket and straightened his tie, glancing at her.

"You don't seem excited, Miss Elizabeth. You know there may be some real theater folks in the audience, too. I intend to spread the word that Brearley is known for its pretty, talented, and smart young women."

"I'm just a little nervous. It means a lot to me." Her parents' faces, exasperated and confused, floated into her awareness. Intertwining and gripping her long fingers, she paused, wanting to flee. Mr. Hemmer sifted through the papers on his desk. His jacket cuffs were frayed. She hadn't noticed that before.

"I started a list of ideas and possible numbers. It's here somewhere. Paperwork," he said, sighing. "My nemesis. Oh well, I'll find it before your next lesson. Then we can talk it over and decide what we want to do. Sound good?" Elizabeth didn't answer.

"Well?" he asked.

"Sounds fine. I'll see you Thursday." She wheeled around, exited into the arched hallway, and gulped air to calm herself.

On the way home, weaving through pedestrians and cracked sidewalks on Park Avenue, she repeated silently, "I want to do this. I *want* to be an actress." It wasn't enough to offset her anxiety about telling her parents about Mr. Hemmer's offer and her acceptance. Gert lumbered alongside, seemingly unaware. Cherry trees were budding. Every block had at least one window box of blooming snowdrops, daffodils, and marguerites, but the sky was stained white and gray. Elizabeth was glad Gert had insisted she wear her camel hair coat and bring an umbrella when they left this morning.

"You ever want something so much you could almost taste it, Gert?" Elizabeth asked, putting a hand on Gert's arm.

"I guess I am mostly grateful for what I have, Miss E.," Gert replied, patting Elizabeth's hand.

"You never saw someone living a fabulously interesting life and thought, *That could be me?*"

"Not really. I mean envy doesn't do much good, does it?"

"Oh, Gert. It's not like coveting a possession. It's the combination of imagination and possibility. That's what I'm talking about." Gert shook her head.

"I don't know what to say. From where I come from, your future always looked good to me."

"There's more to life than marriage and motherhood." Elizabeth continued, "Eventually I might want those but before that, Gert . . . before that—" She paused, high-stepped in front of Gert, extended her arms gracefully while lifting her head, artfully posing despite her heavy overcoat and rain galoshes, "—there's the stage." By that time the two were standing in front of 326 Madison. The heavy front door, rich with brass latticework, opened.

"You're looking well today, Miss Elizabeth," said Fred, bowing playfully and ushering them in. "The duckling is becoming a swan, don't you think, Gertie?"

"None of your fresh talk," Gert admonished him as they swept into the building. "He's right, though. You do look exceptional today. You're almost taller than me now. My da would say you have gams like a thoroughbred filly." Her crackling blue eyes studied her charge as they removed their coats. "You okay? You clammed up as soon as we got home."

"I'm fine. Something came up at school that I need to talk to Momma and Pop about. That's all."

Normally she confided in Gert but this topic seemed like something she needed to handle on her own. After all, ultimately it wasn't just about a school revue.

"Do you need me between now and dinner?" Gert's question derailed her thoughts.

"No, no, I am fine. Just need to do some reading for school." It wasn't quite true but she needed privacy to strategize on when and how to present this latest iteration of the issue.

Before the first dinner course was served, Elizabeth blurted out her news.

"Sounds like this is quite the honor. Congratulations, my girl." Pop lifted his glass of water as if raising a toast. "We'll be there cheering you on, won't we, Anna?" The remark surprised Elizabeth, who was steeled for the usual barrage of questions. Momma gave a strained smile.

"Of course, Elliot, wouldn't miss it."

Frannie's delivery of steaming soup tureens was a welcome interruption.

"Mmm, leek and potato. Excellent choice for a damp chilly day, dear." Pop beamed. Elizabeth recognized his deliberate cheerfulness: it was an attempt to reassure and soothe Momma when she was feeling concerned or anxious.

"Hello, family!" Palmer exclaimed, striding into the dining room and seating himself at the opposite end of the table from his father.

Though sharply dressed in a gray suit and tie, he emanated a faint odor of liquor and cigarettes. Elizabeth glanced at her parents to see if they noticed but they were both already eyeing Palmer.

"Did you let Frannie know you'd be joining us?" Momma queried.

"I stuck my head into the kitchen on the way in. She said there's plenty." He yawned and stretched back in his chair. "Late rehearsals these last few nights. Hey, Pop, is the *Evening Mail* going to cover the show?"

Dabbing his mouth with his napkin, Pop responded in a measured voice.

"I would think so but, as you know, that is not my department."

Before he could continue, Frannie bustled in with a table setting for Palmer and another bowl of soup.

"Smells deeevine, Frannie! Best kept secret in NYC, your cooking."

"Oh, Palmer, you're probably way overdue for a hot meal," Frannie responded though she couldn't resist smiling at his enthusiasm as she exited. Palmer consumed several spoonfuls.

"I could bring a couple of comp tickets to your office, Pop," Palmer offered. "It's going to be quite a combination—song, dance, burlesque, even some rope tricks and blackface." With his thick brown hair falling across his wide forehead, he looked like Huck Finn. Like Huck, he also seemingly haplessly fell into repeated trouble. "Really, the show could use some good publicity. Couldn't you put in a good word for us?"

Dismayed, Elizabeth noticed that Pop's celebratory mood had vanished. Lately it was always thus. Whenever his eldest appeared, Pop retracted into seriousness, his speech labored and forced as if he was trying to impart something but lacked the proper words. She hated seeing her father so constrained. Usually, he skillfully and warmly communicated with everyone from carriage drivers and shoeshine men to his boss and New York's Mayor Mitchell, a member of the Saint Bartholomew's congregation. Everyone called him "Pop" with a degree of familiarity that sometimes rankled Momma, to whom civility and propriety were important.

"Even better, Pop, the show could use another investor or two." Palmer set his spoon down with a clatter as if punctuating his request with an exclamation point.

"You know better, Palmer," Momma said. "No discussion of money, religion, or politics at the dinner table." Her face paled and tightened as it did whenever she disciplined her children.

"Geez, I'm just enthusiastic about the show. The chorus girls are really gorgeous and—"

Frannie swept in carrying a large silver tray.

"Roast beef, Yorkshire pudding, and green beans," she announced, presenting the tray to Elizabeth's mother so she could serve herself.

". . .and talented," Palmer added. "Not to mention the magician and—"

"Let's concentrate on Frannie's delicious-looking dinner," Pop said, maneuvering his helping onto his plate, "and, by the way, you walked in right after Elizabeth shared some good news."

Palmer eyed his sister whom he had previously ignored.

"Do tell, Lizzie."

"Elizabeth," she said, "as I have requested you call me several times."

"It's not so easy to change an old habit. You've been my little sister, Lizzie, for fifteen years."

Elizabeth knew better than to back down with Palmer. *Give him an inch and he'll take a mile*. Gert's warning resounded in her mind.

"Elizabeth is my preferred name." she added. "I am not a little girl."

"Wow, didn't mean to hit a sore spot," he mocked, shrugging his shoulders. "Don't see what the big deal is."

"Actually," Pop interrupted, "our Elizabeth is starring in the Brearley spring revue at her dance teacher's request. She will be his partner."

"Yessir, that is the big time! Off-off-off-Broadway," scoffed Palmer while he voraciously cut his beef.

"Pop, never mind. He's right. It's not a big deal," Elizabeth said, trying to diffuse the situation and the increasing dismay on her mother's face. Momma disliked conflict and rivalry, particularly between her children.

"I think it's an honor bestowed on someone who worked hard to earn it," Pop affirmed. "Who knows? It could be a step or two on the way to Broadway." He smiled at his daughter. *Is he actually supporting my career ambitions?* She didn't dare question him for fear that, under scrutiny, he might backpedal.

Dinner proceeded with uneasy, stilted conversation about the church's upcoming Easter program and their usual summer plan to spend most of July and August at their rental house in Quogue.

CHAPTER 4
THE TRUCE

The sunlight filtering through the glass dome of the Plaza's tearoom seemed translucent. Amid the indoor forest of tall lush green palms and patrons decked out in shades of spring pastels, Elizabeth felt like she was in a Manet painting. Their table was covered with the accoutrements of high tea from delicate Wedgwood cups and lace-edged napkins to a plate full of warm, delicious-smelling scones and silver bowls filled with strawberry jam and heavy cream.

"Oh, Momma, what a treat!"

"I thought a little celebration was in order, my dear." Momma poured two cups of tea carefully, handing one to Elizabeth.

Two days had passed since Elizabeth broached the topic of the revue. She assumed her parents' silence on the matter meant they neither sanctioned nor forbid her to participate in the upcoming production. She was resigned to proceeding without sharing any trepidations or excitement with them, although suppressing her enthusiasm left her feeling isolated with tinges of doubt. The warmth in her mother's voice and brown eyes was therefore quite welcome.

"I agree with your father. Mr. Hemmer's invitation is both an honor and a commendation for your efforts," she said, putting a scone on her plate and helping herself to a dollop of cream and jam. "And it started me thinking." Her fine black eyebrows lifted inquisitively as she regarded Elizabeth, who gripped her chair seat, anticipating what might come next.

"What if we discontinue your Brearley studies after this spring and next fall concentrate on dance, voice, music, and languages?"

Elizabeth, awash with relief and astonishment, was momentarily speechless.

"Ah, that would be fantastic! To concentrate like that would really prepare me well. I promise to work hard. I want to make you and Pop proud."

"We're already proud," Momma said, patting Elizabeth's left hand.

"Yes, but Momma, I'm going to—" Elizabeth self-edited, refraining from use of the word "star." "I'm going to be the best I can be and, hopefully, I can reimburse Pop for the cost of my lessons someday."

"I am sure your father would appreciate your intention but I don't think he expects repayment. I mean what we currently spend on Brearley should be adequate to cover upcoming lessons."

"It's all I've ever wanted." Elizabeth flushed, returning her mother's steady gaze.

Conversation and laughter alternately rose and fell. White-shirted waiters in black pants, vests, and bow ties bore tray after tray of scrumptious delights to the other diners. Overhead, visible through the domed ceiling, big white nimbus clouds paraded across the sky. Elizabeth munched contently on her scone, already wanting to always remember this scene because it was a ceremonial demarcation, an official start to her future.

"Aren't there some girls you'll miss seeing daily?" Momma queried, breaking Elizabeth's reverie.

"Probably Joanie and Isabelle, but we'll arrange to see each other like we do during the summer." *Besides*, she thought, *I will meet other girls at tryouts and make new theater friends not solely concerned with landing a husband.*

Momma patted her mouth with her linen napkin.

"You've been there for two years. I would imagine there were a few aspects you enjoyed."

"Of course, Momma. It has been worthwhile and Mrs. McIntosh is very inspiring." Last autumn Brearley's first female headmistress had assumed the school's leadership. In her firm, soft-spoken way, she enlarged the curriculum to include more physical activities as well as sex education classes for girls from sixth grade up despite some resistance from parents and a few board members. Carl Hemmer's faculty appointment, for which Elizabeth was extremely grateful, had been part of those changes.

"Indeed I don't know how she does it," Momma said. "Four children, a full-time job, and a successful writing career."

"Yes, she makes it look easy, but, Momma, you have a job and a family, too."

"I stay home and fit my lesson schedule around my family life. Not the same. My family is first and foremost, as it should be."

When Momma was adamant, which was infrequent, her dark brown eyes narrowed as they did now, dissuading Elizabeth from disagreeing. She knew her mother's opinion on a woman's proper role in family. What good was an argument? She didn't want to end this celebratory outing on a sour note so she quietly sipped her sweet black tea and feasted her eyes on the sumptuous room and its gaily dressed guests.

CHAPTER 5
NEXT STEPS

The classroom's big windows were ajar, letting in warm air, birdsong, and a cacophony of voices from the street. Elizabeth was having a hard time listening to Miss Hart's lecture about quadratic equations. Lyrics, lines, and dance steps kept intruding. She didn't want to let Mr. Hemmer down. He had gone to bat for her with her parents, helping persuade them to let her immerse herself in a rigorous study of the theater arts, as he called them. He also had convinced them to let her be his dance partner in an upcoming four-week summer road show.

The Brearley School motto—"Seek truth and toil"—was stenciled in dark blue letters above the blackboard on the wall behind Miss Hart. *Is perfecting my ability to dance and sing toiling?* Toil connoted weight, pressure, an onerous pursuit.

"How do we solve a quadratic equation? Let's review, class." Miss Hart, chalk in hand, stood expectantly. "Miss Hines, are you with us?" Elizabeth's face flushed hot against the starched white collar of her uniform.

"Yes, ma'am. There is, ah, um, factoring."

"Yes. Can anyone in the room add some explanation?"

Margaret Steiglitz raised her hand. With her smudged circles under her eyes and her thick lensed glasses, she always looked studious. As she easily resolved the equation to Miss Hart's satisfaction, Elizabeth visualized and counted, *One, two, three, dip, twirl, repeat.* The scraping of desk chairs as the other girls stood to leave alerted her that math class had ended. Elizabeth hastily gathered her belongings. Miss Hart, in a tailored black skirt and gray blouse, stood by the open door, wishing her students farewell.

"Miss Hines, do you have a minute?"

"Yes, ma'am." Elizabeth reluctantly stopped before exiting. Miss Hart closed the door before speaking.

"I just wanted to tell you how much I enjoyed your performance with Mr. Hemmer in the school revue. You are quite talented."

"Oh, I am so glad you liked it," Elizabeth stammered. Despite the fact she didn't enjoy math, she did like Miss Hart, who always treated her students firmly but kindly and respectfully.

"Yes, I heard from Mrs. McIntosh that you are leaving us at the term's end and embarking on a great adventure. You must be excited."

Miss Hart's small pert smiling face emanated concern. Elizabeth nodded.

"I hope you keep up your education," Miss Hart added. "You have an affinity for learning."

"Yes, I'll keep studying languages and reading on all kinds of subjects no matter what else I am doing. I want to be knowledgeable, interesting, and in charge of my own destiny as well as an excellent dancer, singer, and actress."

"I am glad to hear that. The days of women being passive, second-class citizens are ending and you Brearley girls are going to make your mark on history."

Was Miss Hart a suffragette? The thought had never crossed Elizabeth's mind. Somehow the prim, well-spoken woman didn't fit Elizabeth's concept of a political rabble-rouser.

"Well, off you go and do keep in touch if the spirit moves you."

"I'll be sure to. If I ever make it into a Broadway show, I'll send you and Mrs. McIntosh some tickets!"

Elizabeth, elated by the thought of no more math classes in her future, almost danced down the long linoleum hallway. A few peers clustered at the entrance.

"Everything okay? I waited for you." Joanie Farwell hooked her arm with Elizabeth's as they exited together through the heavy doors and down the cement stairs to the sidewalk. Halfway down the block when they were out of earshot of the others, Joanie turned to Elizabeth.

"What was that about?" she asked. "You didn't do anything wrong."

Elizabeth hadn't yet informed Joanie of her news, wanting to ensure that her parents didn't change their minds once they met with Mrs. McIntosh. *Apparently, they were serious. Otherwise, how would Miss Hart know?*

"I am not in trouble but I do have something to tell you," she began, looking into her friend's alarmed brown eyes as they rounded the corner onto Sixtieth Street and wended their way up Park Avenue. "Let's sit."

The two young women, dressed in their ankle-length navy-blue skirts and long-sleeved white bloused uniforms, seated themselves on a bench in the formal garden strip that ran from Fifty-Seventh Street north on either side of the cobblestone street.

"What a glorious day!" Elizabeth exclaimed as she inhaled the scent of lilacs, lilies of the valley, and clipped grass. She removed her hat.

"Almost makes up for the endless winter we had. So come on, spill the beans." Elizabeth realized she had to backtrack because even Joanie didn't know about her secret tango lessons with Mr. Hemmer.

"You know those days I stayed after school since October?"

"Yes, when you were studying piano," Joanie said.

"Not really. Actually, no."

"What do you mean? We didn't walk home together our usual two days a week because you stayed late."

"I know but it wasn't because I was studying piano," Elizabeth began. Her friend's face shifted from confusion to astonishment to a mix of sadness and surprise.

"Let me get this clear, Elizabeth. You're going on the road with Mr. Hemmer in a play called *Oh, Boy!* for most of the summer?" Joanie twirled her forefinger through her tawny curls. "And we won't ever walk to school together after the end of this term."

"Yes, that's true." Elizabeth wanted Joanie to share her excitement. "But it will be my first professional public performance and what better person, along with Gert, to accompany me? Besides, my parents would never let me do this in any other circumstances."

"I see your point and, believe me, I am excited for you. It's just that I will miss you." Joanie's eyes teared up.

"Oh, Joanie, I'll write you regularly and when I get back, we'll find time together, I promise." She put her arm around Joanie's shoulders. It dawned on her that she would miss her friend's cheerful, caring presence as well.

CHAPTER 6
OH, BOY!

Shubert Theatre, New Haven, Connecticut
July 7, 1916

Four weeks into the *Oh, Boy!* run, an exhausted Elizabeth sat on the small musty couch in her hotel room, sipping coffee and picking at the lukewarm scrambled eggs and toast on her breakfast tray. It was a quiet Sunday morning, disturbed only by melodious church bells ringing on the hour or calling parishioners to services.

"God won't mind if you take a day off after all your hard work," Gert assured Elizabeth before she departed for an early service at the Catholic church several blocks away.

Several days earlier, Elizabeth procured some sheets of filigreed pale pink stationery intending to write Joanie, but the show had consumed all her time and energy. Putting breakfast aside, she laid a piece on the tray and picked up her fountain pen.

Dear Joanie,

Here I am delivering on my promise although maybe not as often as either one of us thought or wished!

I can't believe how fast this summer has gone by. Seems like yesterday we were wearing our Brearley unis and commiserating about memorizing *The Song of Hiawatha*. I didn't have to memorize any lines for this production. Thank goodness because my dance with Mr. Hemmer is complicated enough. Sometimes I wonder if I will get it perfectly. The other dancers assure me that he is known in the business for his complex choreography. Innovative but also a classicist, they say. I thought I was in good physical shape before the tour but two weeks of rehearsal and now performing six days a week, twice on Fridays and Saturdays, my legs are as hard as rocks.

Some nights I've been so tired, Gert led me back to our hotel like I was an old dog. I know that doesn't excuse not writing as frequently as I hoped to. You have been on my mind, and on these hot days, I picture you curled up in the hammock on that big shady veranda of your Westport house reading *Sherlock Holmes* or some other mystery novel that you can't put down.

Most performances have been sold out and the reviews favorable. Gert is collecting them to show my parents when we return. I guess I'll have something to show for all this effort beside muscular legs!

Even though I am so busy, I miss you a lot and can't wait to reunite in late August.

Your Aberrant Friend, Elizabeth

The next day, Elizabeth, seated on a stool, was replacing her dancing shoes with her pumps when Mr. Hemmer appeared backstage. Obviously excited, he twirled his black bowler hat.

"Guess who contacted me today?"

"I can't imagine," replied Elizabeth, patting her damp face and neck with a towel. "Wish we had access to swimming up here. These hot steamy days with two shows daily make me miss my summer swims in the cool ocean." Wistfully, she thought of the shady Quogue summer cottage and its winding path across the dunes through beach plum bushes and long grasses to the blue-gray waves and sandy beach.

"I understand but I thought this news might perk you up," he said. His normally austere face beamed. "Henry Savage wants to hire you for his next production." He cleared his throat. "And, ja, me, too, as dance director. There, you have it."

"Excuse me, Mr. Hemmer." Gert peered around the back curtain. "I've come to pick up Miss E." Dressed in street clothes rather than her usual uniform, Gert seemed younger, more lively. Her black hair was swept up under a simple blue hat that matched her eyes.

"Please, Fraulein Gert, you may call me Carl," he said with a small stiff bow. "Did you overhear the good news I was telling our Elizabeth?"

"No, sir. I mean Carl." Gert pushed the heavy stage curtain aside to enter. "I did clip out some of the local reviews of *Oh, Boy!* One *Hartford Courant* reporter said you deserve great credit for originality of the dance numbers and several said Miss E. sings and dances like a dream."

"Ach, I haven't had time to read the reviews. Das is gut!" Mr. Hemmer slipped into German whenever excited or upset. Elizabeth, although exhausted, couldn't help but smile.

"I am keeping a scrapbook of reviews for Mr. and Mrs. Hines so they don't miss anything," Gert announced. "Might as well do something useful during showtimes."

Elizabeth, unaccustomed to the grueling pace of a tour, was grateful her parents had insisted that Gert accompany her. Gert ensured that she ate regularly, given the demanding schedule, and got her to their accommodations as quickly as possible after an evening show.

"You will have a full scrapbook soon," Mr. Hemmer said. He clapped his hands together and then explained that Henry Savage was a well-known producer who wanted to hire Elizabeth for an upcoming show at George M. Cohan's theater in New York City. Suddenly alert, Elizabeth stood up.

"That's Broadway, Mr. Hemmer!"

"Yes indeed. Broadway and Forty-Third, to be exact."

"Oh, my goodness. That's fantastic, but am I ready for that?"

"We have two months after we return to practice," he reassured her. "Besides, your stint here is good preparation. You now know what it takes to be on stage six days a week, week in, week out."

"Does Mr. Savage know that I am sixteen?" Being the youngest in the current cast had been daunting. At first, some chorus girls quipped about her being the teacher's pet. Now, weeks into the production, they treated her like the youngest sister whom they found annoyingly naïve but also endearing and dedicated.

Elizabeth wondered what being in a Broadway lineup would be like.

"That's why he contacted me, Fraulein. He did his research, found out you were my student." Mr. Hemmer never exuded such happiness. Elizabeth was both touched and uneasy.

"Ja, and he said you were the spitting image of Dorothy Dickson. What do you think of that?"

"That is quite a compliment." Dorothy Dickson, a beautiful and accomplished actress and singer, was renowned on both sides of the Atlantic. In addition, she was British, which put her in another category altogether in terms of sophistication.

"This is exciting news!" Gert affirmed. "But we have a tired girl here. I should get her back to our rooms so she can rest up for the last two shows tomorrow."

The three walked the few short blocks to their Chapel Street hotel. The streets' gaslights cast long shadows in the muggy night. Mr. Hemmer and Gert chatted about the run and what the reviews said. Elizabeth listened with half an ear. She couldn't believe that the month of the tour was already over. She had been so caught up in perfecting the routine that she sometimes rehearsed in her sleep. The intensity had been exhilarating and consuming. In a way, she didn't want the show to end because it felt like she was just getting the hang of it.

Endings, beginnings, you better get used to it, she told herself, putting on the white cotton nightgown Gert had laid out for her, applying cold cream to her face, and climbing into the lumpy twin bed. "This is the life you said you wanted."

Dear Joanie,

How pleased I was to find your letter waiting for me at the hotel desk yesterday!

No. I haven't made any new friends. Doesn't seem likely either with the demanding schedule and the fact that I am at least four years younger than everyone in the cast. Not to mention Gert and you know how she can be. Actually, I don't think I would have been able to handle this without her. Even sitting down for a decent lunch or dinner is difficult Gert insists, though. Thank goodness because otherwise Mr. Hemmer would get so wrapped up in rehearsing, we'd never have a break except to change before the performances.

Sounds like you had a good visit from your Boston cousins. That's exciting news about your brother, John, deciding on Princeton University. Your parents must be very proud. I'm sure he'll have his choice of clubs and invite you to some events.

I haven't had time to do much of anything besides practice and perform so I am afraid I don't have much to report. The last show is this upcoming Saturday night. Gert and I will catch a train back home on Sunday. I can't wait to sleep in my own bed and I bet I'll be doing a lot of that when we first get home.

Let's get together as soon as you return.

Love, Elizabeth

CHAPTER 7
BACK IN TOWN

Elizabeth was grateful that her parents insisted on a three-week break before she commenced morning classes in language, voice, and dance, followed by afternoon rehearsals of the new play.

"I want her home for lunch and a little rest before she has to be at the theater," Momma had declared when Mr. Hemmer came to the Hines' home to meet with the three of them. Still adrenalized from her first successful tour and Henry Savage's offer, Elizabeth initially protested mainly because she didn't want to come across as a prima donna to the other cast members.

"Learning to succeed as a performer is about strengthening *and* pacing yourself," Momma stated. "Currently we will help you maintain that balance, won't we, Herr Hemmer?" She looked at him as if to say, *Don't you dare disagree.*

"Ja," said Mr. Hemmer in a muffled voice. He looked like an overgrown schoolboy fearing a scolding.

Pop drummed the fingers of his right hand on the marble fireplace mantel as he leaned up against it.

"Someday, though, you must be prepared to do this for yourself," he said. "Believe me, most producers and directors will try to get as much as they can out of their actors for as little as possible. Isn't that right, Carl?"

Elizabeth, listening intently throughout, had little to add. This kind of negotiation was a totally unfamiliar and somewhat off-putting aspect of show business. By the meeting's end, Pop and Mr. Hemmer were in accord about her contract with Savage and Mr. Hemmer agreed to relay their proposed terms to the Savage organization.

"For the meantime, please tell anyone who asks that I am Elizabeth's manager," Pop declared before proposing a sherry toast to conclude their discussion.

Later that sweltering late August day, Elizabeth fanned herself in front of her open bedroom window as she reclined on her bedroom love seat. It had taken the better part of ten days to recover from the tour. Unable to do much beside sleep, read, and eat Frannie's wonderful meals, she felt weak which worried her, especially in light of what promised to be a rigorous fall schedule.

When she was younger, the New York Aquarium had been one of Elizabeth's favorite places to visit. Sea life fascinated her; she imagined living mostly in water as weightless, free, and easy. She'd also always admired the tiny, reddish brown blenny fish that can breathe air, propel itself on land, or sequester in underwater burrows. *If that little fish can be so adaptable,* she thought, *so can I.*

Buoyed by that thought, she took stock of her room. Despite Gert's efforts, the top of her small desk was buried under unread copies of *Harper's Bazaar,* the *American Woman,* mail, and a few books. Her bedside tables were also untidy and clothes were haphazardly flung over the closet door. She rolled, then pinned, her long blonde hair up at the back of her head. She sighed with relief as the cool air caressed her neck. It was time to make order before the next wave of activity. Humming her favorite John McCormick song, "The Sunshine of Your Smile," she picked up the room before addressing the items on her desk. Gert knocked lightly on her bedroom door.

"Miss Joanie is downstairs," she said. "What should I tell her?"

"That's wonderful!" Elizabeth exclaimed. She flung open the door, startling Gert. "Hooray, she's back! I'll be right down." She glanced in the mirror, slipped on some shoes, and hurried downstairs into Joanie's enthusiastic embrace.

Seated in the coolest room in the house, the bookshelf-lined den, they talked simultaneously and then laughed as they realized their folly.

"Should we draw straws to see who should go first?" Joanie suggested as Gert bustled in with glasses of lemonade and a plate of cookies.

"Fresh from Frannie's kitchen, ladies," Gert said. "Help yourselves."

"You go first," Elizabeth said, "and don't spare the details like you did in your letters." After Gert left, Elizabeth sat back, contently contemplating Joanie's grinning, heart-shaped face.

"Alright, but it was the pretty typical six weeks in Westport," Joanie conceded. "You're the one who had the big adventure."

"There must have been some wonderful celebrations, what with John's news."

"Yes but—" Joanie hesitated. "We're all a bit worried what with the war in Europe and such."

Elizabeth hadn't paid attention to the news while on tour.

"What do you mean? We aren't at war."

"There's talk of building up the army just in case. Father thinks they may initiate a draft."

"Oh but surely if John's already at university, he wouldn't—"

"You know John. He's a stickler for honor and duty and always does the right thing."

"Certainly, not like Palmer," Elizabeth blurted out before correcting herself. She didn't want to spend time talking about her brother. Joanie was well aware of Palmer's escapades. "Isn't going to Princeton University the right path?"

"I suppose that wouldn't be enough for him, especially since all his buddies talk of enlisting." Joanie sighed, her face somber. "I didn't include this news in my letters because I didn't want to rain on your parade, but I am worried, Elizabeth. Not just about John but all the boys we know."

Elizabeth felt deflated. What she underwent on the tour and her news about the Savage production seemed insignificant compared to Joanie's revelation. She leaned forward and put her hands on Joanie's knees as a single tear trailed down her friend's face.

"We'll get through this together," she said. "Maybe America won't have to go to war." She tried to reassure her friend though her words felt inadequate.

By the time the two friends caught up on everything, the oppressive heat had permeated their sanctuary. Spent, speechless, they sat, satiated with the pleasures of friendship and the relief that came from entrusting one another with confidences.

"I should be going," Joanie said. "Maybe meet this weekend at my house? Before life gets too busy. Let me check with Mother and see what the plans are, if any." Joanie put on her straw hat, gathered her purse, and pushed herself upright.

"Yes, indeed. I would like that," Elizabeth affirmed as she walked Joanie to the door. Shutting the heavy front door behind her departing friend, a combination of fatigue and nostalgia washed over Elizabeth as she climbed the carpeted stairs to resume tidying up.

CHAPTER 8
THE BIG TIME

George M. Cohan Theatre, 1428 Broadway, New York City

Joanie requested that the Farwell family driver stop the carriage in the theater district. She and Elizabeth walked around the sunlit corner and found a billboard spanning one entire wall of the George M. Cohan Theatre's granite and terra-cotta entrance on West Forty-Third Street—"The prettiest playhouse in New York City. Thousands turned away nightly."

Joanie squeezed Elizabeth's hand.

"I am so excited, aren't you?" she asked. "I mean, look at this!"

They peered in through the open doors to the lobby where a single uniformed custodian swept out debris from the previous night's performance. When he noticed the two, he tilted his black cap back on his head and gave a tired smile.

"Can I help you?" he asked.

"Oh, yes. My friend Elizabeth is going to be performing here soon," Joanie volunteered. "We'd love to see the inside if it wouldn't be a bother."

"Is she now? And what show would that be?" He fixed his gaze on Elizabeth.

"*Molly O*'," she stammered. "It's a Henry Savage production."

"Ah, the Colonel. What we call him around here. Colonel Savage." He leaned on his broom. "Ain't you a little young to be playing Broadway? I know there are them child stars. He was one of them, grew up in vaudeville, whole family a bunch of actors." He pointed at a life-size photo of a dapper George M. Cohan in a bowler hat leaning on a cane. "But you look like a proper young lady and all."

"I will be seventeen in little more than a month," Elizabeth replied. "The show doesn't open until a week after my birthday."

"There you have it. We started on the wrong foot. Let me introduce me self. You can call me Hank. I'm the behind-the-scenes guy. I build some sets and keep the place clean as I can." He removed his hat with a flourish and bowed to the girls. "Let me make it up to you with a short tour, Miss—?"

"Elizabeth. Elizabeth Hines. And this is my best friend, Joanie Farwell." Elizabeth extended her gloved hand and shook Hank's rough hand.

"Right this way, ladies." Hank lead them into the large main auditorium.

"Oh, what wonderful colors!" Elizabeth exclaimed, taking in the shades of purple, silver, and gray on the elaborate gilded proscenium arch and balcony faces.

"And these are of?" Joanie pointed to the large murals running under the arch and the boxes.

"His self. George M.," Hank gestured. "Those are his greatest hits and these," he said, pointing up the arch murals, "are from his early life, mostly vaudeville. See the whole family. They was all in it together. He was 'Master George' then with his violin."

Elizabeth studied the portrayal of the brown-haired boy, head cocked, nattily dressed in knickers and a bow tie, holding a violin to his shoulder as if he was about to play. There was something both kind and mischievous about his blue eyes.

"He ain't here that much these days. So many of his shows elsewhere," Hank added. "Probably why he let the Colonel rent the place." He scratched his forehead and smiled at Elizabeth. "But don't you worry. We have a good professional crew here to run things, including myself. We'll take good care of you and the rest of Savage's troupe. And now, back to me cleaning and prepping for today's performances, two shows that start at four."

He walked them back to the door, assuring Elizabeth he would be watching for her when rehearsals began.

Since it was a beautiful summer day, not yet torrid, Joanie and Elizabeth walked at least part of the way home. Elizabeth was preoccupied, thinking about the size and grandeur of the Cohan Theatre and the demands of the pending production. Joanie didn't seem to notice. She chatted happily and stopped to window-shop at Dolph's Clothes and other stores they passed as they strolled north. Elizabeth was glad for the distraction though it didn't quite quell her rising excitement and anxiety.

Hank was true to his word. The cast moved out of the dingy rented rehearsal space and into the theater a week prior to opening night on September 23. He came up from the bowels of the building, doffing his black cap with a flourish and bowing to Elizabeth.

"Welcome, Miss Hines," he said. "Anythin' you need, you holler. Even if I looks busy with somethin.'"

"Someone has an admirer." Connie, the unofficial leader of the chorus girls, winked at Elizabeth, who immediately blushed. Connie had taken the youngest cast member under her seasoned wing or so it seemed. When the thirteen other women weren't consumed with practicing the song and dance routines, Elizabeth felt awkward participating in their offstage banter. They all appeared to either know, or know of, each other and discussed prospective suitors, current boyfriends or husbands, and the latest club to be seen at. Connie offered Elizabeth cigarettes at breaks and invited her to join them all for a "cuppa" at the five-and-dime after rehearsal.

Elizabeth apologetically declined most of Connie's offers. She worried about the effect of cigarettes on her singing voice and relegated smoking to weekends. Even then, she smoked sparingly. The few times she joined them for tea or coffee, she found herself relieved when Gert arrived to escort her home for dinner. Most of the female cast members weren't from New York City and lived in boardinghouses or commuted from New Jersey. For them, the city promised fulfillment, a chance to dance and sing, perform for a few years, and hopefully get noticed and wooed by a wealthy patron who'd marry them and establish them in a life of prosperity. Elizabeth felt like an enigma to most of them.

"What, no beau?!" several exclaimed when Elizabeth revealed she had never had a boyfriend and was content with her busy life of music, dance, language lessons, and performances.

Connie cheerfully intervened whenever she heard the others offer Elizabeth tips on how to attract a man.

"Ladies, men aren't the end all and be all," she would say. Then she would regale them with some tale of tragic romantic gossip that supposedly happened to someone she knew. All the while, she punctuated her stories with graceful flourishes of her lit cigarette and throaty chuckles, which drew all the women together companionably.

The day the cast members moved into the theater, Hank lead them all through the main part as some oohed and aahed at everything from the sumptuous colors and murals to the roomy, well-lit dressing room.

"Well, this is about as good as it gets," said Connie as she sat in front of a makeup tables, primping her chestnut-colored hair and reapplying her vibrant red lipstick in the ornate mirror.

Their costumes were already neatly hung on a rack that ran the full length of the far wall. In one corner were two purple velvet settees. placed in a semicircle around a round coffee table. Atop it was a pitcher of water and glasses.

The rest of the women crowded into the room. Some fingered the costumes or plopped down on the couches with appreciative exclamations. Elizabeth's anticipation had increased as soon as they'd entered the theater and now she felt as if she was vibrating.

"The cue-to-cue begins in ten minutes, ladies," announced Mr. Hemmer, standing in the doorway with his arms crossed. His stocky, gray-suited presence reassured Elizabeth. It would be the longest rehearsal so far because the goal was precise synchronized timing with music, lights, action, and dialogue.

"No costumes yet," he added as he exited.

Connie plucked at Elizabeth's skirt to get her attention.

"Elizabeth, once you get out there dancing, you'll be fine," she said. "Believe me, I know. I used to get nauseous before every performance."

"You did?" Elizabeth couldn't believe the beautiful, savvy woman in front of her ever suffered from doubt.

"Yes. Some doctor fella I dated told me adrenalin makes us all jittery. That helped. Knowing it was a chemical—natural, normal."

"Thanks. I'll remember that although I can't imagine ever feeling relaxed before a show."

Connie beckoned her to come closer and whispered in Elizabeth's ear.

"Honey, you've got it all—dancer, singer, actress. You're on your way to what we call a triple threat in this business."

★ ★ ★

Standing in the wings on opening night, before stepping on stage, Elizabeth mentally replayed Connie's reassuring words and tried to relax her clenched stomach with deep breathing. It was her first time as the lead for the chorus line, a role that demanded perfection because mistakes were immediately obvious to the audience. The cluster of dancers behind her quietly fidgeted, adjusting their costumes and hair as the orchestra began to play.

Right on cue, Elizabeth swirled onto the stage under the bright lights, with the troupe following her lead as the audience applauded. It felt like being carried on massive waves of energy that pulsed through her body. After her many hours of practice, her legs and feet moved effortlessly through the routine.

The entire show seemed to pass in half the time it had in rehearsals. She could hardly believe it was over when they finished their curtain calls amid enthusiastic roars and claps. Backstage, Connie threw her arms around Elizabeth, who was trembling from her efforts.

"You did it! No one could ask for a better performance."

CHAPTER 9
PRODIGAL SON

Her parents' voices were unusually audible as Elizabeth pulled on her blue silk robe. She always joined them for Sunday breakfast, followed by a church service, even after the late Saturday night shows. As she descended the oak staircase with its worn blue carpeting, Momma was saying, "We can't turn them away." Pop gave an exasperated sigh then said, "I know, I know."

They stopped speaking when Elizabeth entered. Pop cleared his throat. Momma sipped her coffee. Elizabeth seated herself, looking at her silent parents.

"Are either of you going to tell me what's going on?" Pop threw his crumbled linen napkin on his tablet.

"I was laying out the editorial page when I got a call from your brother yesterday evening. He's coming home. The show in Cleveland is over."

"What's unusual about that?" Elizabeth asked, spreading her napkin over her lap and pouring herself a coffee.

Pop frowned. His eyebrows, when drawn together, gave his face an intense look of concentration.

"Ah, he's met someone. A Cecilia."

"That seems like good news." Women were rarely mentioned when Palmer recounted stories of his vaudevillian life on the road. Elizabeth knew her parents hoped that he might find a woman who somehow convinced him to forgo his wilder ways. She stifled a yawn. *Molly O'* was in its third week, mostly to sold-out crowds. Every night the curtain calls grew longer and more boisterous.

"That isn't the only news," Pop said, frowning. His jaw tightened, as it often did when Palmer was involved. Elizabeth waited as her usually unflappable father composed himself. "It appears that your brother is going to be a father in the near future."

"Really? My goodness!"

"That's not all," Pop continued. "He wants to bring Cecilia home to stay with us because he's joined the army."

Her distraught parents regarded Elizabeth. Despite Momma's silence, her large dark eyes communicated her concern and discomfort. Pop's hands gripped the table edge as if he was trying to steady himself.

"You two are going to be grandparents. What a lucky baby!" Elizabeth exclaimed despite the swarm of emotions she was experiencing. "And I will be Auntie. Maybe Cecilia will be a nice addition to the family, too. Do we know anything about her?"

She acted cheerful although her words sounded hollow. She bit into a piece of buttered toast to peremptorily ward off her frustration. Once again, Palmer's propensity for drama and chaos eclipsed her success and the family's pride in her achievement.

"British vaudevillian and comedian, apparently," Pop answered. "Probably lives on a shoestring like your brother."

"Don't worry, Pop. My show runs six more weeks and I can always get a chorus job if nothing else shows up." Pop instinctively reached out and put a hand over hers.

"Your mother and I will figure it out. You are doing enough already. We are so proud of you." A tired smile softened his stressed face.

"I can add a few piano lessons," Momma volunteered. "Besides, Palmer will get compensation for his service, won't he?"

"Certainly, if he stays—" Pop paused, regarded Momma's worried face, and left his thought unfinished. Elizabeth knew he was avoiding mentioning the possibility that Palmer wouldn't return or, worse, would come home severely wounded like some of the young men with maimed faces and missing limbs who'd begun to appear on New York's streets. "We have a lot to pray about." Pop pushed his chair back and rose. "I have to get ready. We are attempting a complicated piece of music today. Ladies, I'll see you in the pews."

His volunteer job as Saint Bartholomew's choir director never failed to inspire him. Elizabeth often thought her father would have preferred a career in opera to journalism. He loved the medium and had a decent baritone singing voice.

Elizabeth and her mother finished their breakfast, making small talk about the advent of the autumnal weather and the schedule for the upcoming week. Neither ventured to the topic of Palmer's impending arrival.

1918–1921

CHAPTER 10
TRIPLE THREAT

George M. Cohan Theatre

October 4, 1918

When Elizabeth arrived in a taxi for rehearsal, new signs in large red letters were plastered by the theater entrances and exits: "No spitting by Order of the NY Department of Health" and "No Smoking of Cigars or Cigarettes." Despite the autumnal chill in the air, all the theater doors were open. Some cast members, still sporting their coats, huddled inside the stage door entrance. Connie greeted Elizabeth.

"We're waiting until the absolute last moment to take these off," she said. "It's icy in there."

"We might die from frostbite and hypothermia instead of the influenza!" said diminutive, shivering Maureen, rubbing her red gloves together.

"Yes, but the show must go on!" someone exclaimed. They all laughed.

"Hey ladies, though cold we may be, we're the lucky ones," Connie offered. "Health Commissioner Copeland is closing the smaller theaters."

"I agree," Elizabeth affirmed, "and we're in a relatively new theater with good ventilation."

"That's all well and good but some of us take public transportation to get here," added a chorus girl, stamping her cold feet as if to punctuate her comment.

"That's why theater times are staggered as of today. Cuts down on crowding," Connie said. "We're important. We keep the morale up and that's the best defense against getting sick."

"The show must go on!" they all shouted as they shuffled into the empty theater.

News on the influenza outbreak had been spare and slow in coming. When Elizabeth queried Pop about the growing number of placards on residential doors that read, "Quarantine Influenza—Keep Out," he speculated that President Wilson wanted public attention fixed on the burgeoning war effort.

Initially, the *Evening Mail*'s owner had encouraged editors like Pop to print stories enhancing patriotism and all things American, not focusing on a flu that was probably seasonal and therefore short-lived. Despite the expense, Pop insisted that Elizabeth resort to a private taxi for transport to and from the theater and dissuaded Gert from escorting Elizabeth home at night.

"We need to be as cautious as possible. I don't like what is coming over the wires from Kansas," he said. A week prior to the New York Public Health pronouncements, he had warned family members, which now included a very pregnant Cecilia as well as Frannie and Gert, that this influenza outbreak was more deadly than was currently portrayed. Gert spent a few days stitching masks for everyone on the household Singer machine. Frannie somehow persuaded the butcher, baker, and grocer to deliver to Fred, the doorman, who was happy to banter with Gert whenever he showed up at their door bearing packages wearing the mask that she'd made for him.

On the surface, everything seemed okay. However, Elizabeth missed spontaneous walks outdoors, browsing books at Brentano's, and visiting Joanie whose family also sequestered as much as possible. Life was reduced to work and home. She and her new sister-in-law had formed a cordial, comfortable relationship. However, whenever Cecilia brought up Palmer and his "letters from the Seventy-First," as she called them, Elizabeth carefully crafted her responses to avoid casting doubts or dispersions about her brother. Apparently, Palmer persuaded his colonel to let him pull together a music band of his fellow soldiers and write songs and skits to entertain troops returning from the front.

As part of her weekly letter exchange with Joanie, Elizabeth confided:

He never asks her how she is doing or what living with us is like. Nor does he ask about us. Momma and Pop haven't heard from him directly since he went off to boot camp. Cecilia is so nice and lively. I don't know what she sees in him. Oh, Joanie, there I've said it. I don't like my very own brother much. Please bear with me and do not think ill of me for my confession. You're the only person I'd ever tell this to. I miss you. Work (although I shouldn't complain because I love my role as Helen) and this awful influenza have really gotten in the way of our time together! Please tear up this letter after you read it. I don't want anyone else to know how I really feel about Palmer.

The Saturday night a week before the show closed, Elizabeth crowded into the backstage quarters with most of the female cast. She struggled to remove her costume's petticoat and tight velvet bodice without knocking into others when Hank pounded on the door.

"Elizabeth Hines. She back there?" he yelled gruffly.

"She is! Who's asking?" Connie yelled back, winking at Elizabeth across the room.

"I have a note here from George M. himself."

"Really!" Connie maneuvered around the other half-dressed young women, cracked the door a sliver, and reached out.

"I'll be glad to relay it to her. She's getting changed just like the rest of us." Hank hesitated.

"Well, okay, he wants me to give to her directly, but since yous all indisposed, I guess it's alright."

The envelope passed, hand to hand, to Elizabeth, who was tucking her white silk blouse into her black skirt. As if on cue, everyone stopped and waited silently as she carefully opened it. The handwritten scrawl read, "Kiddie, you're nominated. The first suitable part I get, you shall have. Consider this a preliminary contract."

"Mr. Cohan is offering me a part and a contract. I can't believe it!" she said.

"Why not?" Connie threw an arm around Elizabeth's shoulders, giving her a congratulatory squeeze. "What did I tell you? This is just the beginning."

Despite their various states of disarray, the other women clapped, cheered, and offered a running commentary: "Mr. Yankee Doodle, he's the top of the heap. Works his actors hard. Fair, though, treats them like family." Elizabeth, stunned and excited, could barely follow their enthusiastic outpouring.

CHAPTER 11
GEORGE'S GIRL

Too excited to sleep, even after the grueling day of a matinee and an evening show, Elizabeth lay in bed, waiting for night to end. She wanted to surprise Pop with her news before his usual 7:30 a.m. departure for the newspaper office. *Would he be in favor of this monumental opportunity? Why not?* Her mind debated the possibilities until the early morning light shone faintly between a gap in the curtains and she heard the rumble of the milkman's truck and the clank his glass bottles left. Throwing on her robe and putting the note from Mr. Cohan in her pocket, she tiptoed down to the hall toilet to avoid waking Cecilia in the neighboring room. Elizabeth splashed cool water on her face before descending to the dining room.

"My goodness, you're up early," said Pop, putting his newspaper aside, surveying her. "You okay?"

"More than okay." She slid the note out of her pocket and presented it to him. "Look what I received after curtain call last night."

"A note from an admirer, no doubt. You certain you want your father to read this?"

"Oh, Pop, this is much more than that."

"What do we have here?" Adjusting his wire rim glasses on his angular nose, he read, then let out a whistle. "My goodness,

Elizabeth, George M. Fantastic!" He beamed at Elizabeth, standing by his side, her hands clasped in anticipation. He rose and hugged her.

"I am so proud of you," he said. With her cheek pressed against his tweed jacket, she finally relaxed. Pop extracted himself, putting his hands on her shoulders. "Elizabeth, dear, I will contact Mr. Cohan regarding a formal contract. Until we have the terms in writing, I would keep this quiet."

"But Pop." Her voice was shaky from fatigue. "All the women in the cast know already. We were changing when the note was delivered and—"

"The ladies all heard." He finished her sentence. "Let's hope the gossip press doesn't get word of this before I have a chance to meet with Cohan."

"Pop, they said all his contracts are verbal with a handshake."

"That may be but I will offer to write up some terms. As your father and manager, I intend to protect you for as long as necessary."

"What have we here? Elizabeth, an early riser? After such a later night?" Momma entered in a long, quilted robe, her brown hair in a loose braid down her back.

"I don't think our girl slept last night," Pop said, lightly squeezing Elizabeth.

"Not feeling well, dear?" She worriedly scanned Elizabeth, who couldn't refrain from smiling while vigorously shaking her head.

"George M. Cohan—last night, a note to me in the dressing room backstage," babbled Elizabeth.

Momma poured herself a cup of coffee and sat down, looking quizzically at them. Pop, clearing his throat, began in a measured voice to inform her. Elizabeth seated herself. Deflated and somewhat dazed from the intensity of the past twenty-four hours, she appreciated his intervention.

"Goodness, this is happening faster than I thought."

"Don't worry, Anna. I will ensure that our Elizabeth is properly taken care of," Pop said reassuringly. "I will phone Mr. Cohan today from the office. If I reach him, I'll leave a note, Elizabeth, since I won't be home before you leave for tonight's performance. Now, miss, you better eat something and climb back in bed for a few hours." Quickly kissing his wife and daughter on their foreheads and wishing them a good day, he left them sipping coffee and eating toast.

"In normal times this would be cause for a little celebration," Momma offered, breaking the silence. "Sunday brunch with your friends, Joanie and Isabelle, your new chorus friend, Connie, and Mr. Hemmer, too. What with this pandemic, though, you'll have to settle for family. Maybe Frannie and I can get ingredients for and make pecan pie, your favorite—with whipped cream on top."

Elizabeth nodded. Momma's consideration made her simultaneously tearful and speechless.

CHAPTER 12
THE INTERLUDE

Elizabeth sat in the den, unable to focus on the book of Edna St. Vincent Millay's poems in her lap though they usually absorbed her attention. Savage's show had ended with much acclaim by the first week of November. A whirlpool of tremendous relief and fatigue washed over her, combined with a keen bereft feeling she now recognized as the emotional aftermath of being involved in a long running show. Despite the presence of Frannie, Gert, and her immediate family, she also felt an odd loneliness.

New York life had been severely curtailed since September when the Spanish flu began its steady advance from the shipyards. Even though schools, businesses, and the bigger theaters still operated on abbreviated schedules, socializing, even churchgoing, was discouraged. Almost every block had at least one building with a quarantine sign nailed up on the front door. Families isolated, fearing contact with anyone, including neighbors. Church bells for the dead pealed frequently. Ordinarily bustling streets were sparsely populated. Buses and subways were on staggered schedules.

Elizabeth realized she hadn't communicated with Joanie in several weeks and moved to the roll top desk. She chose among the slots of carefully arranged stationary and wrote:

Dearest Joanie,

I was so glad you and your parents used the complimentary tickets to *Molly O'* and enjoyed the show. Sorry I couldn't invite you backstage but the management strictly forbids all visitors due to the pandemic. This flu situation has certainly impacted all our lives. We are being very careful here because Cecilia is on the verge of having the baby any minute. She seems to be in good spirits despite her difficulties sleeping and moving around and the fact that Palmer will not be home from the army in time for the delivery.

I didn't get to tell you that Mr. George M. Cohan was in the audience a week ago Saturday and sent me a note after the show. He wants me to work for him. Can you believe it? He says he's going to write a part in his next show with me in mind. Pop and he are negotiating the terms of the contract. The extra good news is that Mr. Hemmer will also be involved as choreographer and dancer in whatever the next Cohan production is. At least I will have one friendly, familiar face in the cast!

Apparently, Mr. Cohan wants to open in Boston as he often does with a new production but all the theaters are still closed there. I guess it is a waiting game now—waiting for the show to be written, waiting to find out where and when I will be rehearsing. In the meantime, Mr. Hemmer has some producer friends who want me for a major role in a New York show called *Lovebirds* which begins rehearsals in November. It is an amusing, fanciful story in which the shopgirl heroine, Allene Charteris (me), flees from the constant advances of her wealthy boss and ends up captured by an emir and installed in his Persian harem from which her working-class plumber boyfriend rescues her. I hope it lifts peoples' spirits. After the horrid war and this wretched flu, everyone could use some good music, dance and laughter.

At least I will be home to meet my new family member whenever she or he arrives.

I hope you and I get to see each other before I become a full-fledged member of the Cohan troupe. I miss our time together.

Yours always, Elizabeth

The two friends met earlier than they'd anticipated. November was turning out to be chock-full of activities instead of the quiet month Elizabeth had expected. As pandemic numbers subsided, she received a flurry of lunch and tea invitations from friends she'd been unable to see for months.

Since rehearsals for *Lovebirds* wouldn't begin until late November, she planned visits with friends even as she resumed her busy schedule of weekly voice, dance, and language lessons. One day she met Isabelle and Joanie at their favorite Horn & Hardart at Fifty-Seventh Street and Sixth Avenue. As they enjoyed lemon meringue pie and coffee, Elizabeth felt the relief of being reunited with good friends with whom she felt utterly relaxed.

"Now that I graduated, my parents insist that I stay in Manhattan for the coming out season and attend all the parties that I'm invited to," Isabelle glowered. "As if that is important after all that has happened!" Sudden fierceness in her large, hazel eyes dominated her small, delicate face. *If she was a bird, she'd be a falcon,* thought Elizabeth, recalling when she came face to face with a falcon perched on a fence post on a Quogue lane. She and the bird had regarded each other, seemingly for minutes, before it gracefully opened its beautifully striated brown-hued wings and flew across the meadow.

"Oh, Izzy, you could have some fun, you know," Joanie consoled.

"It's the premise of the whole ritual—as if we were brood-mares being paraded and evaluated for generating prize offspring."

"I know what you mean. I don't know how many times I've been asked if I have a fellow or when I plan on marrying," Elizabeth said. "As if my stage career is just whimsy and my real life will begin when I am someone's wife."

"Let's imagine what a woman's life will look like by the year 2000," Joanie proposed. "Maybe Horn & Hardart will still be around?" They laughed, looking at the gleaming linoleum floor and the multi-tiered stations lining the walls. Each was marked with a big block sign reading "Pies," "Drinks," "Sandwiches," "Soup." A steady stream of men in suits and fedoras, workmen in overalls or uniforms, shopgirls, secretaries, and the occasional elegantly dressed woman entered, located the station of their choice, and slid nickels into the slot next to the appropriate cubby to access and remove their choice. Employees from behind the glass stations immediately filled any empty cubby with another plate. Some customers chose to eat at one of the square tables; others carried their neatly wrapped purchase back out the door.

"The pie is great. Tasty and inexpensive!" Elizabeth noted as she placed a forkful of her pie into her mouth.

"Yes, I agree. A Horn & Hardart on every block so women wouldn't have to cook unless they wanted to!" Isabelle exclaimed. "Seriously, though, imagine the positive changes in the future if women could vote."

Women's rights were Isabelle's cause célèbre. Lately, Joanie and Elizabeth both worried about Isabelle's welfare as she became increasingly militant, sneaking out of her house to join in the campaigns and parades of the women in white. Isabelle's parents were bastions of New York society, her father notoriously strict with his children. The suffragette protests were increasingly interrupted by clashing political factions and police arrests, which amplified their concern.

"I bet that women will have a variety of career options by 2000," speculated Joanie, due to enter Teachers College in the spring.

"Maybe women who chose to work like me would not be so stigmatized," Elizabeth said before downing the last delicious morsel of lemon meringue pie.

Isabelle extracted her silver cigarette case from her brown purse and offered them cigarettes, which Elizabeth and Joanie both declined.

"Yes, maybe then women could live independently without getting a bad reputation," Isabelle said, inhaling with a look of deep satisfaction.

"And they could have careers, be wives and mothers without being regarded as negligent—or failures," Elizabeth added.

"I don't see why not." Joanie squeezed Elizabeth's arm affectionately. "I think we should design our own futures accordingly. Elizabeth is already on her way."

Simultaneously, they clasped each other's hands. Isabelle insisted they wait until she finished her cigarette before they pulled on trench coats and cloche hats and stepped into the raw, dank November day.

CHAPTER 13
ACTORS' FIDELITY LEAGUE

The front-page headlines of her father's paper read, "Lee Shubert Violently Against Union" and "Barrymore Speaks Out." Elizabeth put down her teacup, her stomach suddenly roiling. In the past few weeks after rehearsals, cast members gathered outdoors in the sultry late August evenings smoking and discussing the insurrection before leaving for the day. Elizabeth tended to head home immediately after rehearsals, but she overheard fragments of their conversation.

"Lillian Russell is in. So is Jolson and Wynn," affirmed a graying tall man known for his masterful stage lighting. "They've got pedigrees and clout."

Another stagehand eagerly offered, "My brother works at the Hippodrome and they're all planning on striking."

As the newest member of the Cohan troupe, Elizabeth maintained an uneasy silence on the matter around her fellow actors. No one seemed to notice or perhaps they saw her as too young to have a salient point of view. In either case, she preferred her apparent invisibility to engaging in what was an obviously burgeoning conflict.

"I don't like it. How is he going to ensure your safety?" Pop folded his paper, stood up, and circled the breakfast table.

"He's not fighting us," said Elizabeth, buttering her toast and trying to appear nonchalant.

"Yes, but he is potentially setting you and the rest of the cast up against Actors' Equity."

"Everybody knows where George M. stands, Pop, especially anybody who ever worked with him. He won't let any organization, let alone a union, tell him what to do."

"Word is, Elizabeth, the strike will include several marches and close down at least half the shows. You might have trouble getting to rehearsals through picket lines and all—that's if rehearsals continue."

"Pop, we're actors, not soldiers or thugs. We respect each other despite our differences."

Did he know that George M. proposed forming an alternative union, The Actors' Fidelity League, based on loyalty to him? And there was no way she'd jeopardize her first big job with Cohan by refusing to join, even if it meant being called a Fido by the strikers. Pop sat down, shaking his head.

"Sometimes I wish you were happily married instead of—" Elizabeth patted his arm.

"I know, Pop," she said. "You want the best for me, but I've worked hard for this. Nothing means more to me."

Pop had covered some so-called strikes when he was a reporter—well-intentioned groups trying to upgrade the quality of their lives and those of their families. Elizabeth knew they both were remembering his experiences, which he'd shared dozens of times. How quickly the spark of resistance could flare into a brawling aggressive melee, Pop had said time and time again—melees that couldn't be checked until the fire burned itself out, leaving some injured, if not dead.

Momma swept in, her dark eyes sparkling and her rose-scented perfume wafting across the room.

"What are you two up to? You look so serious."

Elizabeth exchanged a quick conspiratorial look with her father.

"Oh, Elizabeth was just telling me about the rehearsals and some cast members she's become friendly with." He stood up and pulled out a chair to seat his wife before seating himself again. "Our girl is really stretching her wings."

Elizabeth hoped Momma didn't hear Pop's forced tone. Momma remained ambivalent about Elizabeth's career. It was as if they consensually agreed not to discuss the subject anymore. After his initial protestations, Pop became Elizabeth's ally. Mr. Hemmer's dedicated mentorship had been significantly persuasive. Her parents trusted him so that when he offered his services to George M. on Elizabeth's behalf, it was of great consolation to them both. *To me as well,* Elizabeth thought as she poured herself more tea. *Mr. Hemmer is a gem.*

"Oh, that's a relief. For a minute there I thought something was wrong."

"No, Momma, everything is going well. Mr. Cohan even complimented me yesterday. He said I am the quintessential Alice O'Brien, the heroine."

"That's wonderful, Elizabeth. I look forward to seeing the show." Anna lightly tapped her soft-boiled egg in its porcelain eggcup as she addressed her husband. "Anything worth reading in the paper, dear?"

"Much the same as yesterday—flu on the wane, more boys coming home," Pop summarized.

To pursue the topic of anything theatrical right now would be folly. Momma simply didn't share her enthusiasm. Over the past six years, Elizabeth learned to abbreviate theater-related concerns or news. It felt like she and Momma had parted ways a while ago, Elizabeth becoming a version of womanhood that her mother wasn't acquainted with or knew how to engage.

She longed to mention that yesterday Mr. Cohan had introduced her as "my ingenue" to a short, dark, fedora-wearing young man about her age named Walter Winchell. Then he'd said, "Kid, I am crazy about you—but not as a stage door johnny; as an actress 'n' girl." Elizabeth scarcely believed her ears. In her confusion she blushed, then curtsied having no idea how to respond. Was his accolade a blessing or a curse? Thank goodness Winchell didn't notice her reaction and resumed rattling away to Mr. Cohan in his staccato voice about vaudeville and the need for better press coverage.

What was involved in being loyal to George M. Cohan besides refusing to join Actors' Equity? What was so wrong with the union, anyway? Actors would be paid for rehearsal time and get an overall pay increase and one day off a week. Her tired legs and feet signaled that more time off would be a welcome boon. Although *Lovebirds* was running for three more weeks, Mr. Cohan had announced that he required her for rehearsals of his newest show, *The O'Brien Girl*, in which she had the lead as Alice O'Brien. She ran from rehearsal to the show, barely having time to eat between commitments, and then dropped into bed in the early morning hours. Gert's cheery "You hoo, Miss E." wake-up call came much too early these days.

Cecilia trundled into the dining room, one hand on her expansive belly as if holding it up.

"I guess I am in training for a few years of no sleep," she said, sitting down heavily before running her fingers through her tousled brown hair. "How did you go through this twice, Anna, and come out so slim and elegant? I don't think my feet will ever regain their former size, let alone the rest of my body." Yawning, she poured herself a cup of tea.

"Don't worry, you're young," Momma said. "You'll bounce back quickly after the birth."

"Maybe it is a good thing Palmer isn't here. He wouldn't recognize me."

"Nonsense. Like many mothers-to-be, you exude a certain radiance that is quite becoming. Isn't that so, Pop?"

"Of course, yes," Pop agreed, clearing his throat, then folding up his paper. "Ahem, I must take my leave, ladies." He stood up, bowing playfully to them before exiting.

Elizabeth couldn't find any radiance in Cecilia's drained face and bloated body. Gaining thirty pounds, not being able to sleep, and having constant dyspepsia was not appealing. Her sister-in-law wasn't one to complain but the vivacious young woman who moved in four months ago was barely evident. Her sympathy for Cecilia was mixed with an intense resurgence of gratitude for her chosen career, a good note on which to launch into another demanding day.

CHAPTER 14
REST IN PARADISE

Elizabeth sat in the window seat in the den and pulled a blue cashmere blanket up to her chest as she turned the pages of *This Side of Paradise*. Fitzgerald's writing was uneven, sometimes breathtaking, sometimes heavy-handed and didactic. The main character, Amory Blaine, embodied what she detested in most Ivy League men—their brash misogyny; competitive snobbery; their aspirations to the artistic European life, free from constructive work, familial, and social convention; and their tendency toward overindulgence and self-destruction.

She sighed, put down the book, and looked out at the cold, rainy Tuesday: the sky was distinctively white, as a New York sky tends to be in mid-December. On the wet street below, people wore galoshes, huddled under umbrellas, and hurried to reach their destinations before they were soaked. She was relieved she didn't have to go to the theater today. An indoor day of rest and reading was perfect. Despite the strike, which caused many theaters to halt productions, hers was going well. Initial reviews of *The O'Brien Girl* had been favorable and she enjoyed playing her part since it required some acting as well as dancing and singing.

My days as a chorus girl are over. The thought was both welcome and nostalgic. Although she missed the comradery, she enjoyed having a say in how her character developed. Mr. Cohan, normally intractable with how he wanted his characters portrayed, listened when she suggested that Alice be more assertive than submissive or manipulative. "Like a twentieth century young woman, not a Victorian!" Elizabeth exclaimed in their early rehearsals. When he looked confused, she walked across the stage, firmly planting each foot, eyes forward—a confident woman who stood up for her beliefs, not abrasively, not in a socially embarrassing way, but as a steady, thoughtful, and discerning lady.

Elizabeth suddenly realized why she had a mixed opinion of Fitzgerald. For the most part, his women characters did not elicit her respect nor admiration. They were caged animals—wild, unpredictable, sometimes vicious. She kept her distance from women like that even if they were esteemed in show business. At a recent gala and dinner party she'd met Tallulah Bankhead, the headliner; Elizabeth was featured as a new talent along with several other acts from current Broadway productions. Even without her cigarettes, which she smoked incessantly, Tallulah smoldered. Elizabeth felt foreboding as soon as they were introduced. Tallulah's gaze raked her and then turned away. Although Elizabeth felt dismissed by their encounter, she also was relieved that she was not of interest to such a powerful, controversial person.

"Elizabeth, teatime!" Her mother tapped lightly on the closed door.

"Coming, Momma." She put down her book and stretched, wiggling her sore feet. Teatime was her favorite time of the day. It was important for touching base with her family since she missed dinner most days. She wondered if Palmer would appear. It seemed like he deliberately avoided family gatherings lately as some sort of silent protest. *If that's the case, what is he protesting?*

Palmer seemed perpetually irritable and dissatisfied. She ceased her attempts to mollify his moods long ago. However, she had hoped that Cecilia and their beautiful little girl, Dorothy, would affect a positive change in his overall demeanor, but they didn't. Whenever he was home, he scowled.

The first week that *The O'Brien Girl* opened at Manhattan's Shubert Theatre, Palmer sat at the breakfast table and proclaimed, "Another lightweight, fluffy Cohan production—just what the world needs." Momma shushed him but his reaction dampened Elizabeth's enthusiasm. She wanted to argue that although Cohan's plots tended to repeat similar comedic romantic dilemmas, the music and dancing were always new. Instead, she resolved to do even better, for what was a better response than success?

"Gert left this out for you, dear," Momma said, pointing to an open page of the *New York Times* as Elizabeth entered the dining room. "She wanted you to see it before she cut it out for your scrapbook."

"Methinks Gert is your most loyal fan, Elizabeth," Cecilia said, grinning and helping herself to shortbread.

"I am grateful," Elizabeth said, "but I don't think I want to know what all the critics say." She seated herself, picked up the paper, and blushed as she read Adrienne Battey's words.

That a girl of such beauty and personal charm should also be able to sing is evidence of nature's lavish hand when she's in a giving mood. Miss Hines's voice is fresh and pure in tone with an appealingly sweet quality and she handles it skillfully. Dancing is another of this young actress' accomplishments.

"I would say this is a favorable review, dear. Nothing to be embarrassed about."

"I know, Momma. I am especially glad he calls me an actress but one good review doesn't mean I can rest on my laurels."

Cecilia gently rocked Dorothy in her arms and sang, "Auntie is an ingenue, an ingenue, your auntie is an ingenue." The baby gurgled at the sound of her mother's voice.

"I don't think I qualify for that status yet!" Elizabeth said, laughing. "It's only my first major role in a Cohan production." The scene before her of the young mother enjoying her infant reminded Elizabeth of the touching intimate quality of Mary Cassatt's paintings.

"With many more to come, from what your father tells me," Momma sighed. "As much I am pleased with your success, I hope this strike resolves soon so Pop resumes his usual work schedule instead of arriving home in the early morning hour."

"I know, Momma. I told him I would be fine traveling to and from the theater but he insisted on changing his shift so he could escort me. Besides, the strikers won't picket us. Everyone respects Mr. Cohan even though he is against Actors' Equity."

"We certainly could use representation and better working conditions," Cecilia affirmed.

"I know some producers are nasty and cheap, but Mr. Cohan takes care of actors," Elizabeth said. "He just doesn't want anyone telling him what to do or interfere with his productions." Lately whenever this subject arose, Elizabeth defended her boss even though she agreed with Cecilia. Mr. Cohan worked hard and alongside his players, doing every dance and singing each song as he crafted a production. He didn't ask of them for what he couldn't or wouldn't also do. His endurance, enthusiastic creativity and vitality, legendary before she came on the scene, were inspiring and irresistible. Under his tutelage, she felt she was becoming the professional she aspired to be.

"Yes. However, many of us don't work for George Cohan or Sam Harris," Cecilia said as she rose to lay an obviously sleepy Dorothy in the crib standing in the arched corner of the room. She reseated herself at the table.

"Speaking of Sam Harris, is it true that he and Cohan broke up their partnership over this strike?"

"That's the word behind the curtain although no one confirmed it to us yet."

"Let's enjoy our tea and company, shall we?" Momma said. "No more talk of strikes and conflict." She passed the plate of shortbread and scones.

CHAPTER 15

THE BOB

Spreading her face and neck with Mineralava cream, Elizabeth luxuriated in her quiet bedroom. Six days a week of performances for the past four months had worn her out.

The gossip was that Zelda Fitzgerald cropped off her own hair, defying Scott and everyone else of importance. *I am ready,* Elizabeth thought as she unwound her coil of golden hair, resenting the effort that good brushing required. Momma would argue.

"Your hair is one of your best features," she'd said. "Bobs are just a fad."

But Elizabeth knew it was time to do something different. Fingering the twisted length of hair, she wondered how it would feel to be free of the weight. The chorus girls had mentioned a French hairdresser, Pierre something, new to the city. He specialized in short hair. Pierre was incurring the wrath of husbands and lovers as women, newly cropped, sleek as seals, welcomed their astonished men home. *I need to get his name and address when I go to rehearsal today,* she thought. *Better do it way before the opening and give the press some time to get over it.*

Although she loved being considered an ingenue because it attracted better roles as well as more dancing and singing, being the subject of the press was annoying. Maintaining boundaries against their intrusiveness was stressful. She didn't want to appear rude or arrogant like Tallulah Bankhead or fawning like some young actresses. Already, some reporters remarked on how she was both talented and nice as if the combination was unusual.

If I cut my hair, what will Mr. Cohan think? His approach to theater was definitively modern but he was quite traditional in his expectations and treatment of women. Seated a few rows behind him and a couple of his male investors at a recent rehearsal, she overheard him say, "Why do women want to vote? Can't they just trust us to make good decisions? If I was a woman, I'd love to stay home and have someone else worry about the state of the world." His male cronies nodded in agreement.

Aghast, Elizabeth slipped out of the plush red seat and tiptoed into the shadows. Pop had encouraged her to educate herself about current affairs and history. She never forgot his words: "Women need to be informed so when the time comes, they can vote their own minds."

She eagerly voted for the first time last November for Warren Harding. It hadn't been an easy decision. She favored some of Wilson's international policies, but the Sedition Act countered her understanding of free speech. Also, she concurred with the popular belief that the war had been a rich man's war and a poor man's fight.

I am no rebel, though, she mused. She hadn't joined the suffragettes, thinking that move would jeopardize her career. On that crisp October day in 1915, though, she, Joanie, and Isabelle had cheered on the marching women for at least an hour before wending their way home, despite the cold wind whipping up Fifth Avenue. The army of women in white, carrying yellow banners and signs filling the street, was still a vivid memory. Elizabeth's favorite sign read, "We talk with you, we eat with you, we dance with you, we marry you. Why can't we vote with you?"

Maybe not a bob but something short, different. But how to convince Momma? Whenever Elizabeth wanted to try some popular trend, Momma reminded her, "You're on the stage but you're also a lady." It was a distinction that Elizabeth appreciated and, in her own way, tried to maintain. Actresses were generally viewed by the public as one step above the ladies of the night of which there were many in Manhattan. Each district had its particular flavor—Italian women on Mulberry, Germans along Second Avenue, and the French ruled Washington Square. In a newspaper interview some visiting dignitary had recently described Manhattan as "sex drenched." Leaving the theater after an evening performance, Elizabeth often saw scantily dressed women gathered under streetlights through the taxi window. Some looked dejected and dirty while others were gaudy and flirtatiously waved at passing carriages and taxis.

She removed all her costumes immediately after every performance, donning street clothes before anyone from the public saw her in what might construed as risqué. That promoted less confusion, especially with male admirers or journalists. First and foremost, she wanted to be regarded as well-bred, respectable, and intelligent as well as talented. Surely a bob would not be a negative strike against her reputation. Besides, wouldn't a shorter haircut be so much easier to maintain?

CHAPTER 16
ASCENT AND CHANGE

The O'Brien Girl played for sixty weeks to a full house almost every night. By the end of the run, Gert, on her own reconnaissance, filled an entire scrapbook of reviews and press tidbits in which Elizabeth was mentioned or featured.

"I knew you were going to be a star," she beamed, surprising Elizabeth by plunking down the red leather book on her desk one dreary gray February morning a week after the show's end. "I thought you might want memories of all this someday."

"Gert, how thoughtful! You shouldn't have," Elizabeth blushed. She put both hands on her forehead in mock alarm. "Oh dear, now I'll have to read what all the critics said!"

"I know you don't like to read reviews but it's all good, Miss E. Don't you worry. Someday you might want the memories. And here's your mail. It came this morning." Gert handed her a light blue envelope. "From a Mister Sam Harris."

"Sam Harris? *The* Sam Harris?" Elizabeth tore open the envelope.

"Do you have a fellow you haven't told me about?"

"No, Gert. If it is who I think it is, it's Mr. Cohan's former partner and best friend."

"What would he be wanting?" asked Gert, lingering to hear whatever Elizabeth was willing to share. At first Elizabeth read the note to herself.

"Oh, how nice of him. He came to the show despite the fallout he and Mr. Cohan had over the Actors' Equity situation." She read aloud.

My dear Elizabeth Hines,

Please may I salute you. You are a darling. I could see George in every movement of the play. I love George and so I loved everyone and everything in his play.

If I were a poet, after seeing you, I would write a rhapsody to the glory of youth. Youth does not appreciate itself. It takes age to do that so with the graying locks trailing in the dust, I salute you.

Sincerely, Sam H. Harris

"This goes in, too," Elizabeth said, slipping the note into the back of the scrapbook. "I can't imagine receiving a note from anyone whose opinion I respect more." She plumped her newly coiffed short hair with her fingers. "You know what else is nice about his letter, Gert?"

"No, Miss E., I didn't even know who the man was until now." Gert circled the room, tidying up.

"Even though he and Mr. Cohan were at odds, he still supports and values his former partner's productions. In a sense they are now competitors but still Mr. Harris enjoyed the show and was nice enough to say so."

She thought of Palmer, who had arrived without forewarning from Camp Meade in mid-January and demanded that Cecilia and Dorothy accompany him within the week to Tampa, where he intended to set up a theater troupe at the Rialto. He barely acknowledged Elizabeth and showed minimal appreciation for their parents' gracious, generous care of his wife and daughter while he was gone for eight months.

"The Palmer Hines Players," he announced on his first night home. "That's what I'm naming it. Got a few army boys to join me down south. They loved the songs I wrote for the army shows, especially this one." He jumped to his feet at the dining table, vigorously singing, "My hope is in March, we'll march home," startling the rest of the family, especially Dorothy, who whimpered in her highchair. Cecilia managed to quiet him down by drawing attention to their daughter's reaction. They all resumed eating as if nothing irregular had happened.

"Wonder how Cecilia and Dorothy like Florida," Elizabeth mused.

"I'm sure it's a good sight better than New York City in winter," Gert volunteered as she finished making the bed. "Things are awfully quiet around here now, though." Elizabeth nodded.

"Still I think it must be difficult to tour as a mother with a young child and no home base."

"Yes, indeed but Miss Cecilia knows the stage life. Knew it long before she met your brother. I do hope the wee tyke gets the attention she deserves," Gert added as she headed for the door.

Gert had clearly enjoyed caring for Dorothy. She consistently offered to take the infant off Cecilia's hands. The baby perked up and oriented her blue eyes on Gert's broad face whenever she appeared. Gert, in turn, incessantly cooed, sang, or talked to the child, regardless of who was around.

Elizabeth attempted to mollify Gert's obvious angst by distracting her.

"By the way, Pop and I already discussed that you're coming with me to Boston," she said. "From what Mr. Cohan shared so far, it seems like it could be a long run."

"Sounds good, Miss E., I've not been to Boston." Before exiting, Gert paused. "This new show have a name yet?"

"*Little Nellie Kelly* and I'll have the lead." Saying it aloud made it more real. "Mr. Cohan said it's his most ambitious show yet. If the rehearsals are any indication, he's right on the money."

Years later, she realized how prescient he had been.

CHAPTER 17
THE FLAPPER

It was late spring before George M,. as Elizabeth now permitted herself to call him, was satisfied with how the songs and dances of his newest production knit together. Meanwhile, she continued her singing lessons with Mrs. Sylvester, Saint Bartholomew's choir director, Mr. Hemmer's dance training, and classes in conversational German and Italian.

Several times weekly, George M. sent word to meet him in a dismal studio in the theater district for a spontaneous rehearsal. The mostly male cast members—Charles King playing Nellie's love interest and Arthur Deagon, Nellie's father—joined them for a run-through of his most recently crafted song and dance number. George M. watched carefully, scribbling notes or jumping in to demonstrate or further edit. Sometimes he wrote lyrics on the spot while simultaneously waving his cane to conduct the piano accompaniment and direct the actors.

After a particularly vigorous rendition of "They Are All My Boys," Elizabeth was mopping the back of her neck with a handkerchief when George M. two-stepped, twirled his cane, and exuberantly announced, "Kiddoes, the patches on this show's pants are pretty thin. There's just one answer. Dance so fast the audience can't see 'em."

Although breathless from exertion in the stuffy studio, they all laughed, even Mr. Hemmer, who helped craft the dances for the chorus and tended to seriousness whenever work was involved.

"We'll open in Boston at the Tremont end of July. Just confirmed it last night," George M. continued. "We'll arrange for lodgings, expect you up there by July 20. Take some time off but don't slack off. A three-hour production requires you all to be in good shape and know your part thoroughly. Oh and a thank you to Miss Hines for bobbing your hair and creating some free advertising for our upcoming show." He bowed to Elizabeth. "As the rest of you may have read, the *Times* named her 'America's Perfect Flapper.'"

Elizabeth's already warm face grew uncomfortably hot as the cast members smiled and briefly clapped.

"Really, I had no idea it was newsworthy," she said. "It's just hair."

"Kiddo, as far as I'm concerned, in the entertainment biz, any press is good press. Attention is attention, doesn't matter where it comes from just so it creates an audience."

Elizabeth thought about his words as her hansom cab bucked and bumped homeward along the potholed streets to Madison Avenue. She doubted she would ever get accustomed to, or even comprehend, the press's prurient interest in the private and banal such as one's choice in dress, exercise, or reading material. Even Joanie and Isabelle now affectionately called her their "trendsetter friend." Increasingly, reporters from various national newspapers wanted to know Elizabeth's opinion on everything from the best face cream to jazz. When fielding their inquiries, Pop prioritized her practice and class schedule, parsing out her spare time to what he considered the most reputable news sources.

When the cab turned north from Fifty-Seventh Street onto Park Avenue, the promenade's wide strips of lawn, blossoming tulips, and hyacinths was so alluring that Elizabeth informed the driver she would walk the rest of the way home. After paying him, despite her tired feet, she stepped out into the fragrant air. Scavenging pigeons scattered, then landed nearby, resuming their bobbing search for anything edible. Large clouds shifted across the blue sky, casting fast-moving shadows. Two men in suits and bowler hats carrying silver-topped canes vigorously debated some topic as they passed her on the wide path. Several children ran exuberantly after a red soccer ball while their watchful mothers sat companionably together and chatted.

Spring walks home with Joanie from Brearley School seemed so long ago now. So much had transpired. Having agreed to the one night of the Christmas Cotillion, Isabelle had successfully avoided most debutante festivities by convincing her father that a two-year attendance at a London art school would benefit her future. Elizabeth recalled Isabelle's impish face when she confided, "Promises of royalty work every time. What my parents would give to have a baron or a duke as part of our family!"

Elizabeth and Joanie surmised that she would quickly affiliate herself with the British suffragettes and prioritize her political activism over any social climbing. Isabelle's occasional letters to her friends confirmed she was pursuing her interests, not her father's.

Joanie had moved into student accommodations near Teachers College, making their get-togethers infrequent and much less spontaneous.

Not to mention my unpredictable schedule, Elizabeth thought. Being at George M.'s beck and call was strenuous but remained exciting and fulfilling. She hummed one of the show's tunes over the last few blocks before the turn toward Madison and home.

CHAPTER 18
THE PALMER EFFECT

Rather than his usual position in the lobby, Fred stood outdoors, doffing his black hat to Elizabeth as she entered the building's small cobblestone driveway.

"Quite the day, ain't it, Miss E.? Almost worth waiting the whole winter for."

"Yes indeed, Fred. Spring is certainly my favorite season."

While making her way to the elevator, lines of an Edna St. Vincent Millay poem crossed her mind:

I will be the gladdest thing under the sun

I will touch a hundred flowers and not pick one

The moody notes of Beethoven's "Moonlight Sonata" drifted from the piano in the living room to the foyer. *Not a good sign. She only plays that piece when she is upset.* Elizabeth set her purse down on the oak side table. Before she could take off her coat, a tight-mouthed Gert appeared from the kitchen.

"The missus got a telegram from your brother right after lunch," she said softly. "She's been in there since." She hung up Elizabeth's coat. "Don't know what it said but I thought I better give you a heads up."

Elizabeth's expansive state, generated by her walk and the delights of spring, deflated—a familiar effect of most news concerning Palmer.

"Thank you, Gert. I think I will wait until Momma is ready to talk."

Not rushing to console her mother was a learned and relatively new behavior. For years, she became inordinately chipper, amusing, and conversational to offset the negative effects of Palmer's actions on her parents. Ascending the stairway to her bedroom, Elizabeth fully realized the full import of the shift she made.

Sometime over the past few years, she had accepted what she clearly could not affect. For incomprehensible reasons, Palmer chose to continually reinforce his antagonistic role with his family members. Elizabeth envied Joanie's relationship with her older brother, John. Whenever she visited the Farwells, she was struck by their obvious enjoyment of and support for one another.

Closing her bedroom door to signal that she was resting, she kicked off her pumps and cracked the window to let in the spring air before nestling into the pillows on the sun-splashed love seat. As she drank in the late afternoon light and soft air, she decided to remain in her room for a few hours until Pop came home from work. He was better at dealing with Momma's upset when it came to Palmer. Besides, Momma took his input to heart whereas she tended to discount Elizabeth's as the ramblings of a naïve youngster who didn't know much about how things really operated in the world.

The Western Union telegram lay face up on the coffee table in the den. Elizabeth, passing by on her way to greet her father, easily read the block letters, "Going directly to Cincinnati to get family settled. Midwest tour all summer. No time to stop in NYC."

Pop sat in his red wing chair. Behind his horn-rimmed glasses, his blue eyes looked almost gray with strain. As Elizabeth stooped to kiss his cheek, he asked, "I presume your mother saw this already?"

"I believe so. She was playing Beethoven when I returned home." Father and daughter regarded each other knowingly.

"Not good news for a devoted grandmother. She was looking forward to time with little Dorothy."

"I know, Pop," Elizabeth agreed. Although she missed Cecilia and Dorothy, she felt somewhat relieved that the quiet household to which she gratefully returned after her intensely busy days would not be disturbed.

Pop took off his glasses and rubbed his face with his hands.

"Maybe Dorothy and Cecilia could join us in Quogue for few weeks," Elizabeth proposed, even as she realized she was, once again, trying to rectify the situation. "If Palmer is busy with the tour and such, Cecilia might welcome a visit East."

"Great idea, daughter of mine. They can easily take a train from Cleveland. I'll even offer to pay their way," Pop said. "Let's go cheer your mother up with your idea and eat one of Frannie's splendid dinners."

CHAPTER 19
BOSTON'S DARLING

"What a pleasure to have the Common so close to the theater!" Elizabeth said, twirling her rose-colored parasol overhead. She and Gert walked along under tall oaks and sycamores. The shadowed paths were a welcome contrast to the searing midday sunlight. "I can come over here when we have breaks."

Flushed from the heat and fanning herself, Gert frowned.

"A well-dressed young lady alone in a city park. Not a good idea, Miss," she said. "What your parents would say if they knew I allowed such a thing?"

"Really, Gert," Elizabeth said, "this is mostly a place for families, children, and lovers." She pointed to several families picnicking, a band of boys playing an informal baseball game, and the couple walking ahead of them, arms intertwined. The woman's dark curls and straw hat were cocked toward her companion as if she meant to rest her head on his shoulder. "Besides, I don't need a nursemaid anymore."

Immediately regretting her tone, she put a hand on Gert's arm.

"I'm sorry. I guess I am a bit wound up," she said. "It's different opening in another city where I don't know anyone. Somehow, I always think some friends are in New York audiences."

"I know, Miss E. How about a little sit?"

"Certainly. Let's." Elizabeth reined in her impulse to keep going. Her face moist with perspiration, Gert was flagging after their exploratory walk north from the Copley Square Hotel to the Tremont Theatre. They had agreed that establishing a sense of the distance and time involved in getting to and fro was necessary.

Yesterday's arrival was a tumble of suitcases and hatboxes. For several days, the planning and packing for the unknown period of the show's run and other contingencies had consumed them. After transporting their personal belongings from home and then on and off the train with the help of porters, Elizabeth again felt gratitude for George M., who provided his actors' costumes. It would have been doubly difficult if they'd also had to bring their own costumes as some producers required.

Still Gert's efforts over the last week obviously had worn her out. Elizabeth steered them toward a bench in the shade of a massive copper beach tree. They sat and regarded a summer scene straight out of a Seurat painting. A yellow balloon drifted high above a wide lawn. Ladies in long, pastel skirts and straw hats occupied neighboring benches, some reading while others protectively watched gaggles of children and dogs playing.

Elizabeth wished she could relax as well but anticipatory excitement over the show was too great. She knew her part well after months of practice, but experience taught her that unforeseen problems could flush up in dress rehearsal and opening night. That possibility had her on edge as did George M.'s propensity for making revisions and additions right down to the wire.

He recently pronounced *Nellie Kelly* not merely a musical comedy but a new hybrid form, "A musical play with a love theme, humor, satire, as well as melodrama and mystery all rolled into one." According to the newspapers she thumbed through at breakfast, Boston was aflutter about a new Cohan production. With five days to go before opening night, there were already lines at the ticket booth and talk of sold-out crowds.

"Your tight lips tell me you are worried," Gert interjected. "I am no expert on theater, but I know you, Miss E. Not only a fast learner but a hard worker and talented at that! Mr. Cohan is lucky to have you."

Despite the humidity and heat, Elizabeth leaned into Gert's reassuring solidity and smiled.

"I think I am lucky to have you along, too, Gert."

They sat in silence for several minutes before agreeing that the midday heat was oppressive, and they'd take a taxi back to their hotel. Upon arrival, when Elizabeth asked the lean, tall clerk for the key, he handed her both a key and a big brown envelope with her name on it in George M.'s signature scrawl.

"Oh dear," she said. "I hope this isn't a major revision." Elizabeth manually manipulated the envelope to ascertain the number of pages as the elevator operator in his navy uniform ushered them into his buffed, gleaming dark domain. Their slow, shaky ascent began.

Elizabeth didn't even bother taking off her hat before opening the envelope. Inside was a note from George M.: "Kiddo, they love you already. Thought you'd want to know." He'd enclosed a few press clippings and advertisements. She blushed as she read through them. Several contained the lines, "*Little Nellie Kelly* with Elizabeth Hines, The Sweetest Girl in America On Or Off The Stage." A full-page photo showed her fingering a long string of pearls around her neck. The caption read, "The Limelight Touches Her Golden Hair."

"Good news, Miss E.?" Gert queried as she cracked one of the windows and turned on the electric fan.

"George M. certainly thinks so." Elizabeth sighed. "It feels like more pressure to me, though."

Gert eyed the clippings on the glass coffee table.

"What you mean, Miss E.? That's a lovely photo of you and it's true—you are sweet."

"I don't feel sweet when I finish dancing and singing for three hours. Heavens, all I want then is a glass of water, my shoes off, and to be left alone."

"Seems to me most everyone understands that you or any actor who puts their heart into a performance needs a break afterwards," said Gert, seating herself on a red velvet couch in the small, elegant sitting room.

"I don't know, Gert. Those stage door johnnies waiting in the alley think we should sign their playbills, converse with them, and date them, not to mention reporters who want commentary on everything from skin cream to motor cars," she said. "As if my opinion or preferences are important."

Elizabeth plopped down in an ornate armchair nearby.

"Disposition or looks don't matter so much as how dedicated and tenacious one is in developing one's skills," Elizabeth said. "That's what I'd like to be appreciated for."

"Ain't you lucky then, Miss E., because you have all those qualities and looks to boot!"

"Speaking of sweet, you're a peach, Gert. Good thing I have Palmer, Carl, and George M. to keep me from getting full of myself!"

They laughed as the afternoon light filtered through the sheer curtains, gilding the room.

As Elizabeth predicted, mishaps were inevitable on opening night. Lights unexpectedly dimmed, then flickered, for most of her primary dance number with Charles King as Jerry Conroy, Nellie Kelly's stalwart Bronx boyfriend. A loud crash erupted backstage during the second act when some carelessly stowed backdrop toppled over. It was one of the summer's hottest nights, too, so by the show's end, the theater was sweltering.

Still, nothing dampened the audience's enthusiasm and energy. After every vigorous song and dance number, people clapped and called out praise from the standing-room-only areas, which were filled to capacity.

The reception amazed Elizabeth. Letters and invitations poured into her hotel mailbox. The abundance of flowers in the hotel room became unmanageable.

"How about giving some of these to the chorus ladies?" Gert suggested as the concierge brought another pungent arrangement to their suite—white gardenias interspersed with red poppies and baby's breath. Elizabeth, wearing her favorite blue silk dressing gown, plucked the embossed card accompanying the flowers and added it to the pile of cards on the cocktail table.

"Mercy, we certainly can't fit any more in here or we'll die of floral asphyxiation!" she said. "Still, I hope whoever sent it doesn't find out that we regifted them. I don't know when I'll ever get to responding to all these invitations, let alone writing thank-you notes for the flowers."

"Soon you are going to need a secretary as well as a lady's maid."

"Gert, I don't think of you as that," Elizabeth replied. "Furthermore, I never want to be the kind of person who needs a staff to function."

"I know, Miss E. You're no demanding prima donna nor one of those cotillion debs I read about in *Town Talk*."

"Whatever am I going to do?" Elizabeth said, picking through the cards on the table. "Maybe write a master thank you and then personalize each one with the addition of their name and my signature?"

"Bonny idea!" Gert exclaimed, sitting down on the settee with a sigh. "Fame isn't all that it is cracked up to be. Seems like hard work, day and night."

"Indeed that is true. Thank goodness, I have had and continue to have such excellent training. Keeps me in good physical shape. And you know, Gert, it's important as well to not get too serious. One doesn't want to lose the joyous spirit of musical comedy. It's a balancing act." Yawning, she extended her arms. Her kimono sleeves hung like silk wings as she arched her chest, inhaling deeply.

"Before I tackle these thank-you notes, I owe Joanie a letter."

"You go right ahead. I'll pick up my knitting again. If I don't get to it, my nephew will be in trousers before I finish his baby blanket." Gert shook her head. "They grow so fast."

Elizabeth laughed, shaking her index finger at Gert.

"Now don't you start with the stories about me when I was four."

She walked to the flat top desk, sat down, and pulled her favorite fountain pen and sheets of hotel stationery from the desk drawer.

Dear Joanie,

So far, the show is a great success. Every night sold out for the next three weeks! We've had a full house from the opening night two weeks ago. George M. is thrilled, of course, especially since he says *Nellie Kelly* is his most ambitious project to date. I guess that is both good and bad news; good because it looks as if the show will have a long run and I'll be employed for quite a while, bad because a long run means I will probably have to go on the road, depending on how the show does here in Boston and what happens if and when we open in New York City in the fall. You know what a homebody I am given the chance!

You must be getting excited about the imminent start of your training.

You are going to make such a great teacher. I just know it. As your friend, I learn from you constantly. You're the only person I know our age who reads more than I do and knows so much about a variety of topics.

The rhythmic click of Gert's knitting needles and the fan's cooling breeze soothed Elizabeth. She looked up at the watercolor on the wall over the desk: three sheep grazed in a verdant rolling pasture while a man in overalls leans on a split rail fence and looks off into the distance. The pastoral scene, though common, still was spacious and inviting. As her tight shoulders relaxed, Elizabeth resumed writing:

Boston welcomed me with open arms. I am unsure what I did to receive such a fantastic reception, nor do I know what to do about the number of invitations I've received not to mention the flowers that keep arriving daily. Gert is a great companion and support but she can't be my front guard if you know what I mean. I must learn how to graciously turn down people—difficult because I hate disappointing people! But I can't possibly perform six days, two shows three days a week, and let people wine and dine me as frequently as they want to. I am sure you would have good advice if you were here. Just picturing your face is making me miss you more.

Sounds like our friend, Izzy, is making the most of her time in England since her aunt is not at all as strict as her parents. That art school has quite the mix of characters from her description. I'm sure she told you as well that she wants to stay there for as long as possible. To quote the Bard, "When will we three meet again? In thunder, lightning or in rain?"

I will let you know when the show plans to move to New York. Hopefully, you and I can carve out some time together even with our respectively demanding schedules.

Sorry! This letter is all over the place. I guess it reflects how scattered I feel living in a hotel and working so many hours.

Love to you, John and your parents,

Elizabeth

"Oh dear, what a mess!" Gert exclaimed as the lapis-colored wool ball rolled off the settee and across the room to Elizabeth's feet. Fumbling, she laid her knitting aside to rise and retrieve it.

"No bother, Gert. Here, let me help," Elizabeth offered. She grabbed and wound up the errant ball of yarn. As she skirted the table following the thread, the "Who's Who" column of that day's *Boston Herald* caught her eye. The first line started with the words, "The history of Elizabeth Hines."

"Now what?" she asked, handing the yarn to Gert before picking up that section of the newspaper to scan the column.

"Remember what your Pop says," Gert cautioned. "No one ever built a statue to a critic."

"I suppose it's an okay article. I just wish they'd stop fussing about how tall I am. Listen to this: 'her success—with a height of five feet and a half—is no mean victory when the vogue of teeny-weeny musical stars is at its height.'"

"I guess they have to fill the page with something," Gert said, settling back down on the settee to resume her knitting.

"I suppose you're right about that. I'm going to take a long soak in the tub before tackling some thank-you notes."

Sometimes she imagined taking a long bath as a restorative ritual. All stress and concerns could be washed away, not to mention the beneficial effects on sore legs and feet after many hours of dancing. As the spacious, claw foot tub filled, she added Epsom salts and steam blurred the vanity mirror. Removing her robe, Elizabeth submerged herself into the warm water, sighing with delight and relief.

CHAPTER 21

HOME AGAIN

Fall was in the air. After so many days of performing in Boston's August heat and humidity, Elizabeth luxuriated in the comfort of her own bed and the cool air pervading her bedroom. Outdoors, the milkman delivered his bounty, the glass bottles clanking down on doorsteps. Rickety produce vans creaked along Third Avenue on their morning rounds.

By popular demand, *Little Nellie Kelly* had been extended an extra two weeks in Boston. Meanwhile, George M. booked a New York run at the Liberty Theatre followed by a tour to Washington, DC, Philadelphia, and Chicago. Now that *Little Nellie Kelly* was an established hit, he visited infrequently, preoccupied with creating his next offering to "the amusement business," as he called it.

Elizabeth found herself missing the small, wiry man in his gray derby, swinging his bamboo cane, and, upon entering, calling out to the cast members, "Good day, kiddoes!" Although intimidatingly precise in his artistic demands, his presence was also inspirational and supportive. When George M. was around, they worked more collaboratively, proposed new dance steps, gestures, and even plot edits, which kept the show fresh even after a long run. But lyrics and their musical accompaniment remained his and only his.

Little Nellie Kelly's success freed Elizabeth in unanticipated ways. She'd believed she owed her parents for their emotional and financial investment in her career. Resolution of that debt had been a major motivator. Now that she generated a relatively stable income, she didn't have to rely on their generosity to fulfill most of her needs.

Just in time, she thought. At last night's dinner, Pop, normally low-key and unruffled, had been obviously upset when he predicted, "Patterson's *Daily News* is going to be the end of the *Mail* and several other papers."

"How could that be, dear?" Momma asked.

"These days people like photos, not so much copy. They want to be fed the story quickly and briefly, even if it is half baked."

"But there will still be people who want to know the whole story and will take the time to do so," Momma countered.

Pop, agitated, ran his fingers through his graying hair.

"Time—that's the issue. These days everyone wants to go fast," he said. "There's the quick lunch, the personal automobile, faster trains and planes. The tabloid format delivers news of the day in a digestible format, two columns instead of eight."

Elizabeth occasionally perused issues of the *Daily News* left in the theater's dressing rooms. Although many photos and lead stories were sensationalist and sexist, showing either grisly murders or scantily clad showgirls, cartoons like *Little Orphan Annie* were wonderful. Additionally, there were also features targeting the concerns of women from cooking to childcare and fashion as well as puzzles and contests. She understood why the tabloid appealed to a wide spectrum of the population.

Before her departure for England, Isabelle had mentioned that the *Daily News* was recruiting women reporters and columnists and promising them the same wages they paid the male journalists. Always intrigued by journalism, Elizabeth briefly considered applying though she didn't admit that to her parents, who were footing the cost of her dance classes and vocal training. The blossoming of her musical comedy career further superseded that idea.

Her current income covered almost everything except Gert's salary. Thank goodness, George M. paid for any travel and expenses related to his productions. She hoped that her solvency eased Pop's fiscal pressure although his dinner pronouncement indicated another potential stressor on the horizon.

Elizabeth lazed in bed, musing. Not that she wanted to be an Astor, a Vanderbilt, or even Isabelle, who had to comply with the implicit rules and expectations of New York high society. She believed in graciousness, kindness, and responsibility whereas upper-class social mores and behaviors often seemed more about competition and backbiting. Better to pursue a career even if it meant discipline and hard work.

A quotation from Maurice Maeterlinck, one of her favorite thinkers, came to mind: "Each man has to seek out his own special aptitude for a higher life in the midst of the humble and inevitable reality of daily existence. Other than this, there can be no nobler aim in life."

Still, she wondered, what would it be like to not have to worry about money?

Liberty Theatre, New York City
November 1922

"Why do you have a steamer chair in your dressing room?" asked Tom Keogh, the *Tribune* reporter, as he sat, pen and notepad in hand. His thick, dark, curly hair was long and on the verge of being unkempt. He leaned forward, toward Elizabeth, his alert, blue gaze scanning the room before settling on her.

The quintessential reporter, she thought as she eyed his well-worn, three-piece tweed suit, which looked like he'd been wearing it for days. She had agreed to do the interview at George M.'s request. Apparently, Tom and he were friendly though there was an obvious age disparity: Tom was obviously considerably younger. *Around my age*, she surmised, realizing she felt awkward being alone with him though she could hear the murmurs and sounds of other people nearby.

"It's like this: A couple of years ago I went to Europe, and I was very ill on the voyage over," she said. "Before starting out, I bought this chair, but it was days before I recovered enough to come out on deck and occupy it." He scribbled as she spoke.

Elizabeth cleared her throat. The memories of the miserable ocean crossing had thankfully receded to the back of her mind. Until now.

"When I finally left my stateroom and came out on deck, it was a lovely day and the chair was so comfortable," she added. "I give it a lot of credit for my convalescence. I was determined to keep it and I have. It is just lovely to sit here between my scenes. I carry it around wherever I go. I guess I am sentimental about the old thing."

"Makes perfect sense to me," Tom affirmed. His slow smile softened his square-jawed face. "You dance up a storm in this show. I can imagine you need a little respite whenever you can grab it."

"Yes, that's true. However, when first on stage, I was a dancer before I began acting or singing." Tom regarded her quizzically, his pen poised in midair.

"What I mean to say is that I know how to keep myself in good physical condition," Elizabeth said. "I also don't have to do very strenuous dances like the can-can. George M. loves the waltz and thinks I do it so well, he always includes at least one in his shows."

She chattered on, unaccustomed to such an attentive gaze from a scruffy but handsome man, seemingly around her age, in such close quarters.

"I like to waltz, but I also like the fox trot and the one-step and I just dote on the tango and don't forget, the tango is coming back," she said. "I predict it will soon displace all other kinds and that is going to happen this very winter. What do you think?"

Tom stopped writing and sat up, obviously perplexed.

"Um, well, Miss Hines, I don't know. I don't dance much myself. Besides, I am supposed to ask you the questions."

Realizing he was uncomfortable, Elizabeth changed the subject.

"Okay, here's a little history: I was born in New York City but spent a lot of time in Albany because my grandparents live there. Albany is where Governor Al Smith lives—you know, the one who signed the repeal of the state prohibition law. New Yorkers all love him for that."

"Yes indeed, they do," Tom acknowledged, apparently relieved to move off the subject of dance.

"For a short time after leaving Brearley School, I went to Albany to sing in a choir and took vocal lessons to strengthen my voice."

"How did you come to go with Mr. Cohan?"

"Oh, George M.—we all call him. He is a fine man to work for. He saw me in a play and thought I had talent. I was fortunate that my dance teacher, Carl Hemmer, introduced me to him. George M. said when a suitable part showed up, he would like to have me. That was *The O'Brien Girl*." *Am I talking too much?* she worried. *Should I wait for his questions?* Elizabeth hesitated, then added, "I have been with him ever since."

"Sounds like you see yourself working for Mr. Cohan for a long time?" Tom asked.

"Can't think of anyone else in the theater business I'd rather work for," Elizabeth said. "Why, he told me the other day that he has another part for me—a new play but not a big one like *Little Nellie Kelly*—just a little intimate musical comedy. It will give me a chance to do some real acting and that is my ambition—to be an actress and play a dramatic part."

"That's some news. Do you know the name of the newest play?"

His eagerness for a scoop was evident. Elizabeth found herself a bit disappointed that he seemed more interested in a story than in getting to know her. She wished that she didn't find him attractive.

"No, George M. has not revealed the name yet," she answered.

"Okay. Our readers probably want to know more about who you are offstage." *O, no*, thought Elizabeth. *Here come those stupid questions about my love life, marriage, etc.*

"I prefer not to discuss my private life," she said, firmly. Tom's face flushed.

"Sorry, Miss Hines, I didn't mean to offend. I meant, how do you enjoy spending time when you're not working?"

"I guess you could say my life is the theater," she replied. "Pretty much everything I am interested in relates to it in some way. When I am not in rehearsal or a show, I am studying or practicing in one form or another: languages lessons, singing or dance lessons, calisthenics to maintain flexibility and strength. Swimming in a pool or the ocean, which I love to do, also keeps my lungs and body fit. Even attending the opera or another play, which I do as often as I can, is also a form of learning and inspires me in how I approach a character, a song, or a dance."

"What you're saying makes me think of an athlete. For example, the best tennis players spend hours practicing their game and off-hours preparing their bodies and minds for the next tournament." He reflected, leaning towards her. "I guess I never thought of your profession in quite that way before."

Really? What did you think? She was defensive about her chosen career. The public tended to view actresses as opportunists waiting to entrap and marry rich benefactors so they could gain wealth and social standing. Tom was smiling at her now, revealing straight white teeth and a dimple, further enhancing his good looks about which he seemed oblivious.

"Beauty doesn't account for much if you're going to have a long career in this business," Elizabeth declared. "Talent helps but dedication and hard work are the keys. Without them, one's career will flounder."

"How does it feel to be a real star?" She couldn't help chuckling.

"I am not quite used to it yet so I cannot tell you," Elizabeth said. "So far, it doesn't make any difference, except that I am being interviewed for the first time and I don't know what to say. You see, I have no theories or convictions that I want to impress upon the public. I have only been on the stage four years, and during this time I've been working so hard, I have not done much thinking about it.

"The thing that appeals to me most about the stage is the atmosphere—the spirit of joyousness, which I suppose is the proper spirit for musical comedy. It is a good thing to lighten the burden of the public and make people forget the humdrum existence of life. People come to the theater to be cheered and to forget their troubles. If musical comedy can do that, it is accomplishing a praiseworthy task—and I try my best to do my part in this, I assure you, and I enjoy it."

"So, if I hear you correctly, Miss Hines, you believe that musical comedy can be somewhat of an antidote for life's difficulties." Tom scratched his head, his fingernails ragged, short, and obviously bitten. There was something about him, a low-level insecurity, that evoked Elizabeth's empathy.

"I suppose you could say it that way although I don't want to come across as minimizing what people have to deal with these days. Look at what we've all had to deal with since I first got on the stage—The Great War and its aftereffects, a worldwide pandemic, huge increases in immigration as well as unemployment, labor strikes, and now Prohibition, which is encouraging an increase in crime and violence. That's not counting whatever personal difficulties people have to face. Yessiree, people could use a little laughter, song, and dance to lighten their loads!"

Musical comedy was her form of activism, she realized, as she sat quietly while Tom scribbled in the crumbled notebook on his knee. He tapped his pen with a flourish when he finished and looked up.

"You are impressive, Miss Hines—talented, beautiful and thoughtful as well. I think this interview will communicate that to our readers and I thank you for your time." He stuffed his notepad in his pocket, tucked his pen in his shirt pocket, grabbed his hat, and stood up.

"I wish you well and hope our paths cross again," Elizabeth said, as she, too, stood. She offered her hand, which he willingly took with his ink-stained fingers.

"It has been a real pleasure," he said, bowing slightly over her hand.

1922–1925

CHAPTER 23
THE TRANSITION

Little Nellie Kelly had three more shows before completing its popular two-year American tour at the National Theater in Washington, DC. Elizabeth eagerly anticipated returning home and enjoying at least a month off. As she and Gert organized their belongings, their hotel suite grew crowded with open suitcases and boxes waiting to be filled.

"Says here this play was the longest running of all Mr. Cohan's productions," Gert said, tapping the newspaper she was reading during a packing break. "If you count the upcoming London production, nine months longer than any other Cohan show."

"I believe it!" Elizabeth said, rubbing cod liver oil into her aching feet as Mr. Hemmer had advised her. It reduced inflammation. "It seems like we've been gone forever. I can't wait to sleep in my own bed and eat some of Frannie's good cooking."

"Yes, Miss E. My little blue bedroom will feel mighty good after the places we've been."

"Some of them quite uncomfortable," Elizabeth replied, remembering their dark, musty rooms in Philadelphia and Chicago and a succession of tight quarters on overnight trains.

"Good thing you wired Mr. Cohan when you did else we might have had dreary lodgings here, too."

"Thank you, Gert. That *was* difficult! I don't like to be demanding, as you know, but I think his manager, Mr. Vion, was scrimping. God knows why since it was such a popular show. In fact, I question whether George M. even knew what was going on."

"I bet you're right, Miss. E.," Gert said, nodding. "That telegram he sent you in response pointed in that direction. What was it he said?"

Elizabeth, somewhat fearful of George M.'s reaction to her complaints, had repeatedly reread the Western Union telegram upon its arrival. She could recite it from memory: "I am very sorry you are unhappy and if you are really unhappy enough to want to go with some other management, I certainly would not stand in your way. As you know, I want you to be happy. God bless you." Thinking aloud, Elizabeth continued. "It's not that I want to leave George M. It's just that he—"

"He's not around much. Once a show is up and running, he's onto other shows, right?" Gert asked as she enfolded one of Elizabeth's dresses with tissue paper before carefully laying it in a large, brown leather suitcase. "That man is always in motion."

"Yes, he's always been a bit that way," Elizabeth said, "but I wonder if quitting acting like he did, to oppose the Actors'

Equity Union, led to the way he operates now. When I first started working for him, he was much more hands on through an entire run. I wouldn't consider any other offer if things were the way they were then." She sighed in exasperation.

"Didn't he break with his best friend over that situation?" Gert asked.

"Yes. Sam Harris. You may remember that letter about *The O'Brien Girl* that Mr. Harris sent me when you and I were in Boston. Anyway, Mr. Harris was on the side of Equity. Some say George M. felt personally betrayed when the actors' strike briefly closed his theater in 1919. He vowed then to defeat his fellow actors."

"What a shame! As my Da says, politics aren't good for most anyone." Gert straightened up and turned. Her plump face was soft with concern. "Miss E., you need to make your own decisions about what next steps are best for you, not for any producer—not even for George M."

The day before they left Washington, Pop telegrammed Elizabeth to meet him beside the information desk in Grand Central Station. True to his word, he waved heartily as she and Gert crossed into the cathedral-like atrium, a red-coated porter trailing behind them as he pushed a cart piled with their luggage. A tawny-haired sylph of a girl stood next to Pop. She waved shyly.

"Why, isn't that Dorothy, Miss E.?" Gert exclaimed.

"I think so but I haven't seen her in a couple of years. My, she is going to be taller than I am soon!"

When the two women drew close, Dorothy curtsied to Elizabeth as if she was royalty. Pop enthusiastically hugged Elizabeth and then sandwiched Gert's hand between both of his.

"Thank you, Gertie, for watching over our girl." He hesitated. "I guess I can't call you a girl anymore, Elizabeth. My apologies. This is the girl in the family now." He placed an arm around Dorothy's thin shoulders. "What a lucky man I am to have such feminine talent and beauty around me!" He beamed as he put his other arm around Elizabeth, squeezing them both against his navy overcoat.

"Oh Pop-pop," Dorothy said, muffling a giggle as she looked up adoringly at her grandfather.

Dorothy's obvious reverence and affection for Pop reminded Elizabeth of her younger self. How she had looked to up to him. But how could this be? Cecilia and Dorothy lived in Akron while Palmer and his company toured nine months of the year. Pop and Dorothy didn't see much of each other.

Pop's hair had grayed considerably in the past six months. He seemed strained, as if he was pushing himself to be cheerful despite circumstances, whatever they were. As he shepherded them and the porter to the Forty-Second Street exit, through throngs of people in motion, Elizabeth reflected anew on the consuming effects of being in a long-running touring show. She had lost track of how her family was faring.

Later, in the cozy confines of her bedroom, Elizabeth, hands behind her head, lay stretched out on her bed, wondering what the truth was. Her parents explained that Dorothy resided with them because Cecilia wanted a better education for her daughter than Akron offered. Meanwhile, Cecilia remained in the Midwest until spring when she would journey to New York on her way to England to visit family.

There was limited mention of Palmer, who apparently was wintering in Tampa and performing at the Rialto Theater with his newly formed troupe of players, The Palmer Hines Musical Company.

Dorothy must miss her parents terribly, Elizabeth speculated. Stability and a good education are important, but at what cost? The once bubbly, playful child seemed unnaturally quiet and reserved. Maybe there will be time for me to get to know Dorothy, show her fun places like the Natural History Museum and the aquarium. I can be like a big sister to her.

The avalanche of unopened mail heaped on Elizabeth's desk tempered that appealing thought. *Ah, yes, but the proverbial show must go on, whatever show it was going to be!* Pop had received several offers from producers other than George M. over the last month. They had yet to discuss them. He wanted her to have a few weeks off to relax before committing to another show. At times, though she yearned to either hire or be her own manager, she felt grateful for his protective prudence.

CHAPTER 24
FIRST ENCOUNTER

On the first day of rehearsal for *Marjorie*, a new Krakeur and Shubert collaboration scheduled for a September opening, Elizabeth literally collided with Roy Royston in the theater corridor. His glittering chestnut brown eyes and handsome face reminded her of a watercolor of an elfin king from her childhood book on Irish mythology. He impulsively grabbed her hands.

"I am so sorry. I cannot believe I almost injured my dance partner before we even had a chance to practice."

"I am fine," she assured him, not wanting to extract her hands from his warm grip.

"Oh, heavens me!" He dropped her hands self-consciously. "I am not myself. I feel like the proverbial fish out of water. This is my first time in the States and on Broadway, to boot." Elizabeth couldn't help but smile.

"I can only imagine what it is like for you to come here," she said. "I know how I feel when I have an out-of-town engagement with actors I don't know in an unknown theater."

"Thank you for understanding," he said, studying her. "Although I feel quite lost in this frenzied city, I promise I won't let you down on stage."

"I'd be happy to show you around when we have some time," she said, though she could scarcely believe that she offered. Usually a day off was sacrosanct for pampering and quiet, unscheduled time.

The rehearsal bell rang. Chorus members jostled them as they scurried to their places. Realizing she was on the wrong side of the stage for her entrance, Elizabeth gave his arm a little squeeze and fled.

"That would be lovely," he called out in his clipped British accent.

The moment he stepped into the footlights, she realized Roy was a consummate pro. Without direction, he constantly repositioned himself to optimize visibility of his fellow actors. Even during more rigorous dance numbers, he adeptly partnered with her as if nonverbally listening to her. He never insisted on leading, as so many male actors did. As a result, Elizabeth relaxed. She let her whole body inhabit her part. His line delivery was seamless, too. Not once did he step on her lines or rush delivery of his own.

At the break Elizabeth stepped outside the alley door to catch a breath of spring air. She found Roy alone, leaning against a brick wall, smoking.

"Care for one?" He offered his dented, scratched silver cigarette case.

"I'd love one but I try not to smoke when I am performing, to protect my voice as best I can."

Amid the smell of gasoline and smoke, a faint flowery fragrance lingered. Strange. She couldn't recall seeing any flowers blooming.

"I smell it, too," he said, stepping alongside her. Silently, they stood side by side, facing the street.

"I'd guess it's those purple flowers. What are they called? My mum grows them in her garden back home."

"You mean hyacinths?" She turned to face him.

"That's it, hy-a-cinth," he said, wistfully. "A nice name for a flower." She wondered if he was homesick. The side door burst open, and the chorus girls poured into the alley, laughing and chattering hastily pulling out cigarettes and lighters.

"Sorry to interrupt your tête-à-tête," said Ethel Shutta, Elizabeth's female costar, running her hand through her damp curls. "We all needed a little pick-me-up. Seems like we've danced for hours." She beamed, then took a long draw on her cigarette.

"By the way, your waltz together was wonderful," she said. "Easy to see why the producers want a waltz number, especially when they have you as one of the leads, Elizabeth." She winked, then turned her attention to Roy. "You're pretty smooth yourself for a former Air Force fella." Somehow, Roy's military service and honors were common knowledge among the troupe members.

"Well, ah, thank you, miss. I'm sorry. I haven't memorized everyone's name yet."

"Call me Ethel. Last name's Shutta. Welcome to the U S of A. We'll have to take you out on the town some night and show you the sights. After all, you're in the city that never sleeps, as they say."

"I say. I am getting some very nice sightseeing offers. I think I'll enjoy being a tourist when I am not working." He grinned at both women.

As the weeks sped by, Elizabeth found herself looking forward to her exchanges with Roy between rehearsals, and dance and vocal classes. She even enjoyed their daily greetings and small talk during breaks and after rehearsal. Although usually disinclined, she joined cast members for post-rehearsal snacks several evenings around a big table at Sardi's where the cast discussed everything from the latest salacious gossip to Prohibition's side effects, such as the rise of bootleggers, speakeasies, and organized crime.

Inevitably, Roy positioned himself on a chair adjacent to hers, his bright eyes following the lively conversation, then periodically fixing on Elizabeth, who remained mostly silent, carefully listening. Roy, being the only British cast member, received a fair amount of ribbing from the other actors, which he parried good-naturedly. When Andrew Tombes bestowed the nickname "Limey" on him, Roy just laughed and corrected his costar.

"You can't refer to me as Limey," he said. "Limeys are sailors originally named for the lime juice they drank to stave off scurvy. I was a pilot."

He also coined the term "Yankee mania" for the American work ethic, which he found absurdly demanding.

"We take things easier at home and seem to get about the same results," he confided to Elizabeth as they strolled to Sardi's after a particularly long, grueling rehearsal. "Don't get me wrong. I am thrilled to be acting in America, especially on Broadway and with the likes of you, sweet Elizabeth!"

Elizabeth didn't know how to respond. As her past four years on the stage had taught her, men tended to be overtly flirtatious with actresses as if such behavior was expected and acceptable. Roy's comments, however, were earnest and personal. He expressed admiration and affection without coming across as lecherous.

She quickly grabbed and squeezed his hand, dropping it before anyone noticed. She had a pact with herself to avoid romantic entanglements with coworkers and maintain her professionalism, no matter what her fellow actors did. As the weeks went on, though, it was increasingly difficult to maintain distance from Roy.

"A charmer": that's what Ethel Shutta called him. *Disarming*, thought Elizabeth, her cheeks flushing as they did whenever she was caught off-guard.

After Roy and Elizabeth discovered their mutual love of choral music, she invited him to Sunday services at Saint Bartholomew's to hear the choir that Pop, as choirmaster, conducted. Roy then attended every Sunday service on his own recourse and ended up meeting her entire family, with the exception of Palmer.

Momma warmed to Roy and encouraged him to come for their traditional post-church lunch one Sunday in early May. When Frannie learned that Elizabeth's acting partner was British, she went to great lengths to prepare a "proper English meal," which she announced as she plunked a large silver bowl of steaming lamb stew on the table. She also set an "English-style trifle pudding" on the sideboard for their dessert.

After lunch, to Elizabeth's surprise and chagrin, Momma insisted that they gather around the piano to sing Verdi's quartet, "Bella figlia dell'amore," while she played the melody and sang her part. Roy didn't miss a beat, deftly assuming the tenor part to Elizabeth's soprano. Dorothy, the sole audience member, obviously delighted, clapped vigorously when they finished.

"When he was your age, your father was our tenor," Momma informed her granddaughter. "We sang together after every Sunday lunch."

"Was Dad as good as Roy?" Dorothy asked, always interested in anything to do with her father.

"Your father was young and inexperienced, dear," Momma said. "Roy is a professional. We can't really compare them." She closed the piano lid, signaling the end of the afternoon's merriment.

"What fun! Quite the musical family!" Roy remarked as Elizabeth walked him to the front door afterwards.

"Yes, we are, except for Dorothy, who can't or maybe refuses to have anything to do with producing music."

"Too much competition, perhaps?" Roy offered. "If I was her age, I would be a bit intimidated by the likes of you all."

"I suppose. She loves to paint and write so maybe that will be her route."

Closing the heavy door behind him, she realized the familiarity and ease she experienced with Roy was pleasurable and also unsettling.

CHAPTER 25
CLARITY AND CONFESSION

Elizabeth and Joanie lunched on cucumber sandwiches in the small garden in the back of the Farwells' stately Park Avenue home. They sat under a trellis draped with fragrant, purple wisteria blossoms. Potted red, pink, and yellow dahlias festively contrasted the dark ivy-covered walls. An abundance of fruit weighed down each apple tree in the two far corners.

"I forgot how lovely it is back here!" Elizabeth exclaimed. "It's your own secret garden in the middle of the city!"

"It has been a long time since we sat here together. We've both been so busy," Joanie said. "Upholding Mr. John Dewey's teaching standards is rigorous and time consuming. Still, I agree with what he says—how teachers must help students develop reflective, ethical minds and imbue them with the skills necessary for contemporary life. Perhaps being an authoritarian teacher who demands docile compliance might be easier, but I so enjoy the lively debates my students have."

Although Joanie's patrician face was wan and gaunt, her blue eyes shone fervently as she said, "I want to be a teacher who inspires, not dictates."

"I don't think you could be anything but an inspirational teacher. Good thing you got a placement in a school aligned with Dewey's ideas."

"Sometimes I think I am only one step ahead of my students. When I am not in the classroom, I read and study. Still, they catch me off-guard. The other day, a student remarked that Jane Austin would have preferred to have her clothes designed by Coco Chanel." Joanie laughed aloud.

"Oh my! How did you respond to that?" Elizabeth asked. "I wouldn't have any idea what to do."

"We are supposed to encourage students to develop both occupationally and intellectually," Joanie said, "so I invited her to design a Chanel wardrobe for her favorite literary heroine and present it to the class."

"Brilliant, my friend." Elizabeth clapped.

"But enough about me. How is life as an ingenue? Your name or photo is in every newspaper I pick up these days."

"Is it that bad? I don't read reviews or society gossip to avoid getting upset. The rumors are ridiculous. Why, I'd be married to at least three leading men so far if the speculations were true! Besides, mixing work and romance has never been my style, lately, though, I don't know. It's just that—" She trailed off and then found herself confiding in Joanie about Roy. Revealing her confusion to her friend clarified her growing affection for him. It was as if a storm-ridden, murky lake was calmed and each stone on the lake bottom suddenly became visible.

"You've done nothing wrong, Elizabeth. For heaven's sake, your feelings make absolute sense to me. He sounds very intriguing. Besides, you work so much, where else are you going to meet anyone appropriate? And I don't mean appropriate by your mother's standards."

"He seems to have won over Momma as well. A mixed blessing, I'd say. Fun, but also fear producing." Elizabeth sipped her iced tea. "It's odd how comfortable I feel with him, both on and off the stage."

"Sounds lovely. Men I find physically attractive aren't the ones I enjoy spending time with," said Joanie, a slight frown gathering on her face. "I keep dodging invitations. The other day brother John accused me of being a teetotaling hermit because I prefer to remain in the city rather than trek up to Westport and attend yet another party with his Ivy League friends."

"For heaven's sake! I would have thought John understood that his sister wants to have a career first and foremost. He always seemed like a modern thinker." Elizabeth sputtered in exasperation.

"At this point, though, I don't see how I could fit anything more or anyone into my schedule and you—well, I am just grateful we carved some time together. By the way, what *is* The Marjorie Walk?"

Elizabeth flushed at Joanie's question. "Oh that. After the dress rehearsal, some reviewer coined that term for the walk I adapted for my role. I thought Marjorie Daw needed a distinctive walk the more she comes into herself, especially as she begins to fall in love with Roy's character, Brian Valcourt, and realizes her dilemma. She wants this man to love her, but for that to be ultimately possible, she has to admit her duplicity to him."

"Wonderful. You actually get to act this time."

"Yes, that's true. Much as I loved George M., his direction was always about capturing his vision with the emphasis on his songs and dances. Mr. Lemaire and Mr. Krakeur like their leads to participate in the creation of their roles. I guess you could say they are more collaborative than directorial."

"I can't wait to see it," Joanie said. "We reserved tickets for the whole family the Friday after next."

"Good. By then all the kinks should be worked out."

"I want to see this Roy fellow in action." Joanie added, smiling.

"I think you'll find he stands out as a performer," Elizabeth said, wondering why she hadn't yet introduced Roy to Joanie. She changed the topic. "It will probably be sweltering since it is August. Hopefully, the play will be a good distraction from the heat."

"If only it could be a day like today, clear, not humid or hot."

"Yes, that would be good. I wish I could spend the rest of the afternoon in your garden," Elizabeth said, enjoying the light breeze wafting across her bare arms. "However, I need to pick up the fabric I ordered for a dress I want to make."

"You still make your own clothes?"

"When I have an idea and get a bit of time to sketch it out and sew. I find it relaxing."

"I suppose, although sewing never relaxes me. Give me a good novel and a comfortable chair."

"Do you want to come with me on my errands?" Elizabeth suggested. "We'd have some more time together."

"If I wasn't so fatigued from days of standing at a blackboard, I would." Joanie stifled a yawn with her hand. "Just need a few more days of rest, I guess."

"Let me take in our dishes," Elizabeth offered. "You stay put." Her friend's pallor and obvious fatigue worried her. She carefully placed their dishes and cups on the silver tray for transport to the kitchen. After kissing Joanie on the cheek, she left the serene garden sanctuary.

CHAPTER 26
THE NIGHTMARE

New York City
October 1924

Elizabeth didn't get to introduce Roy to Joanie. Every day was crowded with interviews and charity fundraisers requesting Elizabeth for a dance or song, each one a good cause she couldn't refuse. Additionally, sellout crowds forced the show to move in September from the Shubert Theatre to the more capacious Forty-Fourth Street Theatre for a six-month run.

One early October Wednesday Elizabeth, home for a few hours between engagements, rifled through the mail stack on her desk when Momma appeared in the doorway.

"Elizabeth, dear, I need to speak to you."

"Certainly, Momma." Elizabeth shifted her chair to face her mother whose brown eyes looked troubled. "Is something wrong?" Momma crossed the room to sit on the bed.

"It's about Joanie."

"What do you mean?" Elizabeth asked, her throat suddenly constricting.

"If I remember correctly, you mentioned she hadn't been feeling well when you two lunched together recently."

"Yes, she told me it was just fatigue from the demands of her teaching practicum. She—"

"I had a long conversation with Mrs. Farwell. Apparently, doctors now think she shows signs of tuberculosis. They recommended the healing cottages in Saranac Lake for a cure. Her parents made arrangements and traveled up there with her last weekend to get her situated."

The news knocked Elizabeth's breath out of her body.

"But she . . . I didn't . . . oh, it's—" Her crying interrupted her speech. "It's not fair, Momma!"

"I know, dear, this is a terrible shock," Momma said, moving closer to Elizabeth to stroke her grieving daughter's hair. Elizabeth let herself lean into her mother, welcoming her familiar rose scent as her fears and regrets began to spin.

"Momma, Joanie loved teaching. What does this mean? Will she ever recover? What if she can't . . . if she . . . " Elizabeth barely mouthed the word "dies." Voicing her worst fear sent her into intense weeping.

"There, there, she may recover. There's much they don't know yet about TB and the disease's course. The Farwells hope getting her treatment quickly will restore her immune system and Joanie will avoid the worst effects."

"I didn't get to say goodbye. How long is she going to be there?" Elizabeth asked. "Can I visit?"

"I'm afraid not, Elizabeth. The risk of exposure is too great. It's lucky that you were outdoors last time you were together."

"Oh, Momma, what can I do?" Elizabeth said, choking. "She's my best friend. I have to do something."

"It is certainly a time for prayers for Joanie and I am sure she would welcome letters as frequently as you can write them."

"Yes, but I want to do more," Elizabeth sputtered.

"Of course you do, and I bet Joanie knows that. However, there isn't much that any of us can do," Momma said. She held Elizabeth at arm's length by the shoulders. "We have to place our faith in the Almighty."

Momma's brown eyes radiated empathy yet firmness. Elizabeth knew better than to voice her personal ambivalence about God's existence to her mother. Why would God infect Joanie with tuberculosis in the first place? How *did* one account for suffering and tragedies? If it was God's will, as she had been taught, God didn't seem at all merciful. Elizabeth sat upright, took the embroidered handkerchief Momma offered, and wiped her tear-soaked face.

"Can I get you anything or do anything for you?" Momma asked.

Elizabeth's mind felt garbled, her body hollowed out by sadness and concern. Initially, a head shake was her only response. Momma resumed her seat on the bed and waited for Elizabeth to contain her tears.

"Does Papa know?"

"Yes. I told him right after I spoke with Joanie's mother. We didn't want to tell you after a show so late at night."

"Momma," Elizabeth said, "I don't believe I can perform tonight." Her admission sparked more tears, which she dabbed while struggling to speak. "How could I make others happy when I am so upset? I can't pretend like I had to, like we all had to, during the Spanish flu. Besides, Joanie is my very best friend."

"I understand, Elizabeth. Due to situations like this, theater producers train understudies as well as leads."

"I've never ever taken a night off."

"I know, but there are times when that is necessary. I can phone your father at work and he can explain to Mr. Lemaire. I am certain Mr. Lemaire knows you would only skip a night under the most extreme circumstance."

"I suppose. The show is going well, especially now that we're in a bigger venue, but I hate to disappoint anyone."

"Wouldn't you hate it more if you got up on stage and realized you couldn't go through with it? This way at least the troupe has time to adjust and maybe practice a little."

"Yes, that's true."

"There, that's settled," Momma said as she stood up. "I will let your father know. He will be glad to do something to help. How about I see if Frannie can muster up something delicious for later?"

"I don't know. I don't feel much like eating."

"Take it easy, dearie. Maybe you'll be hungry by dinner. I'll be in the den if you need me." She shut the door softly behind her. Elizabeth blankly stared out the window.

★ ★ ★

When Elizabeth arrived at the theater two nights later, Roy was waiting outside the alley door, his normally cheerful face pinched with concern.

"Are you feeling better, my dear?" he asked.

"Not really. The problem isn't physical." She hesitated, feeling her grief rise. "I received some bad news about my dear friend, Joanie." Roy waited for her to continue. She teared up. "Best not talk about it before the show."

"All right but I'd like to help anyway I can." He pressed her hand in his before opening the door for her.

The theater bustled with the usual pre-performance fervor. Everyone dashed to and fro, readying themselves and the stage. Elizabeth was grateful people barely acknowledged her entrance since she currently lacked the capacity for witty greetings or chatter. She proceeded to her dressing room. Closing the door, she methodically removed and hung up her street clothes, donned her costume, and applied makeup for the first act.

The night off hadn't helped much. Throughout the evening, during every brief interlude, Joanie came to mind. *Marjorie*'s gaiety and humor seemed frivolous compared to the crisis her friend faced. Elizabeth felt like a wind-up doll that automatically sang and danced when required. Whenever Roy took her in his arms for a dance number, he whispered encouragingly. Ethel Shutta stayed protectively close to Elizabeth's side when they were backstage, ensuring that she didn't have to interact much.

The barrage of flowers delivered to Elizabeth's dressing room after the show felt oppressive. After changing, she collected the gift cards, stuffed them into her purse, and wondered if she would ever have the motivation to respond. Roy tapped four times, signaling his presence outside her closed door.

"Can I accompany you home?" he asked. "Thought you might need a friendly ear and an arm to lean on."

They made their way to the curb where Patrick, her driver, burnished the Model T's black finish with a white towel, a lit cigarette dangling from his mouth. Broadway's nightly ordinarily thrilling parade of multicolored lights and blinking signs irked Elizabeth. Relaxing in the back seat, she was relieved to feel Roy's arm around her shoulders. As the car headed north, he didn't push her to talk. Instead, he exchanged a few words with Patrick about the recent World Series and the fate of the Giants. She admired Roy's ability to converse with everybody, even on relatively unfamiliar subjects like baseball. *He puts everyone at ease*, she thought, closing her eyes and nestling into him.

After they quietly entered the darkened Hines family apartment, Roy insisted on making them tea.

"Some like a dram of good whiskey but I think a properly made cuppa eases the soul better," he said. "Have a seat." He followed her directives to locate tea accoutrements and moving around carefully to avoid waking anyone in the household. Elizabeth couldn't help but smile. She had never seen a man negotiate their warm, aromatic kitchen.

"There you have it, my dear." He set down a tray with two cups, saucers, spoons, sugar, and a porcelain teapot and sat opposite her.

Elizabeth poured them both cups and took several sips, appreciating the sweet milky flavor before confiding her fears about Joanie. Roy drank his tea, too, and listened intently. He did not interrupt her with questions or offer platitudes. When she finished, he reached for both her hands and held them gently in his.

"No wonder you are upset!" he exclaimed. "I am amazed how well you were able to perform tonight, considering this situation."

"You know I can't imagine what I will say in letters to her. I mean I am out here living life and she's confined and facing—" Unable to continue, Elizabeth stopped abruptly, tears welling in her eyes.

"What you feel seems similar to my experience after almost every mission during the war," Roy said. "I'd return, relieved to be intact and alive, only to learn another plane in our unit was downed and the fate of guys I knew was unknown. One could only imagine the worst."

"How did you go on?"

"At first it was difficult. There were so many losses." Roy seemed momentarily far away, his eyes fixed on something beyond her vision. He hadn't spoken of his war experience at length with her or, as far as Elizabeth knew, anyone else. Suddenly, she was aware of the gravity of what he had lived through and how seamless his jaunty public façade really was.

"I watched one of my best friends burn to death. We were getting shelled. His plane caught fire. He couldn't eject—probably tangled in the harness. I was flying alongside him."

As they held hands, acknowledging one another's sorrow, the ticking wall clock was the only sound. Roy cleared his throat.

"At some point," he continued, "I asked myself how my missing comrades would want me to be living. The answer was not in the alternating states I'd immersed myself in for the first year—self-destructiveness and profound grief. I had to live fully precisely because they couldn't."

"Are you advising me to the same regarding Joanie?"

"Yes, to a degree. I don't know Joanie, but I imagine since she's your best friend, she wants the best for you. Furthermore, it won't do her any good if you refuse to flourish." He pointed at the clock. "Now it is time for you to get your rest. I won't say beauty rest because you are beautiful regardless of whether you're tired or not." He grinned.

"Oh, my, it's two o'clock and tomorrow is Wednesday!" Elizabeth exclaimed.

"Yes, two shows, the longest of days," Roy said, yawning. "I best be heading out."

He stood up and bent over the table to kiss her forehead.

"The show—" he began.

"—must go on," she finished.

★ ★ ★

Elizabeth stared at the blaze in the den's fireplace, hoping for inspiration. Several balled-up pages of white stationery lay on the table in front of her. All her attempts to compose a letter to Joanie had been futile. She kept imagining how Joanie felt, torn away from her life, confined indefinitely, her body inhabited by a potentially deadly disease. Not to mention she must be witnessing the travails of other patients.

Gert's stout frame appeared in the doorway.

"Brrr. That's one raw November day out there, Miss E.," she said. "Best bundle up if you are thinking of going out."

"I am staying in. It's been ten days since Momma told me the bad news and I still haven't written Joanie."

"I know but you've prayed and thought of her every day," Gert said. "Besides, she knows how demanding your schedule is when you're the lead in a popular show."

"That's no excuse," Elizabeth sputtered. "What has she got to look forward to up there? I should be writing as often as possible."

Gert stood in front of Elizabeth, her hands on her hips.

"Look here, Miss E. It's not going to help Joanie one bit if you stay sad and sicken yourself."

"I wish Izzy was home," Elizabeth said. "Maybe she and I could figure out the best thing to do for Joanie."

"Izzy is one for ideas, that's for certain." Gert affirmed. "She's full of lofty ideas but I'm not sure how she'd be with a situation like this. Might be good to let her know, though. Can't imagine how she'd find out any other way being as her parents don't associate with the Farwells except for the occasional charity event."

Gert's knowledge of New York's social order always surprised Elizabeth. Once she had asked Gert how she knew so much only to find out there was a lively communication network among staff members of various households, many of whom were Irish. They convened at Sunday mass and, in nicer weather, on benches in Central Park, sharing stories as they watched over their charges skipping rope and playing ball. Elizabeth sighed.

"I don't know where to start, Gert. I don't want to make her feel worse about missing things."

"Why don't you just pretend she's in the room with you? Like you two were just chatting. I'll bring you a tray of tea and some of Frannie's cookies like I do when she visits. Frannie has been teaching Dorothy how to make those oatmeal raisin cookies you like. The girl loves baking. She wants to know all Frannie's recipes, copies them down in a notebook."

"I haven't been a very good aunt these last few weeks either."

"Don't worry. Dorothy knows about Joanie. She won't take it personal that her auntie has been distracted. Now you relax. I'll be right back with some goodies to help prime the pump, as my dear old Da used to say."

After Gert returned with a tray, stoked the fire, and left, Elizabeth conjured Joanie sitting opposite her, her long legs tucked up in the big red armchair she preferred. She began to craft another letter.

Dearest Joanie,

I was and am still shocked by the news of your diagnosis. I can only imagine that you were as well. What an adjustment you must be undergoing! I wish I could be of some help through this travail. Letters seem so unsubstantial, but Momma told me that visits are prohibited. I will have to make do with words and memories of our times together until we can sit together again, perhaps in front of a warm fire in our den, where I am currently.

Yes, with eight shows weekly, interviews, and charity events, time is once again a scarce commodity, but that doesn't excuse me. I promise I will write weekly, if not more. Also, I can send care packages, Frannie's scones perhaps? Anything else you'd like? Is this allowed? Momma didn't ask your mother.

It must be very cold up there in Saranac Lake because it is chilly here. Gert tells me I must bundle up before I leave for tonight's performance. By the way, you were so right about playing Marjorie Daw. It is a chance to truly act. As the show proceeds, I find myself deepening her character by adding a gesture or verbal expression or assuming a different posture at times. A few reviewers have even commented favorably. The other night Roy said I glowed (his words, not mine) when I stepped on stage. Of course, I know he's a bit biased and tends towards exaggeration. Anyway, I would love your input, but I guess I'll have to wait until another show comes along next year and you are fully recovered.

All is well here. Momma continues giving her piano lessons. Now that I have a motorcar and driver, thanks to the Shuberts, Pop is back to his usual hours at the paper although there is talk of possible new ownership. Dorothy is attending Brearley and loves it. Apparently, her school in Ohio was terrible and now that Cecilia decided to stay put in England after her family visit there, Dorothy will live with us.

Palmer and his troupe winter in Tampa at the Rialto Theatre so he's unavailable. I guess divorce is in the picture though we don't speak of it, mostly for Dorothy's sake. Gert and Frannie keep the household running smoothly, bless them!

I hope to hear from you but completely understand if you don't have the energy to write. You must concentrate on your healing and whatever protocols they advise you to follow. Perhaps you can let your mother know what you'd like me to send in addition to regular letters. I will make sure to telephone her now that she has returned.

Much love to you, Elizabeth

To stop herself from editing the letter further, Elizabeth folded it into an already addressed envelope and rewarded herself by munching on a cookie and sipping her tea. Afternoon shadows already stretched across the wide oak flooring beams though it was just two o'clock. The sky, visible from the den window, was the peculiar pearl color that Elizabeth associated with New York winter. The holidays were just around the corner. She promised Roy to accompany him to the inaugural Macy's parade and show him the holiday window displays at Saks, Bergdorf's, and Altman's, but her usual enthusiasm for holiday festivities was lacking. Everything felt precarious and unpredictable.

CHAPTER 27
SCANDAL

"When were you going to tell us?" asked Pop, gesticulating to the newspaper he held. Elizabeth, sleepy and yawning, was jarred awake by her parents' palpable upset as she entered the dining room. They sat at the table, rigidly expectant. Neither had touched their sumptuous Sunday breakfast of scrambled eggs, sausages, fried potatoes, toast, and grilled tomatoes.

"I don't know what you are talking about," Elizabeth replied.

"This!" Pop held up the *Tribune* and pointed to a headline, "Lovebirds on Stage and In Life," accompanied by a caricature of Elizabeth and Roy, intertwined, gazing adoringly at one another. "The article says you and Roy are engaged," sputtered Pop while Momma shook her head and looked down at her hands.

"What!?" Elizabeth, now fully awake, reached for the paper and scanned the column, which claimed that she and Roy were engaged and soon to marry. The author also speculated that the couple probably would elope to avoid public scrutiny. "Jeepers, where in the world? Who started this rumor?" Elizabeth slapped the paper down, narrowly missing the steaming teapot and rattling the cups. "I hate gossip!"

"Are you saying this is the work of a gossip columnist?" asked Momma, pressing her hands together as if unconsciously praying.

"I don't know. Maybe some scamp fed him misinformation." Yet she wondered, *Why? What would anyone have to gain?*

"I suppose it is quite believable, given that you two are frequently in public together," Pop said, stroking his chin thoughtfully.

"And Roy is with us for church and lunch most Sundays," Momma suggested.

"But still," Elizabeth exclaimed, "this is presumptuous and embarrassing! If anyone bothered to ask Roy or me directly, we'd have set him straight."

"If I get the ear of our society editor, maybe he could issue a rebuttal," Pop offered. Elizabeth poured herself a cup of coffee and plunked down in a chair.

"Thanks, Pop. I need to think and talk with Roy before coming up with a plan." What could be done once the fire of gossip was lit?

"We're relieved, aren't we, dear?" said Momma, softly smiling. She and Pop started to converse about the day's ensuing events, but Elizabeth, consumed with her own reactions, barely paid attention. How would Roy take the news? He already questioned the rigorous schedules and demands of working on the American stage. Now he'd have to contend with the country's seemingly insatiable public demand for gossip. Eyeing the bounty of food on the table, Elizabeth realized she couldn't stomach anything more than a piece of toast before readying herself for church and found herself wishing that Roy had opted out of today's service.

★ ★ ★

No such luck. Despite the wintry chill of the overcast morning, Roy was impeccably dressed in a navy blue, cashmere overcoat and black fedora and waiting outside St.

Bartholomew's capacious doors when the Hines family arrived. His wide smile told Elizabeth that he wasn't yet aware of the day's headlines.

"Top of the morning as the Irish say," said Roy, playfully doffing his hat and bowing. They filed in and assumed their usual seats in the third pew just as the massive organ began reverberating throughout the nave, stifling any possible conversation.

Throughout the entire church service, Elizabeth was agitated. Even the choir's melodious rendition of "All Creatures of Our God and King," one of her favorite hymns, didn't soothe her. During Father Gilbert's sermon about hope, she furtively scanned the crowded pews for reporters masquerading as parishioners.

After the service Pop, with Dorothy on one arm and Momma on the other, led the family home along Park Avenue where the summer's flowers, tinged by an overnight frost, drooped. As they left the crowded church, Elizabeth had refused Roy when he offered his arm.

"My dear, is something bothering you?" he asked. "Can I help?"

"Yes, but I don't know how you can help," she said, glancing around. The Washburne family, also leaving church, was close behind them. "Wait until we get home. Then I'll explain."

Once they all entered the apartment and removed their hats and coats, Elizabeth announced that she and Roy needed a few minutes to speak before lunch. She drew him into the library and shut the door behind them.

"Now I am worried," said Roy, his brown eyes wide with concern. As she summarized the newspaper article, Elizabeth's lower lip trembled and her face grew hot and flushed.

"Lovers who intend to elope!" she exclaimed. "I am so angry and sorry about this."

"Darling Elizabeth, there is absolutely nothing for you to apologize for," Roy said. "You are without blame." He crossed the room to put a hand on her shoulder. "The press loves you. That is both good and bad news since they want to know everything about you. I daresay this is a measure of your success."

"Still, it's unfair and untrue. They asked neither you nor I for comment but made up a story and had the audacity to print it. Now they've ruined a wonderful friendship." Roy squeezed her shoulder reassuringly.

"I'm not going to let a romantic fairy tale get in our way."

"That's all well and good but now I fear they'll follow us wherever we go. We won't have a moment's peace." She sniffled. "First, I lost Joanie. Now this."

"You haven't lost me. I remain your loyal friend and the best dance partner you've ever had, maybe will ever have!" he said, a grin puckering his handsome face. "Now can I escort you to lunch, my dear?"

He held out his elbow. Elizabeth stood up and smoothed her skirt before hooking her arm to his.

"Nevertheless," she said, "I would like to find out who started this."

"And then what?"

"I'll demand an apology, maybe a public one."

"That would draw more attention. It's not worth it," said Roy as they passed down the hallway to the dining room. "Let the public imagine whatever they want. They will anyway."

Elizabeth sighed. *He's probably right*, she thought. Still, longing for some clarity and accountability, she silently vowed to uncover whatever information she could.

★ ★ ★

Several days later, before the evening's performance, Elizabeth confided her dismay to Ethel in her friend's dressing room as they partook of tea and some of Frannie's cookies.

"Nasty little men trading in gossip to increase circulation!" Ethel exclaimed. "I agree with Roy, though. To demand a public apology will just make things worse. If we could uncover the source, however, you could confront them personally." Ethel lit a cigarette and slowly blew a smoke ring.

"I have an idea," she continued. "What about asking that reporter who interviewed you to do some sleuthing? You had a favorable impression of him."

"Tom Keogh. I'd be asking him for a personal favor."

"Nothing more fetching than a damsel in distress," said Ethel, winking.

"For heaven's sake, I am not in the market for a beau."

"I know. It's just that I'd like to see something beneficial come out of this for you."

"I don't think that's possible, Ethel. It's the same old, same old. People think romance and marriage should be the ultimate goals for women."

"And if you're not married, something is wrong with you." Ethel finished Elizabeth's thought, emphatically stubbing out her cigarette.

Elizabeth considered Ethel's advice for several days before deciding to call the *Tribune*. The telephone operator answered, "*Tribune*. How can I direct your call?" Her nasal Bronx twang made Elizabeth smile despite her anxiety. She gave her name and asked for Tom Keogh.

"Excuse me," the operator said, "I don't usually do this but are you *the* Elizabeth Hines of *Nellie Kelly* and the *O'Brien Girl*?"

"Yes, I am."

"My sister and I think you're the bee's knees. We've gone to most of George M's productions. I can't wait to tell her I spoke to you!" The woman chuckled. "Now let me find you Mr. K."

Elizabeth waited several minutes before the call went through and Tom Keogh's deep voice resounded over the lines.

"Miss Hines, this is a surprise! To what or to whom do I owe the pleasure of speaking with you?"

"I suppose you could say it is both a what and a whom," Elizabeth replied. "The what is this nasty gossip currently circulating about Mr. Royston and me. The who is the reason I am reaching out to you."

"You are referring to the news of your engagement and future marriage?"

"That's just it. There is no engagement. Yes, we have a great stage partnership and we've become good friends, but that's it."

"I see. Do you want me to help you set things straight in print?" Tom offered.

"What I want is to find out the source of this misinformation and shut them down somehow."

"I can sniff around and see what I come up," he said. "However, we both know that the public hungers for romance, especially when it involves beloved ingenues such as yourself. It could be that some editor, pressured by management to increase sales, directed a reporter to generate the story."

"I've thought of that. Still doesn't make it right, though. It is fabrication verging on slander."

The more they spoke about the situation, the angrier she became. She was grateful they were speaking on the phone so Tom couldn't see the hot flush inflaming her neck and face.

"I'll see what I can do on this end. It may take a few weeks. Shall I phone you or your father when I find any information?"

"Please call me on our home number," Elizabeth said. "I don't want my father bothered any more than he has been already." She gave him the number before they cordially exchanged farewells and hung up. Gulping air, she realized she had barely been breathing during the entire phone call. Thankfully, the household was steeped in midafternoon quiet so their conversation hadn't been overheard.

CHAPTER 28

PROPHETIC

"Come on girl, you need to live a little!" Ethel Shutta told Elizabeth, linking arms with she and Roy as they left a Saturday matinee of *Marjorie*. "You know what they say, all work and no play makes Jackie a dull girl." Horace Liveright, the well-known publisher, had invited lead cast members for a pre-Christmas cocktail party at his Forty-Eighth Street brownstone the following Friday.

"Lillian assures me this isn't one of his usual bawdy Dionysian affairs but an 'A' party, meaning a respectable crowd with good food, good liquor, and smart conversation," said Ethel. She winked at Elizabeth. "Besides, Mr. Liveright is theater struck and is getting involved in writing and producing. You never know!"

Ethel's young friend, Lillian Hellman, one of Liveright's assistants, occasionally popped into their cast gatherings at Sardi's, chain-smoking while vigorously participating in debates on the rights of actors and other workers. Her intensity intrigued Elizabeth, who couldn't imagine herself being so politically savvy and confidently outspoken at age nineteen.

"What do you say, Mr. Royston?" Ethel queried Roy as they rounded the corner away from Broadway's zigzag frenzy of electric advertising signs onto West Forty-Fourth Street. Sardi's appealing awning was in sight.

"I wouldn't want to attend without my leading lady," Roy said, looking quizzically at Elizabeth, who was torn between disappointing her friends and the stultifying despondency that had taken hold of her. Despite writing Joanie weekly, she still hadn't received a response.

Mrs. Farwell's occasional updates so were nonspecific and brief Elizabeth feared exploding with frustration. For the first time in her career, she found performing daily and imbuing her role with vitality effortful. More than once recently, she had asked herself, *Does it all really matter?* She didn't dare share her thoughts, though. They were so negative. Besides, how lucky was she to live the life she was living?

Warm air blasted the trio as they entered the restaurant. The walls were lined with its iconic collection of autographed drawings and photos of famous actors, politicians, musicians, and literati. Some cast members had commandeered their usual two tables in the far corner of the room and already ordered a few pots of tea.

"Come, fair sister!" Patting a neighboring chair, Richard Keane called out to Elizabeth, who played his on-stage sibling. Feeling almost as if she was sleepwalking, Elizabeth complied.

"No incestuous funny business, Mr. Keane," Ethel teased before Roy seated her. Ethel removed her fur stole and gloves and poured tea for everyone.

Richard gently elbowed Elizabeth.

"Winter blues, my dear?" he asked, surveying the restaurant for any Prohibition enforcers before discreetly pulling a silver flask from his suit pocket. "A little dram of brandy in tea can be just the ticket."

He poured a little amber liquid into his cup, then offered her some. For a fleeting moment, Elizabeth considered it. But she remembered Mr. Hemmer's advice about never imbibing alcohol before or between performances, so she politely declined.

As the cacophony of voices swirled around her, Elizabeth smiled wanly at Roy seated across the table although simultaneously wondering how to bolster herself for the evening performance.

By the end of their break, she half-heartedly agreed to attending the Liveright party with Roy and Ethel though she made Roy promise that they could leave if she needed to.

"I enjoy a good party but—" She hadn't revealed much to Roy about Palmer's profligate ways and their effect on her family. They were in their street clothes and seated in her dressing room, decompressing after another demanding work week before leaving for the night.

"Whatever you prefer, darling," Roy said, straightening his tie.

"One of my preferences is not to be in the company of people who are drunk."

"I understand. Not only does too much liquor not bring out the best in most people, but this American Prohibition makes drinking alcohol riskier," Roy said. "One doesn't know what one is really getting half the time. Give me an old-fashioned pub over a speakeasy any day." He stood up, donned his overcoat, and offered her his elbow. "Let me escort you to your car, miss."

It was part of their nightly routine, saying good night on the curb before she departed and he walked the four blocks to the Court Hotel, which housed many actors in current Manhattan shows.

To stave off the bitter cold before their drive, Patrick insisted on tucking a tartan wool blanket over Elizabeth's lap.

"We have to keep our leading lady warm, eh, Mr. Royston?"

"Yes, indeed. Warm, healthy, and happy," Roy agreed, kissing Elizabeth goodbye on the cheek. Sticking his hands in his pockets, he stood watching as the car slowly pulled away while the billboards' glimmering lights played across his face.

★ ★ ★

By the time Ethel, Roy, and Elizabeth arrived at the spacious four-story brownstone, an incongruously elegant oasis in a sea of mostly tawdry-looking speakeasies, the party was in full swing. A gruff man in navy blue livery opened the large front door and took their coats. Lillian, who obviously had been watching out for them, quickly wound her way through the crowd of tuxedos and evening dresses to escort them in.

"Wonderful! So glad you're all here. Let me introduce you to the boss." Lillian leaned over to Ethel and Elizabeth.

"He flirts with every girl he hasn't already met," she said in a low voice. "Thinks he's irresistible like John Barrymore. Just stay at distance so you don't get pinched. That's my solution."

Elizabeth's aversion to lecherous male behavior surfaced. Although she had encountered it often during the past five years, she hadn't become blasé or resigned the way Ethel and some other actresses seemingly were. Roy squeezed her arm, drawing her protectively to his side as if intuiting her reaction.

"Lead on, Lil," Ethel said, smoothing her form-fitted, lapis blue, silk sheath with both hands, then fully elongating as if preparing to step out under a spotlight, formidable yet sensuous.

Elizabeth, on the other hand, fought her urge to leave as they wove through the large reception room, tastefully appointed with Oriental rugs and Italian Renaissance furniture on which a bevy of well-dressed, bejeweled women sat chatting and sipping champagne from crystal glasses. A roaring fire blazed in a large fireplace on the far end. Next to it a long-legged, lean man with a distinctive, regal profile and graying dark hair sat in an armchair. He enthusiastically interacted with a small cadre of men surrounding him.

"What have we here?" he asked Lillian, his piercing black eyes appraising them as they approached.

When Lillian introduced them, Elizabeth felt she was being evaluated and visually undressed. Mr. Liveright slowly stood up, bowed slightly to Elizabeth and Ethel, and shook hands with Roy, saying each of their names aloud.

"A very talented trio meets another talented trio!" he exclaimed. He proceeded to introduce his friends. "My former point man, now competitor, Bennett Cerf; New York's financial guru and art patron, the magnificent Otto Kahn; and the wizard of classy shows, Flo Ziegfield."

Silver-haired Flo Ziegfeld regarded Ethel and Elizabeth with interest while the two other men seemed eager to resume whatever conversation they'd been having. Elizabeth was cautiously intrigued. Ziegfeld's reputation as a producer was stellar but everyone in New York knew of his various affairs with women. The word on the street was that his marriage to Billie Burke had apparently settled him down somewhat.

"Ah, Nellie Kelly, what a pleasure to meet you in person rather than see you from afar!" Ziegfeld said. "George had a way of keeping you to himself."

It wasn't just George M. It was Pop and Mr. Hemmer, too. Good thing they watched out for me. I didn't know how to parry with men like Liveright or Ziegfeld. Nor do I now.

Ziegfeld was the most elegantly dressed of the group in a striking black and dark gray tuxedo, a ruby-colored satin cummerbund, and diamond cufflinks. He had a high, wide forehead with dark, impenetrable eyes and a forceful mouth, tight like a seam. Elizabeth was glad to be standing between Roy and Ethel because her position deterred Ziegfeld from physically insinuating himself next to her, which he seemed likely to do if given the chance.

"What a lucky find you were! Wish I had discovered you. Maybe someday I'll have the right part for you," he mused.

He briefly greeted Roy and Ethel, praising them for their performances before turning back to his colleagues.

"Get some champagne for these hard-working actors and show them around," Liveright commanded Lillian before he, too, resumed his conversation with the men.

"We're dismissed," said Lillian, who flagged down a waiter circulating through the crowd with a tray of full champagne glasses. "Drink up, dears. French. The good stuff."

"How does he get this?" asked Roy, helping himself to a swallow.

"You can get any liquor you desire if you have money—and Canadian contacts," Lillian answered, placing another cigarette in her ebony holder. She lit it, inhaled, and let out a long, satisfied exhale.

"By the way, if you need a glimpse into the future, we engaged a spiritualist for the evening, Mrs. Zara," Lillian said. "The boss's wife thinks highly of her. We set her up in the library. I'm thinking of taking a peek myself. Can't hurt to be prepared."

Laughing, she cocked her bob of thick, dark hair to indicate an arched doorway at the far side of the large room. "Now I must circulate. Boss's orders." She looked at Ethel. "Join me?" Ethel went along willingly.

"Is this what you Yanks would refer to as a swell crowd?" Roy asked Elizabeth as they stood, sipping champagne in a small eddy behind one of the couches, while their two friends blended into the bejeweled crush of satin and silk dresses and black tuxedos.

"I suppose so," Elizabeth replied, studying the crowd. "There are quite a few New York celebrities here as well as some high society folks I recognize from church or charity events I've performed at."

Several seated women seemed to be eyeing and discussing them.

"I fear we are a topic of conversation," she confided to Roy, who was looking around with boyish enthusiasm.

"We are quite the striking pair, don't you think?" he said, smiling wryly.

Rumors in the press about their possible engagement and nuptials didn't bother him the way they affected Elizabeth. He shrugged them off, claiming newspapers made their money on exaggeration, not truth. Roy put an arm around her waist, leading her in the direction of the library.

"Do you want to give them something to talk about?" he asked.

She couldn't help smiling at his insouciance as they entered the cavernous book-lined room. Its relative quiet and spaciousness was a relief.

"One reading or two?" asked the plump matron seated behind a mahogany desk. Her curly, gray hair flowed onto her sequined shoulders. In the warm light cast by the reading lamp, her eyes were a deep indigo against her pale, creamy, ageless face. Laid out on the desktop in front of her were various colored stones of different sizes. A scent like burnt autumn leaves pervaded the room.

"What you smell is sage," the matron explained, as if reading Elizabeth's mind. "I use it to clear the energies between readings. Have a seat." She gestured to the two red leather chairs on the opposite side of the desk. "I am Mrs. Madeleine Zara and you are?"

"Elizabeth and Roy," Roy quickly answered, pulling a chair out for Elizabeth before seating himself.

"Did you want a reading together or separately?"

"We didn't have a plan, actually," Elizabeth said, somewhat apologetically, not wanting to offend Mrs. Zara. "I just wanted to step away from the party for a few minutes and, Roy, well, he helped me escape. I guess you could say we're here by accident."

Mrs. Zara smiled and shook her head.

"There are no accidents, my dears," she said. "One, if not both, of you is meant to be here."

"Hogwash!" Roy erupted, uncharacteristically. "I've seen too many random injuries and deaths in my time to believe that."

"I don't expect you to share my point of view," Mrs. Zara said, apparently unperturbed by Roy's reaction. "How would you like to proceed?"

Roy fidgeted in his chair. Elizabeth knew that meant he was uncomfortable.

"I need a few more minutes, Roy. Why don't you go join the party and I'll come find you shortly?" Elizabeth offered. She didn't want a reading, whatever that was, but she also wasn't ready to leave the calm room.

"Are you sure?" Roy asked as he stood up, holding his empty glass in one hand and glancing first at Mrs. Zara, then back at Elizabeth.

"I will be fine. Go mingle. Keep the rumors alive," she joked. Mrs. Zara asked Roy to close the door behind him.

"We have our answer," she told Elizabeth. "The reading is for you."

Elizabeth found the air around Mrs. Zara to be oddly relaxing.

"I guess," she admitted, "but I have never had a reading nor been drawn to spiritualism."

"Unnecessary. In my opinion, it is better to have no preconceptions. Before we begin, I will light this candle. I will extinguish it when we are through." She lit a tall, thick crimson candle on a wooden stand carved with what resembled hieroglyphs. "We can focus on your specific questions, or I can give you a more general reading. What do you prefer?"

"Oh, dear. I have no idea," Elizabeth hedged. "I suppose I could think of some questions."

"Since you're unprepared, why don't we start with a general reading?" Mrs. Zara suggested. "If a question or two arises, I will be glad to ask my guidance for answers. It is best if I hold your hands for a few moments to begin, if you don't mind."

Elizabeth nodded her consent. Mrs. Zara placed her hands, palms facing upward, on the desk. As Elizabeth rested her hands on top of Mrs. Zara's, both sets of hands increasingly emanated heat. Mrs. Zara's brilliant eyes were now shut and Elizabeth felt as if they were floating in the room and yet somewhere else as well.

She accurately described Elizabeth's years of effort and her recent successes, which Elizabeth didn't find surprising since her journey had been well documented by the press. However, when the medium correctly identified her struggle to be viewed as an educated, independent, and reputable woman despite the lasciviousness and social stigma inherent in the theatrical world, Elizabeth was touched.

"And now, for a bit of advice." Mrs. Zara lightly squeezed Elizabeth's hands, withdrew her hands, opened her eyes, and looked directly at her. "My guidance tells me that there are and will be several men in your life who are not who they appear to be. Remain attentive. Try to see the whole picture and, despite what others say or do, maintain your individuality and morality. Any questions?"

"Can you tell me who those men are?"

"No. They have not given me clarity on that. Now, unfortunately, we only have time for one last question, my dear." Mrs. Zara smiled apologetically. "You see, I must be available to the other guests."

"My friend, Joanie, she is—" Elizabeth sputtered. Mrs. Zara finished her sentence.

"Ill," she said, "but you will see her again in this life. When, I do not know. She, too, is on a journey. The soul evolves in its own time."

"Oh, thank you for that. I hope you're right!" Elizabeth exclaimed as Mrs. Zara extinguished the candle, its sweet, spicy smell filtering across the table.

"Here. If ever you want to meet again." Mrs. Zara handed Elizabeth a cream-colored calling card with her address and phone number in a gilt typeface. "Now get back to that young man before he thinks the worst." She chuckled, pushing back her chair, and rose to usher Elizabeth to the door. Her voluminous, sequined skirts swished, sending points of reflected light dancing along the floorboards and walls.

Elizabeth inhaled deeply before she stepped back into the ruckus, which had increased in volume during her library break. It was going to take some time to locate Roy and Ethel so she could tell them she wasn't interested in staying. Mrs. Zara's advice had resonated, though, preparing her to depart alone if need be.

Despite her prior agreement with Roy, Elizabeth didn't want to curtail his enjoyment if he and Ethel were having a good time, but she would let at least one of them know she was leaving. With that in mind, she picked her way through the gauntlet of chattering people holding a full crystal glass in one hand and a cigar or cigarette holder in the other.

CHAPTER 29

CHRISTMAS DOLDRUMS

"Elizabeth dear, what can I do to put your mind at ease? I hate seeing you so out of sorts," Roy said, grasping her hands. They were sharing a late night pot of tea in the Hines kitchen, their Saturday ritual bookmarking the start of their one day off after another rigorous performance week.

"I wish I could be as cavalier as you are about this gossip!" Elizabeth said. "It feels like the reputation I've worked to establish and maintain has been irrevocably tainted, not to mention the implications now attached to our friendship."

"I wish I could persuade you otherwise. We can't control what other people choose to think."

"Intellectually, I know that," she replied. "I guess it is more complicated for me than it is for you. Many Americans see the theater business as disreputable, not to mention their negative perceptions of actresses in general."

"Yanks. Some are so puritanical, so better than thou!" He withdrew his hands and leaned back in his chair to yawn. "My, it has been a long week. I better be on my way. How about we carve out some time tomorrow to view those Christmas decorations you told me about?"

★ ★ ★

Fifth Avenue was mobbed with strolling shoppers. Though Christmas was only five days away, Elizabeth couldn't muster enthusiasm. Even the carols she normally hummed or played on the piano held little interest for her.

Roy paused in front of a window with a snowy woodland scene, complete with a pair of deer, a variety of birds perched in the evergreen trees, a gnarled dwarf in blue knickers, and a red hat dragging a large pack behind him.

"That poor fellow looks rather burdened, wouldn't you agree, Elizabeth?"

"Oh, yes," she agreed, realizing he was trying to cheer her up. "He looks like he could use help."

"Either that or a break from his duties." He smiled. "His boss must be related to the Shuberts."

The Shuberts had added a *Marjorie* Friday matinee for the duration of the holiday season with minimal compensation for the cast. Roy and several other actors were disgruntled but didn't have any recourse. Working for the Shuberts was a mixed experience. They produced the bulk of successful shows, offering actors in their employ consistent work, but their pay standards, even for star actors, remained on the low side. In addition, the Shuberts worked their actors hard.

"They take advantage because they almost have a monopoly on the production side of things," said Elizabeth. "Actors' rights have always been discounted. That's why Actors' Equity was formed."

"It's different in Britain. Theater work is considered artistic and creative, not just entertainment. Most stage actors are admired and valued unless they exhibit disreputable behavior in their personal lives."

"That sounds like an appealing atmosphere to work in," Elizabeth said. "I'd like to swing down to FAO Schwarz before work to get a watercolor kit for Dorothy. Besides, it is a fantastic store, especially at Christmas—one of Manhattan's gems. You might enjoy it."

"Lead on, Miss E."

A light snow was beginning to coat the crowded streets. They decided to pick up a cab at the taxi stand in front of the Plaza Hotel and make their way south to Twenty-Third Street.

"It couldn't get more Christmas-like than this!" Roy said as they got in. As the cab pulled away from the curb, he used his gloved hand to wipe away the haze on the small window and look on the sights. For a moment, Elizabeth glimpsed the curious, adventurous boy within Roy, endlessly fascinated by the world at large—one of his more endearing qualities along with his humor and scrupulous, attentive manner. Although they had known each other less than a year, somehow, he was as familiar as "an old shoe," as Gert would say. She had never experienced such an easy friendship with a man before. The ease was difficult to describe to her friends, who always inquired about the physical aspects of their relationship. If Elizabeth said, "It's not like that," or declared it a relief to not be pressured into intimacy, they looked askance. If there was one thing to offset her worry about Joanie this Christmas, it was her gratitude for Roy in her life. With that thought, she nestled into him as they jostled along.

When they arrived at the theater, packages in hand, the stage manager greeted them at the stage door, waving a yellow Western Union telegram.

"For you, Mr. Royston. Just came about an hour ago."

"Thanks, mate. Merry Christmas." Roy pressed a dollar into the man's palm. After sequestering in Elizabeth's dressing room and stowing their gifts, Roy opened the envelope. His normally rosy face paled as he read. Elizabeth, purposefully restraining herself from asking what was wrong, sat expectantly on the bench in front of her makeup vanity. When he looked up, it was as if his eyes were unable to focus.

"It's from my brother, Gerald. It's Mum," he stammered. "She's very sick. Lung problems, it seems. Gerry advises me to return home."

Elizabeth spontaneously rose, throwing her arms around him.

"You must go then. As soon as possible."

"How kind and understanding you are," he murmured as they stood, intertwined.

Elizabeth felt his heartbeat and smelled the pleasing lemony scent he emanated. The combination of concern and desire confused her. They had never embraced like this. He broke away, holding her at arm's length.

"Why don't you come with me?" he asked. "You certainly could use a break and the show ends in the new year anyway."

Startled by his invitation and the abruptness of pending changes, Elizabeth hedged.

"I don't know. I can't. I mean I need a few days to figure out if and how I could go with you," she said. "I wouldn't want to leave before Christmas in any case."

"I understand. In the meantime, I will look into what passenger ships are available. We would need to get to Southampton, then take a train to London. And now we need to don costumes." He dropped his hands from Elizabeth's shoulders to glance at his pocket watch.

"To be continued," he said before he spun around and left.

Elizabeth felt as if a small tornado had blown through, upending everything leaving behind questions and unactualized possibilities. She methodically changed clothes while her thoughts coursed. *Will my parents agree to his idea? What about the show? My contract? If I go, when and for how long? Will my savings be adequate? Does Roy want to deepen our friendship? Have it transform into something more serious?* She looked at herself in the dressing room mirror as another thought surfaced. *Will the future of our relationship end up validating the gossip?*

Begrudgingly, she had to admit that possibility even though she still didn't know who started the rumor or why. When Tom Keogh had tracked down the reporter who'd written the gossip column, he had refused to reveal his source although he touted its reliability.

★ ★ ★

Elizabeth broached the topic of England at breakfast. To her surprise, Pop and even Momma enthusiastically supported Roy's idea.

"You have more than earned some time off," Pop said, regarding Elizabeth over the top of his new reading glasses. He placed his carefully folded copy of the *Times* on the table. "I'll argue with the Shuberts if need be, although I don't think they'll object, given your dedication and popular draw. I think it will be a wonderful change of pace."

"Yes, and you can check in on Cecilia which I am sure she'll appreciate and spend time with Isabelle," Momma said. "You should have your own accommodations in London. Roy will be occupied with his mother. Gert will be your companion. I don't want you traveling alone with Roy. There's already enough gossip about you two."

"For you, it will be vacation," Pop cautioned, "but not for Roy. Make plans that don't include him."

"Like go to Paris and elsewhere?" Elizabeth said. Roaming France and Italy had crossed her mind.

"Why not if you're already over there?" Momma said. "I would if I were in your shoes."

Later that morning, Elizabeth, seated at her desk, tried unsuccessfully to complete her correspondence. Christmas preparations, holiday events, and extra shows were distracting enough and now there was an imminent journey to plan for. Her parents even offered to defray some of her trip's costs. However, Elizabeth hoped her savings would suffice. She didn't want to add to their financial burden.

Pop's job status was uncertain although he didn't appear concerned. The *Evening Mail* was being sold and a buyout was imminent. She had condoned her parents' taking in Dorothy and paying for her education and assumed that Palmer's financial contribution to his daughter's care was probably minimal and erratic.

"It will be just like the touring days, you and me traveling, sharing quarters, except we'll be on the other side of the pond," Gert said, carefully tucking newly laundered, folded undergarments into the mahogany chest of drawers. "And you won't have to perform so maybe we can sightsee—visit Westminster Abbey, see the changing of the guard like my dad did before he shipped out to come here as a young man."

Elizabeth couldn't help but smile at Gert's enthusiasm. Her own excitement was modified by concern about her unfolding relationship with Roy, leaving the show, and what her next role might be.

"Anything else you need right now?" Gert asked, straightening up the bed and fluffing the pillows.

"Oh, the usual, someone who writes faster and organizes better than I do."

"You'll get that batch done. You always do. I'll poke my head in later before you get ready for work. Isn't this the last day of two shows before Christmas?"

"Yes, thank goodness. The entire cast is tired out. We're all ready for a break."

Elizabeth had not heard so much grumbling and complaining during any of her previous shows. In the past she had overlooked the stress and soldiered on. This time, though, she found herself empathizing and agreeing with her fellow actors over the need for better working conditions, decent representation, and more satisfying contracts with management. Prior to the opening of *Marjorie*, she had joined the Actors' Equity Union, which had increased in both membership and negotiating power since her days with George M.

After Gert left, Elizabeth decided the stack of cards and letters could wait a bit longer to be answered. What she really wanted to do was write Joanie as a way to imagine her friend's counsel in absentia. So far Joanie's only communication had been a Christmas card with a picture of a brightly colored, small bird incongruously perched on a snow-covered branch. Joanie had handwritten a few lines wishing Elizabeth and her family well and assuring her that she was slowly recovering. Elizabeth had been initially disappointed by the brevity of Joanie's communication until she remembered Mrs. Zara's comment. Visualizing her dear friend, she eagerly put pen to paper.

Dearest Joanie,

Thank you for your card. This letter will reach you after Christmas but know I hold you in my heart and hope that you experienced some holiday joy despite your difficult circumstances. Your mother told Momma that you have to remain upstate and will therefore be away from your family for the duration of the season. It must be so hard to not be with one's family at Christmas.

In fact, I just insisted to Roy that I wouldn't forgo Christmas with my family. He needs to return to England because his mother is quite sick with some sort of lung problem. He asked me to go over with him which, after consulting with Pop and Momma, I've decided to do even though it means quitting the show before it goes out on tour.

I'm a little anxious because I've never pulled out of a show before and hope it doesn't jeopardize my career in any way. Also, I don't know what this means in terms of my relationship with Roy. Not that we'll be travelling alone together! Gert is accompanying me, and we plan to do some travelling on our own since Roy wants to stay put and care for his mother. I do respect him for that.

You might ask why I feel as confused as I do. Yes, he and I do have a great working partnership and a comfortable, growing friendship. In a relatively short time, he's almost part of my family and spends every Sunday with us. It's just that we don't touch in the way I imagine one might with a serious beau, if you know what I mean. He's very respectful, which I really appreciate. There are so many lechers in show business!

Anyway, I guess this upcoming trip will help clarify things between us. I look forward to meeting his younger brother, Gerald, though I probably won't meet his mother. I do intend to catch up with Isabelle in person and spend a few days with her, which should be interesting. I will definitely update you on her British escapades.

Gert and I will have our own accommodations in London and stay there several weeks. We haven't decided where we will go after our London stay but France and Italy are on my list. Some of it depends on what my savings allow as I don't want to rely much on Pop's generosity. He has so much on his plate between the regular household expenses and the addition of Dorothy's upkeep and education.

Gert is a good traveling companion, but I can't help thinking how much fun it would be if you and I were undertaking a European trip together. I promise to pay special attention to sights and events that I know you would enjoy and document them accordingly.

I hope that by the time I return in a couple of months, you will be significantly better and maybe even anticipating release from the Saranac Lake facility. In the meantime, dear one, I send you a ton of good wishes for the New Year.

Your forever friend,

Elizabeth

PS: If there is anything I can pick up for you from across the pond, let me know. I will be glad to send it your way.

Satisfied with her letter, Elizabeth yawned, stretching her arms overhead. Yes, the thought of extended time off and away was becoming quite appealing.

CHAPTER 30
SEASONED

For the first three days, despite its famously large size and classy status for an ocean liner, the RMS *Olympic* was constantly buffeted by the furor of the Atlantic's winter waves. Elizabeth was so nauseated that she barely made it from her bed to the toilet and back. Gert, clucking and fussing like a mother hen, put cool compresses on Elizabeth's feverish, blanched face and petitioned the cooking staff daily for nourishing broths, weak tea, and ginger ale for her charge. She also updated Roy, who stopped by regularly to check on Elizabeth. In her current condition, however, she forbade him to enter.

Restless, achy, and dreading the ship's next heave, Elizabeth thought about the huge discrepancy between her fantasy of their ocean voyage and her current experience. She had pictured walks and shuffleboard on deck during crisp, sunlit days, and leisurely, romantic dinners followed by dancing with Roy to the ship's orchestra late into the night. She felt too weak to laugh or cry though both reactions seemed apt.

It wasn't until the fourth day of their six-day crossing that the sea was calm enough for Elizabeth to don a skirt, a blouse, and her long green wool winter coat, with its matching cloche hat, and venture out. Flanked by Roy and Gert, she strolled on deck. Large nimbus clouds in shades of gray scudded overhead. Periodically, shafts of sunlight sliced through the clouds, making the water shimmer and sparkle. The whole effect was quite dramatic and the tangy cool air welcome after the confines of the cabin.

Men in suits and ties doffed their hats as they passed in the other direction. Well-dressed women grappled with flimsy parasols in the constant breeze as they sought to shield their faces from the occasional bursts of sunlight.

Elizabeth turned her face upward, relishing the light on her face.

"Looks like you may be over the worst of it," Roy said, patting her arm, interlaced with his. "And you, Miss Gert, are notably seaworthy." Gert chuckled.

"Many Celts were seafaring folk, so they say, and don't forget some of us have Viking blood in our veins."

"Yes, I believe Dublin was once ruled by Vikings," said Roy.

Elizabeth had difficulty paying attention to their ensuing discussion about Vikings and Celts. Her mind, seemingly wrapped in gauze, and her usual competent sense of balance compromised, she focused on maintaining her footing on the hard decking. She was so preoccupied with that task, she barely heard the handsome, young blond man striding by, warmly greeting Roy as if they were friends. Roy nodded to the fellow but, uncharacteristically, didn't introduce them.

★ ★ ★

It was mid-morning by the time Elizabeth and Gert exited the Southampton train, loaded their luggage into a hansom cab, and said their goodbyes to Roy, who headed off to his mother's house in North London. Despite the blustery cold, overcast day, Mayfair's quaint, shop-lined streets bustled with pedestrians.

"This is quite the hotel," Gert exclaimed, as they entered Claridge's lobby with its striking Art Deco black-and-white striated floor and luxurious decor.

"Izzy insisted that this is the place to stay," Elizabeth said, surveying the opulent interior and the parade of chic flappers and attractive men passing through the ornate, arched doorways. "At least for the first week or so. Beyond that, we'll see."

"Yes, we'll need lodgings a little less grand," Gert said. "I don't think Miss Isabelle ever has had to budget, do you?"

"You're probably right but we didn't ever talk about finances. It was pretty obvious that her family was of a different social class. We didn't let that interfere with our friendship."

"No, you didn't and the better off you both are for that."

A tall, thin clerk who resembled Ichabod Crane checked them in and motioned for the bell captain to show them to their accommodations.

"Letter for you, Miss Hines," he said, "and the flowers you ordered have been delivered to your rooms."

"Heavens, I didn't order any flowers but thank you."

"Probably Mr. Roy's doing," suggested Gert as they ascended to the third floor in a gleaming mahogany elevator managed by an austere man in a spotless navy-blue uniform with gold epaulets and buttons. Without uttering a word, he accompanied them to their rooms and exited.

"No sirree, this isn't anything like those places we stayed on tour," Gert said, admiringly.

The arched floor-to-ceiling windows opened outward to a stone balcony. A delicately petalled, opal glass chandelier hung like exotic fruit from the sitting room ceiling. Matching wall sconces that looked like single petals were strategically spaced on the cream-colored walls. The floor was a black and white marble zigzag pattern partially covered by a plush burgundy area rug.

"I suppose one could get used to this," said Elizabeth, flopping down on the white suede couch, slipping off her pumps and wiggling her toes. A large arrangement of pale roses, purple lilacs, and forsythia decorated the long black sideboard. Gert laughed.

"You'd get bored soon enough."

"Right now, a little boredom sounds appealing. Just so it's on land and not at sea!" she said, still feeling the effects of the seasickness.

After carefully tearing open the envelope, she quickly perused the note.

"So much for boredom, Gert. Izzy reserved a table for high tea downstairs this afternoon and she sent the flowers as a harbinger of spring. She remembered it's my favorite season."

"Very thoughtful. It's been two or three years since you've seen each other?"

"Three and then some. It was before *Nellie Kelly*. She came home once for a month at Christmas the first or second year she was attending the Royal College of Art. How fast those years have gone!"

"Just you wait, Miss E. They go by faster and faster the older one gets. You two have a lot to catch up on."

"I'll say, especially since Izzy isn't much of a letter writer. If she could draw her correspondence, she would probably communicate more," quipped Elizabeth as she stood up to help Gert unpack and organize their belongings.

CHAPTER 31
WORLDWIDE

Elizabeth, seated at a low, round table covered with a white linen tablecloth, flowered porcelain cups, and silver cutlery, consulted her wristwatch. Izzy was late. She had forgotten Izzy's tendency to be at least ten minutes late for everything, so she alternately gazed at the extensive menu while discreetly studying the people around her.

Matronly women, dressed nondescriptly, sat on couches sipping and helping themselves to small crustless, white bread sandwiches from laden, lacquered coffee tables while quietly talking. At other tables, chic flappers, who Elizabeth guessed were around her age, waved cigarette holders, smoked, chatted, and laughed with meticulously dressed young men. To her left, a patrician-looking man in a gray serge suit and ascot was speaking French with a young woman who appeared to be his daughter. In the background she heard fragments of German, Italian, and what she guessed was Russian.

Elizabeth, so absorbed by the scene, failed to notice Izzy until she was almost at the table. She was swathed in a calf-length, tartan cape in shades of rich purple, green, and brown. Her small face was framed by chin-length chestnut hair, cut on a bias. She wore a green loden hat that complemented her hazel eyes. For an instant, Elizabeth imagined her as a modern-day Artemis, poised in a woodland grove, bow and arrow in one hand, several hounds by her side.

"Darling Elizabeth, let me drink you in!" Izzy exclaimed, opening her arms wide before bending to kiss her friend on both cheeks.

"Heavens, you look wonderful, Izzy. Life in Great Britain must agree with you." Izzy removed her cape and dug her cigarette case out of her purse before seating herself.

"I do feel freer here, it's true," she said, offering Elizabeth a cigarette before contently lighting her own. "I suppose that doesn't make much sense since they still are invested in royalty and titles. Yet I find less jockeying for social standing here. In fact, some of the titled are the most eccentric, freewheeling people I've ever met. Of course, you might not share my reaction. You're in the theater business and I believe actors, singers, and dancers tend to be more liberal and tolerant, not so concerned with social class."

"Really? I believe that is due to our lack of social clout. For one thing, the business is mostly in the hands of Jewish producers and many Americans are anti-Semitic. Secondly, producers are male and patriarchal if not misogynistic. Thirdly, actresses tend to be viewed as social climbers looking for sugar daddies, just a half step above prostitutes and fair game for any red-blooded male."

"That sounds dicey. How do you keep your head above the proverbial water?" Izzy smiled ruefully.

"I was lucky to have Pop as my manager, Mr. Hemmer and George M. as mentors. They respected my work ethic, self-discipline, and I suppose you could say, my overall character."

"But you're not working with George M. anymore," said Izzy, eyebrows arched quizzically.

"True but I integrated what I learned from him and strive to maintain my own standards as well," Elizabeth said. "Also, I've had wonderful cast members to work with and now we actors have union representation."

"And all women in the USA can vote!" Izzy exclaimed. "There is still an age limit in England. Only women above the age of thirty can vote. We're working on changing that, though. Anyway, let's celebrate women's rights and our reunion. It is so good to see you in person, my friend."

A waiter wheeled a multileveled cart to their table. It burst with delicacies from "savory to sweet," as he announced with a flourish.

"Just point out what you'd like, Elizabeth," Izzy said. "He'll plate it for you. I don't think you can choose wrongly. Everything I've had here has been scrumptious. I eat here often because it is on my way home from the Academy, and I am usually ravenous after hours in the studio."

As they spoke Elizabeth discovered that Izzy, once a lackadaisical Brearley student, was now a serious artist with several commissions and pending exhibitions in London and Paris galleries. Although she maintained her suffragette activities, her artistic endeavors seemed to be predominant.

"I can't help asking, Izzy, how is your mother dealing with your burgeoning art career?"

"It has been progressively frustrating for her. The first year she was determined to secure invitations for us to all the glamorous social events and parties. I went just to assuage her. However, at the Royal Academy of Art, the people we met saw me as an artist, not as a socialite or bridal prospect. Poor Mother, all her hopes of a title in the family have come to naught." Izzy laughed aloud. "Defeated by art you could say! Of course, you, of all people, can probably guess I am thrilled with how things have turned out."

"I am grateful that Momma and Pop stopped pressuring me about finding a husband and took my career interest seriously," Elizabeth said, carefully dabbing her mouth after downing a scone lathered with whipped cream and strawberry jam.

"Does that have anything to do with your leading man? I forget his name." Izzy said, apologetically. "I try to follow what the newspapers say about Broadway, you in particular, but I tend to get off track when I am immersed in a painting."

Elizabeth brought Izzy up to date in her relationship with Roy, mentioning her confusion about their status.

"Have you asked him directly?" Izzy suggested.

"I hope this trip together will clarify where we stand. So far, though, circumstances have certainly not been conducive." She briefly described their ocean crossing, her debilitating seasickness, and the health crisis with Roy's mother.

"That trip was quite a trial. Glad you have your appetite back."

"Me, too," said Elizabeth, satiated and warmed by food, strong tea, and Izzy's presence. "I haven't been able to eat much of anything until today."

With their permission, the waiter cleared their table. Izzy proposed a leisurely walk the next day through Mayfair into Hyde Park, weather permitting.

"Invite Gert as well," Izzy said. "We'll make it a sort of informal tour to orient you both to this district. Rest up, dear one, and I will phone your room tomorrow morning. Oh, and Mother would like to know what evening you are free to come to dinner *chez nous* (with us), as the French say."

After Izzy exited the hotel's capacious entrance foyer, Elizabeth, preferring the feel of ground underfoot, walked up the carpeted, curved stairway instead of taking the lift and noting they had not discussed Joanie. How much did Izzy know? Did she deliberately skirt the subject? That and the topic of more affordable housing were on Elizabeth's mental docket for their next rendezvous.

CHAPTER 32
TANGLED

The next day Elizabeth and Gert traipsed all over Mayfair, a flamboyantly dressed Izzy leading the way, peppering them with historical anecdotes.

"Pocahontas visited England in the seventeenth century. Imagine what she must have thought," Izzy said as they entered Gunter's Tea Shop.

"Bet she wondered how anyone survives this damp cold that creeps into one's bones," Gert said, shivering. "I swear it's colder than New York in winter."

"You might be right, Gert. If I remember correctly, she ended up dying here, probably from pneumonia," said Elizabeth, rubbing her gloved hands together for warmth.

"Nothing a strong cup of tea won't fix," said Izzy, winking. She showed them a small silver flask stowed in her interior coat pocket. "Just a splash of whiskey and you'll feel the heat return."

Izzy's suggestion reminded Elizabeth of Roy whose silence she was trying to excuse. After all, it had only been two days since they parted at the train station. He probably needed to establish the severity of his mother's health crisis. Still, she wondered how and when the topic of their relationship, specifically, its future, could be addressed. The length of their London sojourn and their ensuing European tour plans hinged somewhat on what was forthcoming with Roy.

The tea shop's steamy warmth, brightly colored tablecloths, glass canisters filled with loose tea, and delicious, fragrant baked goods was a welcome distraction. Izzy commandeered a round table right next to the shop window.

"We can watch London's finest walk by while we have a cuppa," she said before extolling the pleasures of the shop's baked goods. Gert, who never lacked an appetite, responded enthusiastically to Izzy's recommendations. Dishes laden with goodies arrived before Elizabeth had even glanced at the menu. Izzy appeared to be on a first-name basis with the affable, portly, craggy-faced owner, John, and his wife, who ran from the backroom kitchen to counter and customer seemingly without stopping.

"As you might have guessed, I am a regular," confessed Izzy as Mrs. Gunter placed the last plate of what looked like petit fours on their table. "I am usually voracious after the better part of a day in the studio. Can't make it to dinner without a tea break. In summer they make superb ices in many flavors as well."

"My, Izzy, I believe you've become Britified," remarked Elizabeth.

"Not entirely," Izzy said, slipping a little whiskey into her tea after offering some to Gert, who frowned and shook her head. Elizabeth declined. "I avoid fox hunting, needlepoint, bridge games, and lengthy house parties where men go off hunting and the women stay behind, awaiting their return."

"That sounds old-fashioned, definitely not your bailiwick nor mine," said Elizabeth. "But what do you do for socializing? You are still involved with the suffragette cause but that is serious, not relaxing or fun."

"You mean when I want to put on the glitz? In that case I go to Isa Lanchester's club where artists and literati mingle, put on one-act plays, dance, and of course, drink. It's also a place where single women can show up alone and not be regarded as social pariahs. Occasionally, a few of us from the Academy also meet up there for an evening's fun. In fact, we should go there one of the nights. You, too, Gert."

"Thank you for your invitation but I don't frequent bars or pubs, Miss Isabelle."

Unflustered by Gert's refusal, Izzy continued.

"Please call me Izzy, Gert. Elizabeth, maybe we can get your man friend to join us. I am certain you would both enjoy it."

"Sounds intriguing but I have no idea when or if he'll be available."

"He's got to come up for air sometime," Izzy said.

"True, but by all accounts, his mother is quite ill, and he is as close to her as I am to Momma and Pop," said Elizabeth, omitting her increasing concern about Roy. Had he become more distant the closer they sailed toward England? Or was it her frightful seasickness and imagination that conjured up her sense of estrangement?

"In the meantime, you have a lot more to see in London, which I'll be happy to show you," Izzy offered.

"I'd love to tour the National Gallery and Gert wants to see the Tower of London and the changing of the Guard."

"Preferably not the same day." Gert piped in. "This sightseeing is a bit wearing on the eyes and feet for the likes of me."

"And by the way, Izzy, as much as we love Claridge's, in a week we need to relocate to something more affordable," Elizabeth added. "A place with enough room for Cecilia to come from Sussex and stay for a few days."

"Not a problem. My mother is already canvassing her contacts. I'm certain we'll come up with some suitable place for a month. This time of year, some people retreat to the south of France or Italy and leave their homes empty."

"Can't blame them," Elizabeth said, regarding the dank sidewalks now glistening in a steady, cold rain as people scurried by, huddled under their umbrellas. "Maybe, after our time here, Gert and I will follow their lead. We have ten weeks, including the ocean crossings, before Roy and I are scheduled to begin rehearsing another show for the Shuberts."

"Perhaps in mid-February," Izzy said, "you and Gert can accompany me to Paris for the art show at the Salon Des Indépendants instead of Mother, who prefers avoiding fraternizing with artists. Not her cup of tea, we could say, in the present circumstance." Izzy smiled, then drained her cup. "Now let's get you back to the hotel so you both can put your feet up."

Izzy walked them back through the soaked streets to the Claridge, making them promise to meet at her mother's house the next morning to continue their London tour.

Elizabeth stopped at the front desk on their way up to their room but there was no message from Roy. In her compromised seasick state, she had forgotten to ask for his address or phone number before they parted, which meant she had no way to reach him.

"Don't you worry, Miss E. Being the oldest with one younger brother and no women in the family besides his sick mum, he's probably having a tray full," Gert said, removing her coat and hat and wearily plunking down on the couch.

"I suppose," Elizabeth said, unconvinced. She refrained from pointing out the discrepancy between his New York attentiveness and the behavior she was currently experiencing. "I think I will write Joanie. We'll probably prefer a late dinner tonight, so I'll have enough time."

"I agree. I can't imagine eating for quite a while after that tea." Gert, shoes off, was rubbing her feet.

Elizabeth settled into the leather desk chair, pen in hand, with a couple of sheets of Claridge's ivory stationery.

Dear Joanie,

We've finally arrived in London. I won't bother describing the ocean voyage because I was seasick and couldn't leave our cabin for the better part of the six-day crossing. I can say that I am very grateful that Gert was along and took such good care of me. I felt weak as a kitten for days and am just getting back on my feet.

Good thing too, because our friend, Izzy, has all kinds of plans for showing off what is apparently her new hometown. I say this because she has established what appears to be a full life here. She's such a bad letter writer that I don't know if she told you she was accepted by and is attending the Royal College of Art. Not only is she doing well there but she is beginning to get commissions for her portraitures. She says her mother is not pleased by her artistic success as it hampers Izzy's social and marital prospects. As you can imagine, our Izzy is not at all unhappy about this outcome.

Personally, I am happy that Izzy found a vocation other than suffragette activism. Remember how worried we were about her welfare when she was sneaking out to all those rallies and marches? At least being an artist doesn't tend to lead to beatings or incarceration.

I hope to see some of her work tomorrow when we meet at her mother's house to continue our London touring.

Yesterday, she walked us all over Mayfair and the West End which, even on a cold, rainy day, is so appealing. I didn't dare step foot into the fancy shops with their fetching window displays for fear of slipping off budget so early in our ten-week adventure.

Gert and I are currently staying at Claridge's, which is quite sumptuous, but hope to secure reasonably priced lodging for the month. Izzy assures me that her mother will help us resolve this issue. I would like an affordable place where we could comfortably host a few overnight visitors. I intend to catch up with Cecilia, who is divorcing Palmer (no surprise but my parents want to keep this quiet) and will remain in her homeland.

Roy may need an occasional reprieve from his family crisis as well. I am currently adjusting to not seeing him daily which is more difficult than I anticipated. I guess the old maxim, "absence makes the heart grow fonder" is more truthful than I ever thought.

It applies to you too, dear friend. I sorely miss you and hope I will see you in person again this year.

Sending you much love from England.

Elizabeth

CHAPTER 33
FOR ART'S SAKE

"Elizabeth, I remember when you were a model for a portrait," said Izzy, ushering Gert and Elizabeth into the large drawing room of her mother's house. The walls were adorned with a collection of her watercolors and oil paintings. "What was that artist's name?"

"Max Nordell. Pop said the painting *Young American Girl* is in the Corcoran Gallery in Washington now. I guess he kept in touch with Mr. Nordell." Elizabeth looked around her and deliberately diverted the conversation from her celebrity to Izzy's portraits.

"Izzy, these are stunning! Where do you get your models?"

Women in Izzy's paintings were engaged in various tasks—arranging flowers, drawing water for a bath, fixing their hair, reading, knitting. Children and pets played in the foreground of some. All exhibited a definite Impressionistic influence, their mostly pastel colors verging on hazy if one stepped too close to a painting but strikingly clear and vibrant at a distance. Most exuded a serene, tender intimacy.

"I mostly draft friends and friends of friends," Izzy said. "A few were models in the studio classes at school, but I prefer naturalness to a more posed picture."

"Isabelle, did you offer your guests any refreshment?" asked Mrs. Armour, pristine in a navy-blue jacket and ankle-length skirt as she briskly entered the room. She acknowledged Elizabeth and Gert with a tepid smile. A large brooch of what looked like a lapis hummingbird with diamond eyes and a gold beak was fastened over her left breast. Although she had the same dark hair as Izzy, their resemblance ended there. Mrs. Armour's face was sternly impassive while Izzy's face was a constant kaleidoscope of expression. Izzy had a lithe dancer's body while her mother was curvaceous, squat, and solid like the Venus of Willendorf.

"Not necessary, Mrs. Armour. We had much too much to eat and drink at Claridge's just before we came here," Elizabeth said, hastily. "Thank you for thinking of us, though. Izzy kindly offered to be our London tour guide so we're taking her up on it."

"She should be good at that. She's been running all over the city since we arrived here," Mrs. Armour said. "Although I don't approve of young women going out in public alone, I've given up trying to keep track of her."

"Oh, Mother, I am very careful and, most of the time, Charles meets me and we go places together. Today I am accompanied by these two ladies," she said, beaming at Elizabeth and Gert.

"Huh, Charles! Is that young man ever going to make a move?" Mrs. Armour scoffed. "You two have been socializing for almost two years now." Izzy grimaced.

"Mother, I don't want to discuss this subject right now."

"I hope your sensible friend, Elizabeth, will be a good influence."

Elizabeth, taken aback by Mrs. Armour's declaration and the considerable tension between Izzy and her mother, intervened, enlisting Gert to change the topic.

"We are excited to see the sights, aren't we, Gert?"

"Yes indeed, Miss E.," Gert agreed, assuming the deferential tone she used around imperious people like Mrs. Armour.

"I am so pleased to see some of Izzy's fabulous artwork. She is quite talented," Elizabeth said, in an effort to defuse the situation. "As her mother, you must be quite proud."

"I am but art won't provide for her future and her father isn't willing to fund an overseas household forever."

"Don't worry, Mother. Everything is working out. Now, ladies, let's get a move on. The taxi is outside, and we have a lot to see," Izzy said, pinning on her green hat and slipping into her cape before planting a perfunctory farewell kiss on her mother's cheek.

"Okay, tell me, who is Charles?" Elizabeth asked after they settled into the hansom cab's worn leather seats.

"Charles Wilson Fleet, a fellow art student, youngest son of a very proper British family—landed gentry and all. The family has a huge estate in the Lake District. Charles was expected to graduate from Oxford and then become a lawyer, but he dropped out in favor of the Academy and an art career. His family was none too pleased about his choice but haven't disowned him yet."

"And are you two—? "

"Really just friends but don't tell Mother," Izzy said, quickly glancing at Gert, who sat in the front passenger seat looking out the front window. She lowered her voice to confide in Elizabeth. "Charles and I have a little pact. I'll tell more when we're alone."

"Here's Piccadilly Circus," Izzy loudly announced. "We're on our way to Buckingham Palace for the eleven o'clock Changing of the Guard." She then outlined their day's itinerary while Elizabeth wondered what mischief Izzy and her friend, Charles, were involved in.

"Alfred Gilbert's *Eros*. Gorgeous, isn't he?" said Izzy, pointing to a delicately wrought, winged statue armed with bow and arrow poised on a pedestal in the middle of the traffic circle.

Mrs. Mullen, Elizabeth's Greek teacher at Brearley, had said the Greeks invented *Eros* to express the acute nature of desire and longing. At the time Elizabeth found the creation of a God for such a purpose hyperbolic, but because of her current situation with Roy, she better understood what the statue represented. Roy's importance in her life hadn't fully dawned on her until this trip and her newfound awareness was profoundly disconcerting.

Eros, erotic: was that the nature of her feelings for Roy? If it was, should she express them?

The questions kept resurfacing despite the Guards' pageantry, a visit to the queen's lovely chapel, and a stroll around Saint James's Park, followed by a prolonged late lunch. It wasn't until after Izzy dropped them off at teatime, promising to return in the morning, that Elizabeth realized that she was left with several important unanswered questions about Roy and that Izzy hadn't followed up on the topic of Charles.

"That was a splendid day!" Gert said, laying a protective hand on Elizabeth's arm and steered her toward the concierge's desk as they entered the bustling lobby.

"The operator took a call for you, Miss Hines." He handed her an envelope along with the brass room key on its red velvet loop.

Elizabeth tore the envelope open as soon as they reached their room and scanned Roy's note: "Mother diagnosed with pleurisy. We are organizing care. Hope to visit with you this upcoming Saturday. Will phone to confirm time. Fondly, Roy"

An address was included, which was a relief, but the note's brevity was unsettling.

"So?" Gert asked.

"Not much news. His mother has pleurisy. He may be able to visit on Saturday if he can arrange care for her."

"There you go. Mr. Roy has a lot on his plate. Can't imagine healing from pleurisy in this climate is easy." Gert took a handkerchief from her coat pocket and vigorously blew her nose, as if for emphasis. "Heavens, I am glad our rooms are so warm and cozy."

"I agree. I hope we find an equally warm place to rent," said Elizabeth, shivering involuntarily as she removed her coat. Although it had been an exciting day of sightseeing, her legs and feet felt as if they had absorbed the cold from the many stone surfaces they walked.

"A good soak might be just the thing tonight," Gert suggested.

"Followed by room service, gin rummy, and some reading," Elizabeth added. The gas lamps along the street outside their living room window were already casting shadows. Nights seemed to fall more quickly in London than in Manhattan. They also lingered longer into the dawn hours.

A flurry of communication punctuated the next morning's breakfast in the dining room. There were telegrams from her parents wishing them well and from Cecilia welcoming them to England. Also, Izzy phoned proposing a visit and announcing good news regarding housing. She suggested meeting at the National Gallery of Art in Trafalgar Square at noon.

"We can take it a bit slower this morning, Gert," Elizabeth said after reading Izzy's message.

"That sounds good. Mmm, Brits must prefer their toast dry and cold," Gert commented, disdainfully removing a piece of toast from a silver toast caddy and placing it on her plate. "I like my toast soft and warm, if possible."

"One of many adjustments we'll have to make traveling in different countries," Elizabeth teased.

"Let's hope the rest of them aren't more challenging than this," Gert said, spreading her toast generously with butter.

★ ★ ★

"This is one of my favorites!" Izzy said, standing in front of a sensuous painting of a supine naked woman viewed from the rear as she looks into a mirror held by a chubby Cupid. "Not only do I love Velázquez as an artist but the back story on this painting is close to my heart."

Elizabeth waited expectantly for Izzy to explain.

"You can't see the marks now because of the excellent restoration but in 1914 suffragette Mary Richardson smuggled a meat cleaver into the National Gallery and slashed this painting to protest another arrest of Emmeline Pankhurst, founder of the Women's Social and Political Union in Britain."

"What a shame!" Elizabeth exclaimed. "Why vandalize a master's painting for politics?"

"Mary was quoted as saying she tried to destroy the picture of the most beautiful woman in mythological history to protest the government's attempts to destroy Mrs. Pankhurst, the most beautiful woman in modern history!" Izzy said defiantly. Suddenly her small face was fierce and tight as it had often been during their school years.

Elizabeth had stopped arguing with Izzy about women's rights years earlier. She agreed that women should have equal voting rights but advancing her career demanded some conformity to existing theatrical norms. Izzy either didn't understand, or outright rejected, any form of compliance.

After Gert, obviously disapproving of such destructive action, wandered off to sit and rest in the adjoining gallery, Elizabeth saw an opportunity.

"What is it you were going to tell me about your friend, Charles?"

"Promise not to tell a soul, not even Gert or Joanie," Izzy sternly requested.

"I promise," Elizabeth said, wondering what she was getting herself into.

"Neither Charles nor I want to marry and have children, but our families are pressuring us so much, we made a pact."

"A pact to marry each other just to satisfy your respective families? That doesn't sound like you, Izzy."

"Sort of but not exactly." Drawing Elizabeth into a corner of the large gallery, away from the few visitors viewing paintings, Izzy addressed her friend in a hushed tone. "It's more a pact to keep our freedom, freedom to be artists and have whatever relationships we desire." Elizabeth was perplexed.

"I'm not certain I understand. You mean you two might marry? Then what? Have lovers?"

"I suppose I might if I was interested, and the man didn't get in the way of my painting."

"Wouldn't Charles get jealous if you had an affair?" Elizabeth probed.

"No, he wouldn't." Izzy surreptitiously glanced around before continuing. "He's not interested in women, if you know what I mean."

"Oh, I can't say I—" Elizabeth sputtered.

"Don't get me wrong, Elizabeth, Charles and I enjoy each other's company but we're never going to live conventionally. We'll go through the motions of having the proper festivities and all that but once we're on our own, we'll live under the same roof but separately. There you have it."

Risky, fraught with possible disasters, thought Elizabeth. Izzy's revelation had taken her aback. She found herself longing once again for Joanie's sage presence. Between the two of them, they usually found ways to get Izzy to modify her radical stances. Disputing Izzy's plan now, though, probably would increase her reactivity.

Over their next few weeks together, Elizabeth opted for a few strategically asked questions inviting Izzy to consider the long-term effects of her plan rather than focusing on the more immediate relief from social and familial expectations.

"Ahem, that is a novel plan," Elizabeth said hesitatingly before changing the subject. "Shall we round up Gert? She doesn't have the stamina for looking at art that we have and I imagine we could all use a late lunch."

CHAPTER 34

RESTRAINT

After another full day of sightseeing, Elizabeth and Gert returned to find a note from Mrs. Armour, who, true to her word, had secured them a house for a month south of Hyde Park in the Knightsbridge section.

"We pay just the wages of the cook and housemaid. No rent. What a relief!" Elizabeth exclaimed, removing her hat and coat before prying her pumps off her swollen feet.

"That is good news. Your father will be pleased."

"Both of my parents will be glad that we have a home base for the rest of our stay in Britain. And, as you well know, Gert, I prefer a home to a hotel any day. If I ever play a long run somewhere other than New York, I will definitely rent an apartment or house if I can afford it. I guess I am a bit of a homebody."

"Nothing wrong with that, Miss E., excepting when you're touring like you did for Mr. Cohan."

"That certainly was demanding."

"I think that manager of his always scrimped on the actors' accommodations so he could pay himself more," said Gert, frowning.

"I could overlook anything then because I was so excited to have a role instead of being in the chorus. I wouldn't settle for those conditions now, though."

Elizabeth briefly recalled a blurry sequence of dank, dimly lit rooms, musty-smelling costumes and crowded changing rooms. Stardom brought benefits though the amount and quality of attention it drew was often irksome. Vacationing abroad had relieved those pressures. No one in England wanted her to endorse products, appear at some charity function, or give an impromptu interview. The only sources of disquiet were maintaining a reasonable budget for their ten-week trip and figuring out how to proceed with Roy.

As if mind-reading, Gert, also now shoeless, stretched out on the couch and asked, "Isn't tomorrow the day Mr. Roy said he was coming?"

"Yes, but we won't know for certain until tomorrow," said Elizabeth, who had tried to ignore her increasing uneasiness by focusing on Izzy and their London experiences. For that reason, she deliberately avoided further conversation with Gert on the topic of Roy for the rest of the evening.

★ ★ ★

Sunlight cascaded through windows and snaked through the narrow side streets, highlighting the intricate ironwork on the balcony and the carved doors of the surrounding buildings. It was the first clear day since their arrival. Elizabeth, alone outdoors on their small balcony, studied the scene below and contemplated how best to organize her day. Gert was out exploring the neighborhood for a place to buy postcards.

Izzy and her mother were eager to show Elizabeth the rental house on Montpelier Street and Roy had proposed meeting at the Claridge's at noon. Gert begged off on sightseeing for a day, preferring to write postcards and wander over to Hyde Park when and if it became warm enough.

Asking Roy to lunch, and afterwards to accompany her to Knightsbridge, gave them some casual time together and an opportunity to introduce Roy to Izzy and her mother, which would resolve Izzy's questions about him. Besides, Elizabeth enjoyed the idea of Izzy and Roy meeting since she'd been unable to introduce him to Joanie before her illness. It seemed like a reasonable plan although she realized she didn't know how much time Roy could spare.

Meanwhile, Elizabeth decided to telegram her parents to let them know the good news about their lodgings and ask the hotel operator to connect her to Cecilia's number. To have more than a day or two of spontaneously scheduled time was so foreign yet such a treat. She leaned back against the brick façade, listening as two pigeons, perched close together on a neighboring railing, clucked and cooed enthusiastically. For a few moments, all apprehension about Roy quelled.

Elizabeth carefully chose her wardrobe to look feminine yet assertive and independent. Wearing her one-piece, pleated tailleur with a matching jacket, yellow-and-white-patterned silk blouse, and her new taffeta hat, she regarded herself in the mirrored wardrobe door. She thought she'd achieved what she'd hoped for.

She was sporadically reading Somerset Maughan's *The Painted Veil* in the sitting room adjoining the hotel lobby when she heard Roy's voice. Curtailing her urge to run out to embrace him, she rose, deliberately walking slowly and casually into the main foyer. *This is when being an actress really pays*.

As Roy tended to do with strangers, he chatted with the concierge. She was almost by his side before he noticed her presence. When he turned to face her, she saw his normally vibrant countenance looked sallow, his normally bright eyes, dull.

"Elizabeth, my dear." He took her right hand and bent over to kiss it in a playful, theatrical way. Elizabeth, adopting Izzy's style of greeting, kissed him lightly on each cheek, refraining from throwing her arms around him.

"You look much more yourself than when I left you five days ago," commented Roy as they were seated for lunch in the elegant Art Nouveau dining room.

"You mean I am no longer pallid shades tinged with blue?" Elizabeth said. "Believe me, it was a pleasure to regain an appetite and enjoy food again."

"Poor dear, it was a wretched trip across for you."

"I already fear the return trip," Elizabeth admitted. They briefly consulted the menu and ordered before she asked about his welfare and his mother's condition.

He ran his fingers through his abundant, wavy brown hair several times, as if trying to recall and summarize events.

"It's a bit of blur, really. So much needed to be addressed and has transpired since my arrival," Roy said. "Not that Gerry hadn't done his bit, but Mum is stubborn in the best of times and when she's sick, which is rarely, she digs in her heels even more. Besides she's lived alone for sixteen years since Dad died. She fought all the doctor's recommendations, so we drew a line in the proverbial sand—either she accepted a live-in helper and regular nursing care, or she'd have to be in the hospital. Even though she can hardly breathe, she's angry with both of us right now but at least she's in her own home."

Elizabeth had never seen Roy so dispirited. Usually, when he was flustered or irritable, the state was short-lived. He had an uncanny ability to rebound quickly and make light of uncomfortable difficulties. He didn't wallow in negativity and self-absorption like Palmer. Nor was he prone to bravado and self-aggrandizement. The obvious change in his demeanor contributed to her sense of a growing distance between them. The congenial ease she generally felt with him was lacking. She hoped her proposal for the afternoon together might be restorative, so she broached the subject after he finished telling her about the events since his return home.

"I would love your input on this house, and it would be a treat to have you and Izzy meet," Elizabeth said, tracking his tired face for any enthusiasm.

"I intend to spend this afternoon with you. I left Gerry on duty. It's the least I could do, given I lured you and Gert over here and then had to forgo hosting you two in my hometown for the past week. I guess I underestimated how ill Mum really is," Roy said, glumly. "I'm afraid it will be catch as catch can right now until Mum's health improves."

"Don't worry about us, Roy. Izzy is a splendid tour guide and it's been three years since she and I spent time together," Elizabeth said, nervously chattering on about Izzy, her burgeoning success as an artist, and her conflict with her mother. Given Roy's state, she decided to avoid discussing their relationship and where it was headed until he was in a better frame of mind.

CHAPTER 35

HOME AWAY

When Elizabeth and Roy arrived at the four-story brick and stucco house, Mrs. Armour and Izzy were already there. Mrs. Armour, in a dark gray suit and matching hat, opened the paneled door, waving them through into the small marble-tiled foyer. As she ushered them into a cream-colored den with moss green Edwardian chairs and a patterned sofa, a breathless Izzy slipped in behind them.

"I think it is perfect!" Izzy exclaimed, kissing both Roy and Elizabeth on their respective cheeks. "I've run up all the floors for a look-see. The bedrooms are quite cozy. There's a wonderfully deep clawfoot tub in the upstairs bathroom, several fireplaces, and the kitchen is spacious, not that you'll spend a lot of time there. There's so much we need to do while you're in London. I hope you don't mind if I co-opt Elizabeth while she's here, Roy. It's been so long since we've been together."

"I suppose I'll have to share her," said Roy, stroking his chin before breaking into a dimpled grin. "Actually, Miss Armour, I am grateful that you are an enthusiastic host and tour guide for Elizabeth and Gert, given my current situation with my mum."

"Please, call me Izzy, not Miss Armour."

"Izzy, for heaven's sake, Mr. Royston is appropriately proper," said Mrs. Armour. "After all, you've just met."

"Mother, since we left New York, he's practically become a Hines family member."

Elizabeth blushed, embarrassed to hear her own words come out of Izzy's mouth.

"Yes, it has been a lucky adoption," Roy affirmed, without skipping a beat. "The Hines' friendship has made all the difference in my American stay. I don't feel like a stranger in a strange land, which can be such an uncomfortable experience."

"Why don't you look around for yourselves?" said Mrs. Armour, sitting down heavily on the couch. "I'll stay here. My arthritic knees prefer to avoid stairs whenever possible."

"Let's start at the top and work our way down," suggested Izzy, leading them to the central staircase. Elizabeth and Roy dutifully followed, passing large, painted portraits of regally dressed men mounted on the walls. Some stood with one hand resting on a book on a small table. Others were seated, looking as if they were somberly viewing something or someone in the distance.

"You'd think their only ancestors were men," Izzy said over her shoulder to Elizabeth as they ascended.

Elizabeth, aware of Roy behind her, avoided engaging with Izzy in another potentially political discussion. The rest of their conversation revolved around the spacious, well-appointed rooms and other amenities, from the abundant electric lights and radiators to the charming second-floor balcony overlooking the wide street and small tree-lined square below.

"Wonderful! Thank you so much for finding this place for Gert and I," Elizabeth exclaimed to Mrs. Armour when they rejoined her in the den.

"Good location as well." Roy added. "Easy to get to the Soho, the West End, and Mayfair from here."

Elizabeth, noticing the omission of his location, wondered what that indicated.

"So I will let the Maxwells know that you would like the house for a month with the cook and housemaid?" Mrs. Armour asked. "The cook lives elsewhere but the maid resides in the top floor bedroom."

Elizabeth confirmed the arrangement and her willingness to pay the staff during their stay.

"Now that that is settled, I think we should have a celebratory evening out after you and Gert move in. What about it, Roy?" Izzy asked as they let themselves out the front door.

"Certainly Miss Izzy, good idea," said Roy, clamping on his bowler hat and turning up the collar on his tweed coat. "Elizabeth, would you let me know a few days ahead of time as I need to ensure that I have coverage for my mother? And now, I must bid you ladies adieu and be on my way." He bowed and spun on his heels, striding away northward along the cobbled street.

"By the time we get home, it will be time for tea," Izzy announced.

"I could use some warmth after sitting in that cold house. I must admit, though, I will always prefer coffee to tea," Mrs. Armour confided to Elizabeth.

"A genuine British tea is so delicious, though!" Izzy exclaimed.

"Yes, I know you're enamored with everything British. Elizabeth, we'll give you a ride back to Claridge's. It is on our way."

"That's very kind. Thank you, but I'd like to make my return on my own so I learn my way around," said Elizabeth, preferring navigating unfamiliar streets to the ongoing tension between Izzy and her mother.

"Absolutely not, Elizabeth. Your parents would think me remiss if I let you wander London by yourself. Now come along."

Mrs. Armour signaled to her chauffeur, who sprang out to open both doors of the Armours' burgundy four-seated Daimler parked in front of the house. Elizabeth capitulated, clambering into the back seat with Izzy. The driver tucked a large wool blanket over their knees before starting up the motor, which sputtered and shuddered before erupting into a loud constant purr that, thankfully, limited conversation.

Elizabeth simultaneously felt excitement and gratitude over securing such an agreeable, affordable London lodging and relief and doubt about her time with Roy. They had easily fallen back into their familiar repartee. Roy told humorous anecdotes about his return home and reunion with his brother, which prompted Elizabeth to recount her adventures with Gert and Izzy, emphasizing the moments that made her smile. Yet she felt an ambiguous absence more keenly than ever. Exact words to describe it eluded her, but she knew it had something to do with physical touch or, to be more accurate, the lack thereof.

Initially, Roy's gentlemanly comportment and restraint were a welcome contrast to the many flirtatious physical advances from men she had fended off during her career. Now, though, she longed for more than hand-holding or quick kisses on the cheek. The return ride to the hotel sped by. When they arrived at the entrance, Elizabeth's thoughts were more garbled than ever, the path out of confusion no clearer.

She disclosed the good news to Gert, who had peremptorily ordered a tray with tea and scones from room service. The stack of Gert's written and stamped postcards on the side table prompted Elizabeth to write Joanie after she finished her tea. Imagining Joanie's considerate, wise input might put things in another perspective. She often found that writing a letter took her further into herself than casual conversation did.

Dear Joanie,

I hope you're rounding the corner health wise and beginning

to experience some glimmers of spring and rebirth. It is mighty damp and cold here but there is no snow so at least the streets are clear and walkable if one bundles up. No wonder the British love their tea and whiskey. If I had to live here forever, I might become a convert like our good friend, Izzy, who appears to have taken to London habits and life like a proverbial duck to water.

Actually, Gert and I will be residents for at least a month. Mrs. Armour found us a lovely house in the Knightsbridge part of London south of Hyde Park with easy access to most of the places I want to frequent or explore in London. It is a four-story, brick and stucco house right on Montpelier Square so I will be able to look out on some trees from my window like I do at home. Apparently, the owners winter in the south of France and welcome the idea of having Gert and I in residence and paying the wages of the skeletal staff left behind. They're not even charging us rent.

Izzy has been a terrific tour guide so far. Thank goodness because Roy has been consumed with his mother's health crisis. Although we've been here a week, this afternoon was the first time we could get together. Pop warned me that this might be the case, but I was hoping for more than half days once a week. I don't want to be demanding especially under these circumstances but . . .

How I could use your sage advice, dear friend! I realize that I have been a bit cavalier about how I feel about Roy. I guess you could say he's more important in my life than I was willing to acknowledge. As you know, I always prioritized my career over any possible relationship with a man and truthfully, it wasn't ever an issue before. I thought getting away from work and traveling together might clarify what we mean to each other and how we want to proceed but so far, I feel I am treading water.

Oh bosh. You are dealing with a much more critical situation and shouldn't have to concern yourself with my silly drama.

I don't know what we will be doing yet for the next eight weeks. Izzy has a few paintings to be shown in a Parisian gallery show and would like us to accompany her. I do like the idea of a week in Paris perhaps followed by traveling to the South of France to hopefully milder weather.

As you probably surmise, some of what happens next depends on the Roy situation. I intend to see more of Europe while I am over here with or without him. We are scheduled to begin rehearsals of another Shubert production, *June Days*, in April so I need to return at least two weeks prior to that.

In the meantime, Momma and Pop send a weekly package of my correspondence to Mrs. Armour's house here. If you feel up to writing, best to use our Manhattan address.

I will keep you informed and continue to pray that we reunite this spring in Manhattan or upstate New York if that is our only option.

Sending you much love,

Elizabeth

Isa Lanchester's nightclub bustled. Every seat at the long zinc bar to the right of the entry door was occupied. Waiters, juggling full trays, squeezed between the black and white tiled tables, their patrons brandishing cigarette holders and glassware differing in size and contents. The small wooden stage in the far corner, however, was empty excepting a black upright piano and a garland of multicolored festive lights strung overhead.

"No worry. I reserved a table," Izzy reassured Elizabeth and Roy. "Besides, there's Charles." A patrician-looking, blond man, dressed entirely in black, vigorously waved from a table on the far side wall. He leapt to his feet, pulling out two chairs for the women as they approached and nodding welcome to Roy.

"Afraid Isa's is becoming too popular if this crowd is any indication," Charles said in a deep bass voice that was surprisingly incongruent with his lanky, adolescent bearing.

Piano hands, Elizabeth thought, as she observed his elegant, long fingers. With his chiseled facial features, large brown eyes, and long dark lashes that would be the envy of most women, Charles was remarkably handsome. She had expected someone somewhat effeminate like the few obviously homosexual actors she worked with in the past, but he was anything but.

"I ordered a bottle of bubbly to celebrate your presence in our great city." He drew a bottle of Veuve Clicquot from a silver ice bucket and poured them all glasses. Clinking his glass against each of theirs, he made a toast: "To Broadway royalty in our midst!"

Elizabeth's face flushed in embarrassment when the people at the surrounding tables lifted their glasses in acknowledgment. She enjoyed the anonymity London had provided thus far and was not eager to lose it. Ray grasped her knee under the table, as if affirming his empathy. Winking at Roy and Elizabeth, Izzy took a large gulp, then wound her arm around Charles's shoulders, pulling him close to whisper in his ear. *What does she have up her sleeve?* With Izzy, one could only be sure of one thing. Whatever mischief she caused, it would never be spiteful or caustic. As a result, although Izzy tended toward eccentricity and unconventionality, she inspired loyalty and affection in a wide range of friendships.

"You know anyone can offer a reading or song here," she said. "That's the whole point. Isa wants it to be a place for creative expression and experimentation, not just the usual nightclub. Isn't that right, Charles?" Charles enthusiastically seconded her. "I left New York before you two started to perform together. Any chance of a song?"

"I suppose," Roy said. He turned to Elizabeth. "If my leading lady is game."

"I suppose," Elizabeth said, "if we sing something relatively new, something fun." Roy scratched his head as he sipped more champagne.

"I have an idea," he said, triumphantly. "*No, No, Nanette* is opening at the Palace soon. What about a song from that musical?"

"Perfect. I love 'Tea for Two.' I started to learn it on the piano before we left New York. Do you know the lyrics?"

"I do!" Roy said.

"I think I can remember them," Elizabeth said, reciting the words to Roy.

Having taken it upon himself to introduce them, Charles thread his way up to stage and clinked his glass with a knife to alert the crowd. "Fresh from a successful Broadway run—" he began.

Once Elizabeth seated herself. Roy stood, casually leaning an elbow atop the piano. As Elizabeth relaxed, her fingers easily remembered the chords. She pretended they were singing together after Sunday dinner at home in Manhattan, as they often had. She was so successful at blocking out the venue that when they finished, the thunder of applause startled her. Roy extended his warm hand to help her up from the piano stool. Simultaneously, they bowed before returning to their seats.

"What a treat to see you two pros together!" said Izzy. "However, I don't know how you keep a straight face with those lyrics, Elizabeth. Something about baking a sugar cake and raising a boy for you and a girl for me. God, save us!"

Thankfully another bottle of champagne arrived at the table, courtesy of Isa Lanchester, derailing Izzy from another exposition on the drudgeries of conventional family life. Since Elizabeth had previously warned Roy about her friend's political activism, he skillfully turned their conversation into a discussion of favored performers and plays. As it turned out, Charles was an avid theater buff and much more knowledgeable than Izzy in this regard.

The following morning, Elizabeth recounted the evening's events to Gert as they breakfasted on freshly baked bread; thick, delicious Irish butter; and strawberry preserves provided by Mrs. Dawson, the housekeeper, at the oak table of the capacious kitchen.

"We had a splendid time although I didn't expect to perform," Elizabeth said, omitting that she hadn't gained further insight into her relationship with Roy. Perhaps he avoided the topic because

Izzy and Charles had accompanied them all evening. Both of them had commented on how much they enjoyed Roy's company and suggested another outing as soon as one could be arranged.

"Glad to hear Miss Izzy has a beau," Gert said, picking up their empty plates to transport them to the big metal sink for washing. "A sensible man who tames without her knowledge would be good."

If you only knew, Elizabeth thought. Charles had struck her as knowledgeable, sophisticated, and well-read, yes, but with no interest in curtailing Izzy. In fact, he seemed to enjoy her outspoken, frank expressiveness. If anything, his appreciation might embolden Izzy to further breach convention. Elizabeth grudgingly admitted to herself that she could imagine the two of them crafting a life together—behind closed doors, of course. It wouldn't resemble what Mr. and Mrs. Armour pictured for their daughter. Elizabeth sighed. Izzy, who'd previously either defied or avoided planning, had a clearer vision of her future than she did.

"Isn't Cecilia arriving today?" Gert asked, drying her hands and putting the clean dishes back in the cupboard.

"Yes. According to her telegram, she'll be arriving at King's Cross station late afternoon. We'll meet her and bring her back here. I've asked Mrs. Dawson to prepare dinner and leave it for the three of us."

"I bet she was happy about your request," Gert replied. "She misses planning and cooking meals for her people. She says, 'Four months is too long a vacation for me.' I understand. I wouldn't know what to do with that much time meself." Hands on her wide hips, Gert regarded Elizabeth. "And what would you like to do in the meantime today?"

"Stay in until we go to meet Cecilia," Elizabeth answered, yawning and looking out the window at an overcast day that seemed to be verging on some form of precipitation. The pleasantly warm kitchen and her late breakfast evoked lethargy. Besides, Izzy had relayed a thick packet of letters, cards, and newspapers from home that she was eager to go through. Somehow it felt like she, Roy, and Gert had been gone longer than two-and-a-half weeks.

★ ★ ★

Cecilia, clad in a conservative tweed skirt and matching jacket, no longer resembled the ebullient vaudevillian or the harried young mother of Elizabeth's memory. Although she had departed the United States only two years prior, the woman who sat at the dinner table with Gert and Elizabeth was almost prim. Her tawny hair was arranged in a French twist and she lacked lipstick and makeup on her pale, heart-shaped face. Elizabeth forced herself to overlook Cecilia's disconcerting physical changes in order to listen as the three of them reminisced.

"I miss my little girl, but I thought she would be better provided for by her grandparents," Cecilia said. "I didn't know what I was going to do. I couldn't depend on your brother and with motherhood, my acting career had to end." Cecilia pulled a linen handkerchief out of her purse and dabbed at her tearing eyes. "Ach, I knew I was going to get a little emotional seeing you two again. Apologies."

"There, there . . . " Gert clucked, sympathetically. "You were in a tough position."

"Yes, and I didn't want to burden your parents any longer with my upkeep, Elizabeth. They had already been so generous."

"If it is any consolation, Dorothy is a much-valued family member. I think of her as my creative, thoughtful younger sister and Pop adores her. I think he hopes she'll become a journalist or a writer of some sort."

"She spends much of her free time reading and writing." Gert affirmed. "Loves to cook also, assists in the meal preparation and baking whenever Frannie will let her."

Cecilia smiled weakly, obviously torn between her grief and her desire to know more about her daughter.

"And what is your work now?" Elizabeth asked, hoping to steer Cecilia onto less emotionally painful ground.

"My father loaned me money to attend secretarial school, which I did for three months. Now I am the secretary to the president of the biggest real estate company in Sussex," Cecilia explained. "The job allowed me to pay him back and move into a flat with a girlfriend. Not exactly exciting, but I am grateful for the regular income and the boss is training me to make sales of my own eventually. By next fall I hope to have enough money saved to bring Dorothy over here to visit during her summer vacation."

Cecilia dolloped mint jelly on her lamb chop and cut it into bite-sized pieces. The three of them ate, chatting about work and life until last bit of pudding was consumed, and they adjourned to separate bedrooms.

Lying alone in the quiet room, its far wall awash with pale light from the gas lamps on the street below, Elizabeth replayed their conversation, especially Cecilia's remarks about motherhood and a theatrical career. She had wanted to dispute that motherhood and career were mutually exclusive but the more she thought about it, the more complex the issue became. A congenial partner and adequate support, financial and otherwise, was crucial, none of which were available to Cecilia. To no avail, Elizabeth tried to recall meeting anyone in her line of work who pulled off being both a good mother and a successful actress. She fell asleep reassuring herself that she had exceeded people's expectations before. Why not in this case?

CHAPTER 37
TRUTH OR DARE

Cecilia's three-day weekend visit passed quickly. Elizabeth was sorry to see her leave. With her self-deprecating humor and expressive, warm presence, Cecilia was great company. Their shared love and knowledge of theater and dance lead to much conversation about playwrights, plays, and actors—the kind of conversation she rarely had with anyone except Roy. On a whim, they got last-minute tickets to a matinee revival of *The Pirates of Penzance* at one of the West End theaters, which they thoroughly enjoyed though they'd both already seen it.

Cecilia also insisted on visiting Harrods. Though neither could afford to shop there, they pretended they could, sampling perfumes and free food tidbits and ogling designer dresses in the couture department.

"I haven't laughed that much since we left New York," Elizabeth told Gert, after Cecilia boarded her train and they waved until the caboose became a distant red speck.

"She's a peach," Gert said. "Master Palmer made a big mistake abandoning her."

"I am sure he would never admit that." said Elizabeth as they passed through the station's main rotunda. The pale sunlight, fractured by the large, bracketed arched windows, resembled shards on the glossy floor.

Cecilia was not the only one abandoned. Dorothy would grow up without seeing either of her parents regularly. Palmer's contact was mostly in the form of hastily scribbled postcards from Floridian beach scenes, a present for Christmas and birthdays, monthly phone calls, and occasional short visits to New York. How long could Palmer leave behind waves of upset without having to face any consequences? *Seemingly endlessly*, Elizabeth thought, although she also dreaded the fallout should that day ever come. Pop and Momma were dedicated and caring substitutes, but they weren't getting any younger. In addition, the heated, aggressive rivalry between Hearst and Pulitzer threatened the status and circulation of other New York newspapers as well as the livelihoods of their staff members like Pop.

"Have a bee in your bonnet, Miss E.?" Gert asked, as they halted on the pavement next to the line of taxis, their motors chugging as they emitted small clouds of exhaust.

"Just thinking about Momma and Pop," she said, preferring not to worry Gert.

"Ladies?" asked the tartan-capped taxi driver at the head of the line. He bowed and opened the back door of his taxi. With bushy eyebrows, ruddy cheeks, sea blue eyes, and a red beard, he looked as if he belonged in the Highlands, not the throes of London.

"Yes, thank you," Elizabeth said, climbing onto the cracked leather back seat. The interior smelled faintly of tobacco and something woody she couldn't identify.

"Is that a small bit of heather hanging from your mirror?" Gert asked, settling next to Elizabeth.

"Tiz. Good guess," he acknowledged with a toothy grin. "How'd you ken if you're American? I'm guessing meself that is where you two beauteous ladies hail from."

By the time they arrived back at Kensington Square in midafternoon, Gert and Duncan Campbell, as he introduced himself, had briefly exchanged their life stories. He offered his services as a driver while they were in London and also to take them to an authentic Scottish pub. The lively repartee and Duncan's brogue were the perfect amusing antidote for Elizabeth's somber thoughts of family and future.

Everything was coming together for their London sojourn. The only nagging loose end was Roy. They hadn't communicated since Cecilia arrived. He'd said he thought it best that Elizabeth enjoy uninterrupted time with her sister-in-law, especially since her visit was so brief and he and Cecilia had never met. At the time, Elizabeth thought Roy was considerate. Now she wondered if he was being avoidant. Regardless, when they entered the house, she silently affirmed her determination to enjoy her British experience even as she picked up the envelope the housemaid had left on the hall table. It was written in Izzy's unmistakable scrawl.

"This seems to be my week for frequenting London's best department stores," Elizabeth said, scrutinizing Izzy's invitation to lunch at Selfridge's the following day and her mysterious request for Elizabeth to come alone.

Thankfully, Gert preempted a possibly awkward situation by declaring, "If you don't mind, I will stay put tomorrow. Cecilia's visit was a treat but now I am ready for some knitting and a day of rest."

★ ★ ★

"Actually, I think it is rather hideous," Izzy said. She and Elizabeth stood on the sidewalk, contemplating the iconic Gilbert Bayes sculpture, *Queen of Time*, looming over the entrance to Selfridge's.

"Well, there's no overlooking it," Elizabeth chuckled. "That's certain."

"Into the halls of trade, my friend," said Izzy, linking her elbow with Elizabeth's as they joined the bevy of mostly women streaming through the ornate doors into the store. Smartly dressed, coiffed women, and some men manned pristinely decorated kiosks offering scarves, purses, jewelry, hats, and other accessories. Piano music wafted from somewhere and mingled with the hums of moving elevators and multiple conversations as people eyed and discussed the wares. The colorful, lively scene reminded Elizabeth of *National Geographic* photos of Istanbul's bazaar.

"I have something to pick up for Mother after we lunch. Let's walk up to the restaurant, so you can see more of what capitalism has to offer," said Izzy.

Once they were seated in the airy, white-pillared dining area with its monogrammed, white linen tablecloths and matching napkins, Izzy burrowed into her capacious purse and pulled out a wrinkled section of the *Daily Mirror*, which she smoothed out on their table.

"Okay, when were you going tell me about this?" she asked, pointing to an article titled "Sweet Romance: Elizabeth Hines is Engaged to Roy Royston," and read aloud. "A romance that had its inception backstage in a New York theatre will soon culminate in the marriage of pretty Elizabeth Hines, star of 'Marjorie,' to handsome Roy Royston, leading man of the same musical show."

"That's hearsay, Izzy," Elizabeth interrupted in exasperation.

"But dearie, it goes on to say that you confirmed the rumor in an exclusive interview with their paper. Why would they lie?" Obviously, Izzy, savvy in many other ways, wasn't familiar with the wiles of gossip columnists and tabloid newspapers.

"Because they can and rumors about the personal lives of stars sell," Elizabeth answered.

"You mean there's absolutely no truth to this?" Izzy's eyes bored into Elizabeth who squirmed uncomfortably under her stare.

"Not exactly. I suppose there's a smidgen," Elizabeth said, begrudgingly. She went into detail about her perplexing relationship with Roy.

For once, Izzy listened without interrupting or editorializing until Elizabeth took a long drink of water.

"There you have it, such as it is," Elizabeth said. "You could say this is my truth but as to the actual truth, that's currently unknown."

"Poor you! I see why you're confused although if I were in your place, I think at this juncture, I'd be angry more than anything else." Izzy rested her chin in her hand and regarded Elizabeth thoughtfully.

"How can I be angry? His mother is very ill with pleurisy, and I want to be supportive, not demanding," said Elizabeth, cutting into the herbed omelet cooling on the plate in front of her.

They ate in companionable silence. When finished, Izzy leaned back in her chair and lit up a cigarette.

"I wish I could help you unravel this knot," she said.

"Oh, Izzy, you're helping by being my friend. I haven't spoken about this to anyone, even Gert, although I am sure she knows something is up. Besides, in addition to being my confidante, I couldn't ask for a better tour guide."

"If Roy were to ask, would you want to marry him?" The directness of Izzy's question threw Elizabeth.

"I don't know," she stammered. "We've barely touched in an intimate way. I do find him physically attractive; it is easy to be with him and my family loves him." She was thinking out loud. "It is an incredible idea, isn't it? Choosing to be with a man for a lifetime. I had no qualms about wanting to be an actress but marriage and family, well, they always seemed like evolving future decisions."

"If one wants to pursue that path," added Izzy, snuffing out the remains of her cigarette in the crystal ashtray. "Personally, I don't want to be a mother. I want to bring art into the world, not children."

"I envy your clarity on this subject, Izzy. Your courage to do things differently, too, although sometimes—"

"Sometimes you worry I'll go too far off the track," said Izzy, grinning mischievously.

"Yes indeed. Joanie and I feared you'd get arrested, beaten, or both. Not to mention incur more of your father's disapproval."

"Dear Joanie. There's nothing I can do to help her currently but there may be something I can do for you," Izzy said. "I'll give it some thought."

"Oh, please, Izzy. I am not asking for aid. Roy simply may be distracted in a way that I've never seen him before since he is now home and around his family." Even as Elizabeth was speaking, she realized she didn't quite believe this interpretation. However, lacking a satisfactory understanding and slightly embarrassed by confessing her upset, she ended their conversation by proposing to pay for lunch so they could proceed with their afternoon plans.

CHAPTER 38
BUT A DREAM

With fragments of a dream lingering, Elizabeth lay under the warm blankets in the damp, cool early morning, piecing together what she could remember—a regal man resembling Prince Edward held out his hand to her, but she hesitated out of caution. Or was it aversion? During the time she balked, the man mutated into an arthritic, stern old man authoritatively waving her away. She could recall no more though lines from a Maurice Maeterlinck poem surfaced:

> *Here are the old desires that pass,*
> *The dreams of weary men, that die,*
> *The dreams that faint and fail, alas!*
> *And there the days of hope gone by!*

Dreams and what they conveyed interested her. The summer before Joanie got ill, they had made a pact to read and discuss Sigmund Freud's *Interpretation of Dreams*. A challenging task, it led to many questions about the existence of the Freudian "id," wish fulfillment, and what they agreed was his excessive emphasis on sexual interpretation. Still, Elizabeth found some dreams emotionally impacted her even hours after waking. The odd transformation of the obviously princely man disturbed her. So did Maeterlinck's lines.

She admired Maeterlinck's work, particularly *The Blue Bird* and *The Mayor of Stilmonde*, and it was common knowledge both his longtime female companions were actresses, his first wife, Georgette Leblanc, well known in Europe and his current wife, Renée Dahon, thirty-four years his junior. Was that the thread in her dream? Or was it reading an interview where he discussed universal consciousness and the perennial truths inherent in all religions? Gert's cheery voice interrupted Elizabeth's musing.

"Miss E., I brought you a cup of coffee just the way you like it!" Dressed in a pleated wool skirt and sweater, Gert entered carrying a small tray. "Eleanor, the housemaid, makes a good cup of tea, but coffee is another matter for these Brits. Brought myself one up, too." She placed Elizabeth's cup on the bedside table, seated herself in the wing chair by the bedroom window, and took an obviously satisfying long sip.

"What's on the schedule for today?" she asked.

Elizabeth rousted herself and sat upright. The coffee's delicious fragrance wafted through the room.

"Need to take a few sips first." She reached for the steaming blue and white cup. "Hmmm. That's better. Merci beaucoup, Gert." She leaned back against the pillows, holding her cup in both hands, appreciating the heat.

"That is French for 'thank you,' correct?" Gert asked.

"Perfect."

"I bought myself a wee French phrase book when I was out and about—the kind they recommend for tourists to stash in their pockets or purses," Gert replied, her blue eyes sparkling. "Thought it might come in handy in Paris, especially when we meet Isabelle at the gallery show March seventh. Besides, we have a lot of time in the city—a whole week before we go to Provence."

"If you want to explore Paris a bit on your own while we're there, I agree, study the book," Elizabeth said. "The rest of the time, I can get us around. I've kept my French up over the years since I studied it at Brearley."

"By any chance, is Paris less damp than London?"

"I don't know. I'd guess not much, if at all, since they are close in latitude," said Elizabeth, downing the rest of her cup. "One thing I do know is that the French like their coffee!"

"That leaves us with a couple more weeks here so we best plan accordingly," Gert said. "Don't want to have any regrets about missing something we want to see or do."

"I wonder if a day in Oxford would be possible," said Elizabeth.

"We still haven't seen the Crown Jewels and don't forget we have a date with our taxi driver, Duncan Campbell, for a visit to a true Scottish pub," Gert said.

★ ★ ★

Downstairs in the spacious kitchen, Elizabeth, fully dressed, and Gert, sat at the table, enjoying a late breakfast of soft-boiled eggs, sausage, and toast with marmalade. Each shared sites to visit before their imminent departure.

"Westminster Abbey," Gert said.

"We could attend one of the Abbey's daily services," Elizabeth suggested. "That might be an interesting way to visit it."

"I suppose," Gert replied, "though I've only been to Catholic masses."

They discussed the differences between a High Episcopalian service and the Catholic mass when Eleanor, the demure house-maid, poked her head around the kitchen door.

"Miss Isabelle is here, Miss Elizabeth," she quietly announced.

"Heavens, I didn't expect her! I was going to phone her later this morning. Please show her into the living room. I'll be right there." Elizabeth hastily folded her napkin and began picking up her dirty dishes.

"Let me do that, Miss E. You go find out what your friend is up to," Gert said, shooing Elizabeth out of the large kitchen. "I'll be up in my room after I clean up here. Just give me a shout."

When Elizabeth found her, Izzy stood facing the leaded glass windows overlooking the street.

"I couldn't stay away any longer. I hope you had a nice visit with your former sister-in-law," she said before turning and purposefully striding across the room to bestow a quick kiss on each of Elizabeth's cheeks. "I want to hear all about it. Are you busy today?"

"Not yet. We were just discussing what we want to see before we leave but we hadn't decided on a plan for today yet."

"I am free so if you don't mind, I'd like to join you, but right now, I have something to tell you. Mind if I close this door? It's for your ears only." Izzy closed the door, took Elizabeth by the hand, and led her to the couch. Once they were seated side by side, Isabelle spoke in a low, measured voice.

"When we were last together, I said I wanted to help you with this Roy situation in any way I could. Charlie helped. He is so well connected, travels between many worlds here in London."

Had Izzy revealed her concerns about Roy to Charlie? Elizabeth's cheeks flushed as they always did when she felt embarrassed or vulnerable. They'd only met once that evening at Isa Lanchester's club.

"After our night out together, Charlie asked if you and Roy were engaged. See, I am not the only one who reads the tabloids! Anyway, I set him straight, told him the real story. When I summarized the situation, he told me something he noticed that night at Lanchester's. It may mean nothing, but I thought you should know. Have you ever heard of Parlyaree?"

Elizabeth, mute with anticipation, shook her head.

"I hadn't either, but Charlie informed me that it's a secret slang language that actors, circus performers, sailors, and homosexuals use to communicate with each other, especially if they don't want anyone else to know what they're saying. When Charlie was leaving the men's room at the nightclub, he overheard Roy say a few words in Parlyaree to someone."

"Roy has been in British theater since he was in his early teens," Elizabeth said, perplexed by Izzy's revelation. "It is likely that he would have run into that language. Maybe he was greeting an acquaintance from his past."

"Perhaps, but I thought it might be a clue."

"A clue to what, Izzy?" asked Elizabeth, simultaneously confused, concerned, and irritated.

"A clue to why you two don't have much of a physical relationship."

"I see. You think—You're insinuating that Roy might be of Charlie's persuasion?" She couldn't bring herself to say the word.

"Isn't it a possibility?" asked Izzy, digging into her purse to offer Elizabeth a cigarette before securing one for herself in her ivory holder. Stunned, Elizabeth accepted. She wanted to dispute Izzy's suggestion but had to admit that she could be right. Tendrils of gray smoke encircled them as they sat, quietly smoking.

"I still don't know how to proceed," said Elizabeth, breaking the silence. "I mean if he hasn't said anything to me, he obviously doesn't want me to know."

"From what Charlie has told me, it is difficult to come to terms with. For one thing, to have such proclivities is considered a crime in many countries. And who knows how one's friends and family will react once they know? One of Charlie's oldest friends refused to continue their friendship after Charlie confided in him."

"Weren't you upset when he told you?"

"Not really. I don't have romantic feelings toward him." Izzy uncrossed her long legs and took another drag on her cigarette. "I love and admire him as a friend, companion, and fellow artist. However, I've never been inclined to devote myself to one man."

"Maybe that is why Charlie could tell you."

"Perhaps. Fact is, there are a lot of men out there leading double lives," Izzy said, tipping her head emphatically toward the windows.

"I know there are many men who have extramarital liaisons. More than half the show girls I know have a big daddy. I've *never* wanted that arrangement."

"Why would you? That's a covert form of prostitution, if you ask me. Besides you have a supportive family and a successful career." Elizabeth saw the affection in her friend's eyes. "But if you eventually desire the wife and mother role, Elizabeth, you need to broach the topic with Roy."

"I guess you're right since he hasn't said a word. He tells me how lovely and considerate I am but that's it. I always thought initiating discussion of commitment and marriage was more of a man's responsibility."

"Not so much these days," said Izzy, extinguishing her cigarette stub in an ashtray. "Anyway, that's all I have to report. I told my driver to wait so if you two want to tour something, we don't have to wait for a ride."

CHAPTER 39
HEART OF THE MATTER

Their guide had regaled Elizabeth, Gert, and Izzy with the sordid and often violent intricacies of British politics over the past thousand years as he led them from one London site to another. They even traipsed through the large complex of buildings that made up the Tower of London and viewed the Crown Jewels, all in one afternoon.

By the end of their tour, even the irrepressible Izzy was lagging. After her driver dropped off Elizabeth and Gert, she immediately departed for home.

"As Mum used to say, my goose is cooked," Gert said as they walked in the door. She headed to the red leather armchair and rested her stocking feet on its matching ottoman. Elizabeth went straight to the couch where she lay prone.

Eleanor addressed Elizabeth.

"While you were out," she said, "Roy telephoned and suggested getting together."

Since her morning conversation with Izzy, Elizabeth had committed to speaking with Roy, but she preferred a circumstance in which they could be leisurely as well as alone together. Given the sensitivity of the subject matter, privacy was necessary. Besides, she was unsure of her reaction to whatever he might reveal.

"If you and Izzy are planning another escapade tomorrow," Gert said, "I think I'll bow out."

"I think Izzy had her fill of sightseeing for a while," said Elizabeth, propping herself up on her elbow. "Actually, I am going to suggest to Roy that we spend the day in Oxford. I've always wanted to see the Oxford campus. Maybe we can even visit the Bodleian Library, if we can get in."

If Roy agreed, it seemed like an ideal plan for her purposes. Oxford might provide anonymity and more tranquility than London. She decided to bring an overnight bag, just in case.

★ ★ ★

Roy met Elizabeth at the entrance to Paddington Station, as they had agreed. Though the day was brisk, the bright sun exuded a modicum of the spring warmth to come.

"What a wonderful idea for an outing, and for once, the weather is cooperating," he said, kissing her cheek and then holding her at arm's length by her shoulders. "Mmm, I have never seen you look so well rested, my dear."

"Probably true. I haven't been on a long vacation since I started on the stage."

Roy, on the other hand, despite his meticulous dress and jaunty manner, looked more haggard. She refrained from commenting on his appearance, hoping their time together might be restorative for him despite what she intended to bring up.

"I already bought our tickets. Let me guide you through the masses to the platform," he said, offering his arm, which she was happy to take as they entered the cavernous wrought iron and glass structure crowded with travelers in constant motion, often with luggage and children in tow. Trackside, the great engines purred and belched steam like waking dragons. Uniformed conductors in navy hats piped with gold waved passengers onto their trains. Roy and Elizabeth settled themselves, facing each another in an empty compartment. Elizabeth felt awkward and uneasy.

"Tell me, how is your mother?" she asked. Roy sighed, almost imperceptibly.

"She seems to be on the rebound. Yesterday, despite being bedridden, she told me how to cook oatmeal as if I didn't know already. So, yes, I'd say she is recovering. I've been on duty whenever the nurse's aide isn't there. While I am around, I want to give my brother Gerry time with his family after work. It's the least I can do, given that he is Mother's caretaker whenever I am elsewhere." He hesitated, his normally lively brown eyes muddied.

"The thing is, though," he added, "I don't think she realizes that she isn't likely to recover her former lung capacity and, therefore, the strength she previously had."

"And that will impair her ability to live independently," said Elizabeth aloud, finishing his thought.

"Exactly, and that in turn affects me," he said, "because I would feel badly leaving Gerry with the bulk of her care." The train began to chug out of the station. Elizabeth instinctively reached out and lightly squeezed his knee. She immensely valued his concern for his family, loyalty, and sense of duty even as she simultaneously realized the situation would affect their future, whatever it was to be.

"Enough of my life," Roy said. "Tell me what you, Gert, and Izzy have been up to."

To lighten his mood, Elizabeth deliberately peppered her narrative with humorous anecdotes. She relayed Izzy's outspoken outrage at the Tower guide's suggestion that Henry VIII had hired a professional French swordsman to give Anne Boleyn a quick, clean execution, illustrating the king's affection for her. And she told Roy about Gert's fascination with the Tower ravens and the Raven Master's job. The hour sped by as Elizabeth caught Roy up on her London adventures and relevant communications from New York.

Oxford, with its spacious lawns and craggy stone buildings and walkways, seemed more peaceable than London. Pedestrians and bicyclists outnumbered cars and horse-drawn carts on the streets, imbuing the city with a sense of leisure that Elizabeth found soothing.

"If I had the means and desire to go to university, this would have been my choice," Elizabeth said as they took a midday break on a bench overlooking Magdalen College. "What an appealing place! It just breathes learning."

"If you ever wished to return to school, Oxford would be lucky to have you," said Roy, taking off his bowler hat and tipping his face upward to the sunlight with closed eyes. "It's not too late should you decide to go that route, you know."

As she did before stepping onstage, Elizabeth inhaled deeply and exhaled slowly.

"Is that an invitation of sorts?" she asked.

"An invitation?"

"You said earlier that you wouldn't be able to stay away and leave Gerry with all your mother's care, so I assume you're preparing to spend more time here than in the States."

"I am considering how to proceed, given the situation. I do intend to fulfill my contract with the Shuberts for our next play together but then—" He looked off into the distance thoughtfully. Unable to contain her emotions anymore, Elizabeth burst out.

"What about us?" she asked.

"I would miss you dearly and hope to find times and ways we could reunite in the future."

Much to her chagrin, tears trickled down Elizabeth's cheeks. She fumbled in her purse for a handkerchief.

"Did I say something wrong?" he asked as she patted her eyes.

"It is just that I thought we were more than—" Roy, his eyes now wide open, faced her, alert but silent. Elizabeth steadied herself with a few breaths. "I thought we were more than friends and stage partners."

There I've said it. She felt relieved. His jaw was slightly flexing which Elizabeth knew signaled his stress. Several minutes went by as they sat silently, stranded in a sea of kempt green hedges and lawns.

"I wish I could give you more," Roy began. "It would be you if I wasn't—I always believed I hadn't met the right woman. You are the right woman but I—" His voice trailed off as he clasped her hands in his cold fingers. The conversation was obviously as difficult for him as it was for her. His handsome face was pinched, his cheeks blotched.

"I couldn't abide the life your friend Izzy is proposing to live with Charles," he said. "I know how important family is to you. You'll want children someday and I can't go down that road." He stared at her imploringly. "I never meant to deceive you or misrepresent myself if that is what you think."

Elizabeth withdrew her hands from his and instinctively crossed her arms, embracing herself to maintain some composure. She suddenly felt chilled with an odd floating sensation. Dark blue-gray clouds amassed behind the majestic stone ramparts of Magdalen College. What had been a light breeze was ramping up to a gusty wind.

"We best get to some cover," Roy said, picking up her overnight bag and holding out a hand to help her rise. Out of habit, she took his hand and followed behind as he led them across the expanses of lawn into a warren of winding streets. Big raindrops fell just as they ducked into a smoke-filled pub with grimy windows and well-worn wooden chairs and tables. They commandeered a corner table. Roy went up to the bar where a few obvious regulars sat smoking pipes, drinking, and talking. He returned with a pot of tea for her and a pint for himself.

Elizabeth had nothing to say. Polite conversation was effortful and seemed ridiculously incongruent. This man, with whom she had shared so much in the last year and a half, was not who she thought he was. Furthermore, they were not who she thought they were. She sipped the musky strong black tea, hoping its sweet liquid warmth would ease her stunned, wooden feeling.

"Would you like something to eat?" Roy asked. "They probably have a few food items to offer, standard pub fare—bangers and eggs, maybe shepherd's pie or potato soup."

She shook her head, wondering how he could think she might be hungry. Sheets of rain rattled the windows as the wind moaned through the nooks and crannies of the old building.

"We were lucky to find this place and not to get caught in that."

"Yes" said Elizabeth. It was the only response she could muster. she recognized that Roy was trying to make contact.

"It should pass in an hour or so," he said. "Then we could go the Bodleian Library, just as you said you wanted to."

She drank slowly, praying her tumultuous emotions would settle so she could decide what her next step would be. She wanted to ask, *Were you ever attracted to me?* She wanted to know how he first realized, then reconciled to, his preference. However, this was not the time or place. Not only would discussion in this setting endanger Roy but she was contending with a knot of anger and embarrassment over how her desire had blinded her to the reality of their relationship. So they sat, the men's voices rising and falling while the rain steadily thrummed outdoors.

In the end, she opted to forgo the Bodleian tour to return to London, hoping that the intense ache Roy's presence elicited would decrease with distance. They parted ways at Paddington Station without proposing another get-together. As usual, Roy courteously escorted her into a taxi at the station and lightly kissed her on the cheek before helping her into the car. While the taxi bumped and swayed along under an overcast sky, her feelings amplified, coalescing into a profound, alien loneliness she had never before experienced.

"You are home earlier than I expected. I was just going to—" said Gert, scrambling to her feet when Elizabeth entered and set down her belongings. "Oh dear, Miss E., what the devil?"

The warm parlor with a fire cheerfully crackling in the fireplace and Gert's broad, concerned face were too much. Elizabeth, unable to tamp her emotions down any longer, crumpled onto the couch and quietly sobbed. Gert sat down next to her, stroking her hair lightly just as she had comforted Elizabeth when she was a child. "There, there," she mumbled. "It's going to be okay."

Even in her compromised state, Elizabeth wanted to deny Gert's well-intentioned words. It was not going to be okay. In one day, her relationship with Roy had irreparably changed and beyond the next Shubert show coming up in May, her future resembled a bottomless abyss.

CHAPTER 40
BUT NOT FOR ME

On the train back from Oxford, she'd passed quaint stone houses, their chimneys breathing white smoke trails, while pedestrians, horse-drawn drays, and the occasional car moved about their business through the cobbled streets. As she looked at the scenes, she speculated. Up to that juncture, she hadn't thought much beyond the next role and perfecting her skills as an actress. Her dedicated focus, coupled with rapid success, had shielded her from the ambiguities inherent in courting and the life choices to which it led. The loss of her illusions about Roy was painful but secondary to the vast unknown she now faced.

"Did you and Mr. Roy have a fight?" asked Gert. Elizabeth's crying had petered out to sniffles. She sat up, rubbing her tired eyes.

"Not really." She realized she had to come up with some explanation to mollify a perplexed, alarmed Gert. "More like a clarification. We're not going in the same direction. After the run of our upcoming show, *June Days*, he intends to spend more time in England to help his brother care for their mother."

"Oh, now I see. You're going to miss him. They say absence makes the heart grow fonder. I'm sure that he'll miss you, too. You're both young and anything could happen."

Anything has happened. Besides, I am almost twenty-five. Elizabeth stifled her retort and appreciatively patted Gert's hand.

"Did Mrs. Dawson leave anything for dinner? I'm famished. Couldn't eat a thing earlier."

"I'm sure she left us a store full. She was here most of the day. We had a nice sit and chat before she left. I'll check while you put your things away and then we can decide what we'd like to heat up."

★ ★ ★

After a night of fractured dreams and light sleep, Elizabeth decided writing Joanie might offset her increasing despondency. Envisioning her friend and imagining her responses had become a reassuring ritual in the many months since Joanie had been away. After breakfast, Elizabeth closed her bedroom door and settled herself in the window seat with a pad of paper and pen.

Dearest Joanie,

I hope this letter finds you on the mend and signs of spring beginning to show in Saranac Lake. Here in London, the sun seems warmer and brighter. Sycamore trees in the small park outside our rental house are budding and we haven't had frost in several weeks.

With Izzy's help, Gert and I visited most all our proposed list of places and completed the activities we wanted to do, from shopping at Harrod's, touring the Tower of London, seeing some West End plays (*No, No Nanette* is not to be missed!) to visiting several splendid museums and venerable churches probably bigger than even St. Patrick's or St. Bart's.

Early next week we will accompany Izzy to Paris for the art show at the Salon des Indépendants in which two of her paintings will be displayed. Our Izzy is indeed making a name for herself in the art world over here.

That is the good news. However, I imagine your dark eyebrows lifting as they do when you, with your quiet, steady voice, invite me into deeper inquiry, saying something like, "I am interested in how you are feeling, not just what you're doing."

You've always had a way of bringing what has heart and meaning to the forefront, dear Joanie. It is one of your many gifts which I sorely miss, especially in my current confused, upset state. Let me proceed as if we were together lunching in your garden, which, hopefully, we will do this upcoming summer.

As you know, Roy and I spent a great deal of time together in the past year, both as stage partners and friends. He is a big hit with my family and tended to spend most Sundays with us as well as holidays. He has been consistently affectionate, considerate, and supportive so I began to inadvertently consider a committed relationship with him (something I had not entertained with any other man). This idea gained ground when he invited me to accompany him to England on his return here to visit his ailing mother.

Although I knew he would be somewhat preoccupied with his mother's care, I didn't foresee that we would see so little of each other. Also, I had overlooked the lack of physical touch in our relationship, probably because I was relieved to not be forced to fend off roving male hands for once! In any case, I chalked up the absence of petting to his courteous demeanor and my reluctance to initiate since I didn't want to come across as unladylike (old school of me, according to Izzy).

While we were alone yesterday in Oxford for the day (our first full day together in almost a month here), I finally got the courage to address the subject. The topic of our respective futures arose spontaneously so I took the opportunity to get clarification as to his intentions and begin to reveal my thoughts. First, he announced that he will return to England for an unknown amount of time after our next Shubert show. When I responded by voicing my reactions, he declared that he loved me but had also consequently realized his incapacity for pursuing conventional marriage and family.

I'm sure you can read between the lines and understand what I am referring to. I can't say the word yet to describe what his relationship preferences are. I guess I am somewhat shocked as well as massively disappointed. Please keep all this confidential. I will only confide in you and Izzy, who already suspected the truth of the matter. To everyone else, including Gert and my parents, I will attribute the apparent change in my relationship with Roy to the fact that he is moving back to England.

The whole situation has spurred me to think about so much. I suppose when one's world tilts unexpectedly, that is natural. You have probably gone through your share of second guesses and doubts after your diagnosis and during your treatment. When you have the time and energy, I am eager to hear about your inner journey.

In the meantime, I will send some picture postcards to keep you abreast of our travels and perhaps provide some amusement.

Much love, Elizabeth

Satisfied with her effort, Elizabeth put down her pen and paper to gaze out the window onto the park below. White-barked sycamores seemed to glow in the morning sunlight. An aura of spring green tinged several bushes. Two seated women chatted together on a bench as each rocked a baby carriage. A small boy in knickers determinedly kicked a soccer ball around on the grass. It was all so peaceful, so normal. She sat clasping her knees, trying to shake her bereft feelings.

CHAPTER 41
ONWARD

Nice, France
February, 1925

Several days before they left for France, Elizabeth was preoccupied with packing up and mailing home packages of English marmalade, tins of fruitcake, soft wool scarfs, and sweaters for everyone at home. She attended final dinners with Mrs. Armour as well as Izzy, Charles, and their friends. Thankfully, Roy declined all their invitations, so she was spared seeing him. However, his brief farewell note arrived the day before they left. He affirmed his deep, abiding affection for her and voiced regret at any "undue upset," as he phrased it. The note ended with his exclamation: "Looking forward to waltzing together in *June Days*!"

His cheerful, idiosyncratic sign-off depressed her. Obviously, what she perceived as a major rupture didn't hold the same import for him. His continued courtesy made it difficult for her to be angry at him. Instead, she alternated between fury at her self-delusion and immense sadness, which she tried her best to conceal, especially from Izzy, who was increasingly animated about the upcoming exhibit and its attendant events.

The daylong trip to Paris was a trial of getting themselves and their luggage on and off the requisite two trains and the ferry. The sonorous French language, which Elizabeth normally relished hearing and speaking, didn't hold much allure. By the time they stepped off the train from Calais in the Gare du Nord, she wished they were instead disembarking at Grand Central Station so she could see her family.

"Oh my, isn't it gorgeous!" Gert exclaimed as their taxi crossed onto the Pont Neuf over the green, gray Seine. Small red boats clustered on the river's banks while some hardy, well-clad pedestrians walked along the stone sidewalks under gas lamps sparkling in the twilight. Despite the encroaching darkness, Notre Dame's spires were still visible in the distance. "I can see why they call it the City of Light."

Izzy turned to them from the front seat.

"There is some debate why the city is known as that," she explained. "Some say the name refers to the Enlightenment and not to light, per se."

"C'est vrai," confirmed the taxi driver in his quintessential black beret. He nodded approvingly at Izzy, who beamed.

Gert and Izzy proceeded to query the driver as to how much English he spoke. The ensuing conversation was such a humorous banter of French and English that Elizabeth's mood lightened. After they exited the bridge, they drove onto a wide boulevard running alongside the river.

"Et voilà, mesdames, la Rive Gauche," the driver said, pointing out the Left Bank. The boulevard was lined with what Elizabeth assumed were four-story houses as elegantly detailed as any Park Avenue mansion. By the time they pulled into their hotel's small courtyard through what looked like a hole in the wall, the city was alive with streetlamps and interior lights diffusing its velvety darkness.

After they settled into the Hôtel de Varenne, they went to a brasserie down the block where a black-vested waiter, a white towel folded neatly over one forearm, showed them to a table. Izzy ordered a bottle of Veuve Clicquot to celebrate.

"Don't worry, Elizabeth," she said. "Mother booked our suite at the hotel and intends to pick up the tab for our ten-day stay."

"Such unexpected generosity! I must get her a thank-you gift for you to take back."

"I don't think generosity was her motivation. She was just relieved she didn't have to chaperone me. After all, you are the sensible one and Mother thinks Gert is quite proper and trustworthy."

Izzy winked at both of them, then drew on her lit cigarette. Elizabeth began translating the menu for Gert, who regarded hers with a look of forlorn dismay.

★ ★ ★

According to Izzy, the exhibition's opening promised to be an extravagant affair. A multitude of European aristocrats would attend, having conceded for one night to mingle with established as well as upcoming artists and assorted gallery owners. In view of that company, Gert appointed herself as their ladies' maid and arranged with the hotel manager for their evening clothes to be pressed, a hairdresser to come to their suite, and transportation to take them to and from the Grand Palais.

Gert zipped up Elizabeth's sequined silver, ankle-length gown and stood back, beholding her. Hands on her generous hips, she admired her handiwork.

"Look at you two!" she exclaimed. "You will certainly turn heads tonight even if you don't have one of them long titles."

"I'd rather they admired my paintings," Izzy said, smirking at Gert's comment. She looked fabulous in a dark purple sheath trimmed with small pearls around its delicate, scoop neckline. A matching velvet and pearl headband, ornamented with a clutch of peacock feathers, accentuated her facial contour and sheen of dark hair.

For two days Elizabeth and Izzy had wandered through shops along Saint-Germain-des-Prés, admiring French fabrics and fashions and idling at the Les Deux Magots, where Izzy hoped but failed to glimpse the café's notable regulars—Picasso, Fernand Léger, Henri Matisse. Elizabeth still felt like she was sleepwalking. This evening was no exception. Roy's absence was highlighted, in fact since she had grown accustomed to having him by her side at events. Never one for large parties, she realized anew how much she relied on his social acumen and easy wit. *I'm here for Izzy,* she reminded herself as they put on long satin gloves and coats and gathered their clutch purses before descending to the lobby.

Paris at twilight is at its most magical, Elizabeth thought. The glow of the sun's waning rays intermingled with lengthening shadows. Every narrow, winding street they passed became a pastiche of light and dark. As their taxi approached the Quai and its corresponding bridge leading to the Right Bank and the Grand Palais, Izzy, who had been unusually quiet during the ride, clasped Elizabeth's gloved hand.

"I am so glad you are with me," she said. "I didn't realize how nervous I'd be. I've never been in a show of this caliber." Elizabeth squeezed Izzy's hand reassuringly.

"I am no art expert but from what I've seen, your work holds its own and deserves to be seen."

"It would be a coup if I got gallery representation out of this."

"You mean it might convince your mother that you are on the right path?"

"My mother will never be fully convinced that I am doing the right thing," Izzy said, sighing. "In her eyes, a woman should primarily aspire to be a wife, mother, and social doyenne."

The Grand Palais lived up to its name. The monumental outdoor staircase led up to the huge nave of glass and intricate ironwork. Its entrance flanked two long wings, each pillared with tall columns. The dome radiated the indoor lights, casting rays into the inky night, an effect both alluring and intimidating.

"There you are!" exclaimed Charles, regally handsome in a tuxedo and brandishing a silver cane. He sauntered over to greet them as they entered the vast building.

"Heavens, I didn't know you were coming," said Izzy, momentarily flustered by his unexpected appearance.

"I managed to procure an invitation. I wanted to be here for your big European debut." He bowed, kissed them on both their cheeks, murmuring something about the French way, and then offered each a copy of the striking, geometrical black and red exposition catalogue. "Ladies, let me escort you."

Charles positioned himself between them, linked his elbows with theirs, and led them into the exhibit.

The paintings, organized by nationality and grouped alphabetically, hung on canvas-sheathed walls. So many people were circulating through the high-ceilinged rooms that it was difficult to stand in front of a painting and fully take it in without getting jostled or blocked from the view altogether. Izzy and Charles flitted from one painting to another, excitedly discussing painterly techniques and subject matter. Wanting to go at her own pace, Elizabeth agreed to rendezvous with them later in the English and American wing and detached from them.

As she progressed through the selection, Elizabeth realized she lacked an informed eye for contemporary art. Where was the beauty in bottles and machinelike objects grouped with guitars; barely recognizable, distorted human features; or dark cityscapes with industrial overtones? The colorful Impressionist-style paintings, whether still life, human, or landscape, were much more appealing although she wondered if her taste was too prosaic since she overheard many positive comments about the abstract art. Whenever the crowd flow allowed, she paused, studying each piece for any intriguing aspects.

Absorbed in the task she had set out for herself, she was surprised to be entering the American wing, having fully completed the European selection. Izzy and Charles were in animated conversation with a couple in the far corner of the first room where Izzy's two paintings were grouped.

As Elizabeth approached them, Izzy gesticulated.

"My dear friend and star in her own right, Elizabeth Hines," she announced. "Elizabeth, may I introduce Count and Countess Maeterlinck?"

"We are honored," said the tall, majestic, dark-haired man, taking her hand in his large, rough one, and bowing. Elizabeth recalled the popular epithets for Maurice Maeterlinck—the "Belgian mystic" and the "Belgian Shakespeare."

"Heavens, I am the honored one," Elizabeth exclaimed. "I've read some of your work, saw *The Bluebird* in New York, and cheered you on in the 1920 ticker-tape parade when you visited the city."

"Did you read my work in French or English?" he asked in heavily accented English.

"French. I prefer reading in an author's native language if I can."

"Splendid. Most English speakers don't take the time and I fear some of my nuances are lost in translation." He shook his leonine head in disapproval. "What other languages do you read in?"

"Italian and German, although my German has been mostly limited to opera librettos, not literature. I aspired to be an opera singer before I became an actress."

His beautiful, petite, redheaded wife, considerably younger than the count, eyed Elizabeth with her startling green eyes.

"Vous êtes un actrice? (Are you an actress?)" she asked.

Elizabeth's affirmative answer apparently pleased her. After establishing they were the same age and started acting professionally at the same time, the countess requested that Elizabeth drop the formalities and call her Rénee.

"We are quite interested in Isabelle's work," said Count Maeterlinck. Elizabeth assumed he was speaking English for Izzy's benefit since her French was obviously limited. "We are building a house in Nice and want to purchase some paintings for it and this one is perfect."

He pointed to the painting of a woman in a long nut-brown skirt, almost prone on a maroon couch, with a book in hand. Her discarded blue shoes lie on their sides on the floor like small animals. The walls behind her are draped, floor to ceiling, as a soft filtered light permeates throughout. It looked as if the woman was merging into her surroundings as she read. A slight blurring of the rich colors at the edges of the woman's clothing and other objects in the room enhanced the overall effect.

After admiring Izzy's paintings, the five of them circumambulated the rest of the exhibit, their conversation alternating between French and English. Izzy, beaming from the Maeterlincks' enthusiastic response to her work and a prospective sale, practically danced her way along. Elizabeth was pleased to notice Charles periodically touch Izzy's arm or shoulders and exchange a few words with her, thereby interrupting Izzy's intensifying mania. In the past, Elizabeth and Joanie had collaborated to ground Izzy whenever she was emotionally overwrought. *Joanie would appreciate Charles's instinctual care for Izzy*, thought Elizabeth, again regretting Joanie's absence.

Before they parted company for the rest of the evening, the Maeterlincks made Elizabeth promise to visit them if she and Gert traveled south. Renée was most adamant in her invitation, stressing how rare, and therefore special, it was to meet another successful actress her age who was "si gentille, si cultivée (so kind, so cultured)."

CHAPTER 42
MEETING WITH THE MASTER

The Count—or Maurice, as he requested Elizabeth call him—freely announced that, although he was an atheist, he believed strongly in the godlike virtues of compassion, wisdom, and integrity.

"I also firmly believe in death," he added as they sat on the terrace under an arbor of what Elizabeth speculated were grape leaves. The Mediterranean's aqua waves dulcetly lapped on Nice's sun-seared rocky shoreline below. The cloudless sky seemed to stretch away without a perceptible horizon.

His comment perplexed her.

"Could you say more about that?" she asked.

Renée, glamorous in a red shift, dark tortoiseshell glasses, and a broad-brimmed hat, laughed.

"Of course, Maurice can say more! It is what he does. N'est-ce pas, mon cher?" She stood up and kissed him lightly on the cheek. "While you talk, I am going to bring us some refreshments."

As Renée exited up the stone stairs to the house, Maurice kept talking.

"Death teaches us how to live," he said. "Unfortunately, we view death as an enemy and seek to banish, overcome, or deny it. The sicknesses we attribute to death are really a form of nature and life. Therefore, it is not death but life we must act upon." His gray eyes shined with fervor as he went on.

"Death shares the aspect of infinite incomprehensibility with God. That is, if God exists. Reason and understanding can't prove that, so we resort to faith. Really, we are incapable of knowing what He is or if He is. So, too, with death, we know only that the physical body ceases functioning. Beyond that, we have no idea what awaits us."

"Do you believe there is life after death?" Elizabeth asked. During the flu pandemic and war, she and Joanie often discussed the topic without coming to a conclusion.

"I am strongly persuaded by the studies of William James and the Psychical Research Society that it is likely," he said. "Though, what kind of life is it? Do the dead retain some form of consciousness? How is it that they can relay details of their former lives through mediums? Why, in fact, can they only speak through mediums? Why not to dear friends and family members? There are so many questions lacking substantial answers."

"I also wonder how some psychics know the future," Elizabeth added. Her brief reading with Mrs. Zara and the psychic's cautionary words about men not being who they were suddenly came to mind. Was Roy the man who the psychic intuited would disappoint her?

"Yes, the psychical ability for prediction highlights questions about the nature of time itself," agreed Maurice, sweeping back the wave of dark brown hair that continually fell across his broad forehead.

Her mind spinning, Elizabeth was relieved to hear Renée's footsteps coming down the stone stairs.

"Chére Elizabeth, has my dear Maurice been—how do you say it in English?—bending your ear? Such a funny expression!" She put down a tray with a bottle of water, three glasses, lemon wedges on a small plate, a bowl of olives, an oozing wedge of soft cheese, and a sliced baguette.

"I admit I am currently particularly excited by these questions as I am currently writing about them," he said before popping an olive into his mouth.

"I understand. I periodically think about some of these ideas and even discussed them with my close friend until—" She unexpectedly choked up.

Maurice and Renée regarded her with concern as she, embarrassed by her sudden emotional upsurge, reached into her purse for a handkerchief. After dabbing at her eyes, she briefly told them about Joanie's situation.

"This is absolute tragedy," said Maurice. "An obviously intelligent, competent young woman crippled by that monstrous disease, just as she had found her calling. Circumstances like this make absolutely no sense to the rational mind. No wonder you are grieving." He rested his chin on his clasped hands as he regarded Elizabeth's tear-stained face.

That is only part of it. She refrained from revealing anything about Roy although it felt as if a bottomless pit of oceanic sorrow and disorientation had been inadvertently uncapped. She struggled to regain composure.

"Perhaps we need something stronger than water, Maurice," suggested Renée, pulling her chair closer, resting her small, manicured hand sympathetically on Elizabeth's.

"Bien sûr. I will return with some wine," said Maurice, hauling his large frame out of the chair and trudging back up the stairs.

"I am sorry for such a display," Elizabeth said, sniffling. "I guess the train trip from Paris was more tiring than I thought. I really can't sleep on trains no matter how luxurious they are."

"I have the same problem. The train is, I don't know how you say in English, *perturbé*." Reneé took off her dark glasses and fixed her green eyes on Elizabeth. "There's more to this isn't there, Chérie? I know I am a new friend but if you want to talk more, I listen well. One could not stay married to, and in love with, Maurice unless that was the case."

"Thank you for your kindness. I fear if I start talking, I won't stop crying. I haven't told anyone the details of what recently happened."

"No matter. Just relax. When you are ready, I am here." She lightly squeezed Elizabeth's hand before letting go.

Maurice returned with an uncorked bottle of white wine in a silver ice bucket and three glasses. He poured them each a glass. Elizabeth calmed herself by inhaling the fragrant ocean air as the palm fronds melodically rustled in a slight breeze.

"What plans do you and your companion have while you are in Nice?" Maurice asked. "We might have some recommendations."

"And I might join you some of the time," Reneé said. "When Maurice is consumed by a project, I try to stay out of the way until late afternoon. Lately, however, the renovation of Villa Orlamonde, our new place east of the old part of Nice, has required many interruptions to our usual regime."

"That would be lovely. Gert and I didn't plan anything yet," Elizabeth said. "We are just grateful to be here soaking up the sunlight, greenery, and mild weather. London certainly has its attractions, but the weather isn't one of them. It is so pleasant to sit comfortably outdoors in the fresh air."

"Exactly why we chose to live here, my dear," Maurice said. "Both of us had enough of the interminable overcast, damp, cold weather." He playfully toasted Elizabeth's comment with his glass of wine.

As they discussed the merits of Nice and its environs and sipped the delicious wine, Elizabeth's tension seeped away. Later, after bidding the Maeterlincks goodbye, she walked back to her hotel along the Promenade des Anglais, admiring the expansive, white sandy beach and pastel-colored buildings. Narrow roads snaked across the ragged mountains and rose abruptly beyond the town to the north. Gulls and pelicans arced and wheeled over the shoreline, casting shadows across the turquoise water. While some children played in the sparkling shallows, several women, shoes in hand and skirts lifted, wandered the beach barefoot.

Elizabeth, deciding to do the same, descended to the beach, strategically reaching under her skirts to detach her stockings from her garter belt and roll them up into her removed pumps. She meandered, relishing the warm, forgiving sand underfoot. For the first time since leaving New York, she felt fully present, not preoccupied with confusion or concern about Roy.

CHAPTER 43

ADVENTURE

When Elizabeth came back to their hotel quarters with sandy bare feet, jubilant and enthused, dangling her shoes, she proposed a North African tour. Gert, who was writing postcards, paused.

"Why would you want to visit a non-Christian country full of Musselmen?" she balked.

"You mean Muslims," clarified Elizabeth.

"Musselmen, that's what we called 'em at home, though Da had some other choice names. In any case, they aren't trustworthy, and the husbands can have as many wives as they want. Can you imagine?"

"Both countries are heavily influenced by Europe, particularly France. In fact, Algiers is touted as an incredibly beautiful, international city with spectacular surroundings and views. I think it may be a very interesting motor tour. Besides, when will we ever have another chance to travel there?"

"I suppose, but you'll never convince me that God wants men to have multiple wives."

The next evening, at dinner with the Maeterlincks at their favorite restaurant, Elizabeth voiced her dismay at Gert's reaction. Maurice's big head shook sympathetically.

"Fear combined with righteous religiosity are the underpinnings of prejudice," he said.

"I knew she was a devout Catholic, but I didn't know she was prejudiced. I guess we were never together in a situation where it became so obvious."

"Chérie, we actresses are accustomed to working with a variety of people, n'est-ce pas?" Renée added.

"That is very true," agreed Elizabeth. Performers like George M., Bessie Smith, Will Rogers, and Jay C. Flippen came to mind. She had shared the stage with all of them. She always had appreciated how George M. treated his cast members with respectful equanimity despite their skin color, religion, or personal quirks, unless they underperformed or betrayed him in some way. In fact, she followed his example in her dealings with casts and crews.

"Travel to other countries and cultures is also a great antidote to prejudice if one goes with an open, curious mind and doesn't impose one's values on others," Maurice said. "Then one sees that humans have multiple ways of living in this world, perhaps some more foreign than others. When it comes down to it, however, aren't we all trying to find contentment, ease, and meaning?"

As they continued to discuss travel and education, Elizabeth munched on her grilled, locally caught fish, roasted baby potatoes, and asparagus. She occasionally commented although she was mostly content to listen to Maurice expound and Renée add her insights.

★ ★ ★

In the following two days, after much discussion with a reluctant Gert, an exchange of telegrams with Pop, and a long consultation with the local Thomas Cook travel agent, the plan for a North African motor tour was settled upon. Elizabeth felt she'd won a victory against a fair amount of opposition and celebrated by thoroughly exploring the old part of Nice, following Renée's suggestions.

She and Gert wandered the winding cobbled streets, admiring the flower boxes, their contents spilling over balcony lips. In one courtyard, they came upon what appeared to be an outdoor spice market. Under blue striped awnings, mounds of spices filled large wooden flats, exuding rich aromas in an array of colors from ocher and lime green to chestnut brown and black pepper.

"Our Frannie would love this," said Gert, eyeing the wares. A woman stood behind the flats, her weathered face seamed and darkly tanned, a colorful kerchief wrapped around her head. Silently, she watched them with piercing black eyes.

Gypsy, surmised Elizabeth although she had never knowingly met a Gypsy. The woman resembled the illustration of the witch in *Hansel and Gretel* in her old copy of *Grimm's Fairy Tales*. In an instant, Elizabeth regretted that, much like Gert, she also had stereotyped a stranger.

"Let's buy some for Frannie and send it home with our other purchases," Elizabeth said. "Only problem is, I don't know what's what."

"I don't know, either, although this looks like paprika," Gert said, pointing to a beautiful rust-colored pile.

"You like?" asked the Gypsy, her face wreathed in a mostly toothless smile.

"Yes, I mean, *oui*," Gert replied. They discovered that if they pointed to a spice and used their hands to indicate the desired amount, they could communicate with the woman, who obviously didn't speak much English and whose heavily accented French dialect was beyond Elizabeth's capacity to understand. The spices they picked were put into small, filigreed tins, each unique and pretty.

Delighted with their transaction, both decided that tea in the hotel garden would be the perfect finale to their outing.

In the garden a marble fountain tinkled merrily in the background. As they waited for their tea, Elizabeth took in the statue of a mermaid pouring water from a jug into the pool of water. Lavender bushes along the garden's perimeter lightly perfumed the air.

"After tea, it's time for me to write a letter to Joanie and a few postcards," said Elizabeth. "It's been so relaxing here; I haven't had the gumption. Besides, I imagine the postal service is slower from North Africa, so I better get to it before we leave."

"Yes, and a week of touring will go by fast, and heaven knows what conditions we'll face," Gert said, dabbing moisture off her forehead with a handkerchief.

Elizabeth took off her straw hat and turned her face toward the warm sun, deliberately not responding to Gert's doubt-ridden comment. The upcoming trip arrangements were as comprehensive as could be accomplished from afar. Gert had been informed about every stage and told what measures were in place for their comfort and safety.

After their tea break, Elizabeth was ready to compose a letter to Joanie. Gathering some hotel stationery and a pen, she situated herself on their small balcony, shaded by a massive palm tree.

Dear Joanie,

I find myself in probably the loveliest place I've ever been to date. I suppose others more well-traveled than I might refer to Nice as quintessentially Mediterranean. Since I haven't been to any other coastal areas, I have no experience with which to compare. The landscape is gorgeous; steep, tree-covered hills drop to a large tourmaline-colored bay with white sand beaches. Temperatures are mild, the air fragrant with the smell of the sea mingled with the blooms of plants mostly unknown to me. The sun shines daily which, after the penetrating cold and damp overcast weather of London and Paris, has been a welcome respite.

I was fortunate to meet Renée and Maurice Maeterlinck in Paris at Izzy's showing and they extended an invitation to visit them here. When we first met, I was a bit intimidated by Maurice (you may recall he won the Nobel Prize for Literature in 1911), but in addition to having an amazing intellect and being a brilliant speaker, he is a thoughtful, caring listener with a good sense of humor. Therefore, he is easy to talk with. Renée, who is my same age, is delightful, lively, and an accomplished actress on the European stage. We swap stories and discuss the difficulties we had establishing ourselves as professional women in the theatrical world.

By now your eyebrows will be raised in that quizzical way I know so well as you wait for me to address the fraught topic of Roy. There isn't really much to say beyond what I covered in my last letter. He isn't capable of loving me in the way I want to be loved by a man. That is the bottom line. He wasn't and isn't intentionally deceptive and manipulative. In fact, he is truly fond of me and hopes we resume our friendship when we meet again in the States. Currently, I am uncertain if I can or would want to do that. Regardless, I will see him again, at least professionally, because we have the lead roles in a Shubert production scheduled for a June opening in Chicago.

The whole situation has been quite emotionally upsetting. However, my spirits are beginning to recover. I am not revealing the true reason for the rupture in my relationship with Roy to anyone other than you and Izzy, who suspected what the real situation was. Yes, I am somewhat embarrassed but, more importantly, I don't want to endanger Roy. Personally, I don't care if a man prefers loving another man. In my opinion, cultivating a respectful, caring love relationship with all its attendant benefits is an enviable goal. Unfortunately, we live in a society which, to a degree, dictates then enforces parameters on how and whom we love and criminalizes those perceived as aberrant.

I apologize for waxing philosophical. Maurice's influence, I guess. We've had some interesting conversations about culture, religion, death, and science you would have enjoyed. I have been prompted to think deeply about several subjects, including my future, although I haven't concluded much yet. My French, however, is immensely improved!

I do hope you have found some people there in Saranac Lake whose company is as simulating and comfortable as mine with the Maeterlincks. Good company makes such a big difference in one's state of mind.

This may be my last letter for the next few weeks as I've decided to spend the latter part of this vacation on a North African tour, which I am excited about. I have never been anywhere seemingly so exotic. However, Gert isn't thrilled with my choice so I hope the travel arrangements are more than adequate. Otherwise, I may never hear the end of it!

I imagine the snow is almost melted there and crocuses and snowdrops are appearing. May they improve your health and lift your spirits. I miss you so much and pray we see each other in person soon.

Much Love, Elizabeth

Clouds scudded and danced over the Mediterranean, a tapestry of blues in aqua, turquoise, lapis, and grayish blue. Elizabeth spent the daylight hours of the two-day trip on the steamer deck reading her copy of *Baedeker's Guide to North Africa* or watching the peaceful sea shift in texture and color. The water became murky as the ship pulled into the Port of Algiers. Brightly colored small fishing boats threaded in between coal barges. Some larger cargo and steam ships were at anchor while others, docked at the long piers, were being unloaded by squadrons of brown or black men who used carts or the occasional crane to lift an automobile or large containers onto the shore.

"Guess we've arrived in the land of the infidels," Gert joked from her seat under the boat's eaves. She stuffed her latest knitting project into the bag she reserved for that purpose and rose to join Elizabeth at the railing.

Purplish mountains etched with silver slivers of snow rose to the west of the city. Its sprawl of gleaming white buildings was punctuated by minarets, domes, and occasional clusters of palm, eucalyptus, and other trees. A string of green hills framed the other edges of the town, which, were it not for the ornate arches constructed around its perimeter, appeared to nearly slip into the ocean.

"There's an Arab saying that Algiers is like a diamond set in an emerald frame," said a tall man in a white linen suit, leaning his elbows on the railing. His straw hat shadowed his angular face. His accent was slightly British although Elizabeth detected intimations of American English as well. He tilted his head in their direction.

"How do you do?" he said. "Name is Frank, Frank Warton, and you two are?" His gray green eyes unabashedly studied them. "If I was to bet right now, I'd guess you're American."

"The odds of us being anything else are rather small," said Elizabeth, smiling and gesticulating to the other passengers on the deck. They were all male with the exception of two heavyset older women in monotone Western garb, firmly holding the hands of young children, and one woman in a breathtaking red caftan embroidered in gold. Her face was veiled with lace. A stern-looking, older man in an impeccably white shirt, ornate vest, baggy trousers, and a red fez closely accompanied her.

Gert and Elizabeth introduced themselves to Frank, but the ferry's creaks, clanks, and shudders as it maneuvered into place dockside made ongoing conversation impossible.

After the gangplank was put in place, the passengers descended into a cacophonous melee of shouting porters and drivers, horse-drawn carriages, open carts being loaded with baggage by the ship's crew, and a few automobiles, their chauffeurs in livery standing nearby attentively. Elizabeth spied their hotel name on one car and was able to steer herself and Gert to it through the crowd.

"Mohammed, at your service, mademoiselles," said the bowing chauffeur. He opened the car door for them and called a wiry man in shabby clothes out of the shadows to wrestle their luggage up from the dockside carts and load it onto the back of the car. It took quite a bit of time to secure everything before they could get underway. As they slowly made their way through the narrow streets, Mohammed called out the names of mosques. He also pointed out the Casbah and other important buildings. The streets were lined with shops, open air fruit and vegetables kiosks, veiled women in flowing robes doing errands with children in tow, and pockets of seated men talking and sipping what Elizabeth surmised was coffee from small cups.

"My heavens, I don't think I have ever felt heat like this before," said Gert, fanning her damp, flushed face as their car bumped along. "New York can get humid and hot in the summer, but this is something else altogether!"

"It is certainly an argument for loose-fitting, light-colored clothes, brimmed hats, and sandals," said Elizabeth, noticing that many natives wore open toe sandals or flimsy slippers or went barefoot, like the man who loaded their luggage. She was thankful she had followed Renée's advice and purchased some sport clothing in Nice that was specifically designed for equatorial climates.

The road widened as they ascended a slight hill through an enclave of pretty villas surrounded by flowering bushes, yuccas, and other tropical plants with large fleshy leaves that Elizabeth didn't know by name.

"Mademoiselles, we are now in the area of the most beautiful garden in all Africa, the Jardin Botanique," Mohammed proudly informed them in his heavily accented French. "It is thirty-two hectares and has more plants and animals than you've ever seen."

"How big is a hectare? Do you know?" Gert asked Elizabeth.

"Almost two-and-a-half acres."

They passed through shadows cast by a row of stately palms on the garden's perimeter. The visible interior was a lush jumble of blooms, cacti, and bushes with winding alabaster-colored stone paths.

"And here, here is Hôtel Saint-George D'Alger, the most famous hotel where you will stay." He pulled into the semicircular drive where several doormen, who looked like marionettes in navy uniforms with heavy gold piping, stood at attention in front of an expansive portico with large columns.

"Dear me, it looks like we're staying in a palace!" exclaimed Gert.

The building was much more impressive than Elizabeth had anticipated. As they entered the lavishly ornate lobby, she wondered if the Cook travel agent in Nice had ignored her expressed desire to stay within the financially reasonable estimate she calculated to cover the remainder of their trip. She didn't want to ask Pop to loan her money if that could be avoided.

More apartment than hotel accommodation, their suite had two big bedrooms, each with its own bathroom, and a large opulent parlor with glass doors that opened onto a spacious veranda overlooking a series of well-kempt terraces below. A fantastically colorful array of cut flowers stood on the ornate sideboard in the foyer. Elizabeth opened the white envelope with their names written on it. The card inside read, "Welcome, my fellow Americans. Hope our paths converge again. Frank Warton."

"I'd say you have an admirer," said Gert, winking.

"I'd like to know how he ordered flowers so quickly and found us. It's not as if we dawdled getting off the ship. Besides, we didn't tell him where we were staying. And I need to point out that the card is addressed to both of us."

Elizabeth apprehensively regarding the assortment of red and white calla lilies, freesia, and unidentifiable purple flowers and greens. Disconcerted, she walked to the filigreed doors and threw them open. Air tinged with a jasmine scent wafted into the room.

"Your father would say the man is resourceful," Gert continued.

"I'm not interested," Elizabeth said. "I came here to adventure and see things I will probably never see again, not meet a man."

"What's wrong with the possibility of both?"

"Really, Gert, I don't understand you sometimes. You've always encouraged me to be an independent woman and yet here you are matchmaking."

"Oh, Miss E. Don't get me wrong. I am just talking about you having fun, nothing serious. You've been upset a lot recently. Even though you don't talk about it, I know you well enough to know that."

Gert stood alongside Elizabeth as they both looked out on the vista—gardens in the foreground, the blue seam of ocean and undulating hills in the distance.

★ ★ ★

As it turned out, Mohammed was not only their appointed driver but also their guide to Algiers. After escorting them from the hotel into the black car, he drove them into the Casbah and haphazardly squeezed the black car into a parking spot in front of his cousin's shop.

"It is the best shop in all Algiers," he said.

Mohammed's cousin, a taciturn, lean, raven-haired man in impeccable white robes stood in the arched doorway and bid them, "Assalum alaikum," before withdrawing into the shop's dark confines.

"My apology, mademoiselles, but automobiles no good here," he said, instructing them to walk single file through the labyrinth of narrow steep alleys of what Elizabeth's guidebook referred to as the "High Casbah." The stone streets were alive. Women walked by with baskets on their arms. Donkey or horse-drawn carts carried panniers of produce or dry goods. Mangy dogs prowled. Bands of barefooted urchins tried to beg only to be chastised by Mohammed and shooed away. While they wandered, he recounted an abbreviated history of the ancient city, starting with its inception as the Phoenician city of Icosium and leading up to its present status as a French colony.

Between his raspy voice and grammatically convoluted French, Elizabeth struggled to translate for Gert. Occasionally, they stopped to admire some gorgeous mosaic punctuating the seemingly endless array of white-faced buildings.

"Our guide appears to have a supply of cousins," Gert remarked while they lunched on herbed omelets and salad at an open-air restaurant in the Lower Casbah. The place was run by a portly, squat man with a bushy mustache whom Mohammed introduced as a cousin. He did not at all resemble the shop-keeper cousin they met in the High Casbah. While they ate, Mohammed disappeared into the back of the restaurant along with his cousin.

"That does appear to be the case," Elizabeth said. "Perhaps he refers to anyone he does business with as 'cousin.'"

A steady stream of people in all manner of dress were passing by—Berbers in burnooses; turbaned Muslims; Sephardic Jews in their long-striped robes and traditional headdress; the perennially slender, pallid French; ruddy-faced Englishmen in suits, ties, and hats; and the occasional tall, majestic Negro. It was a virtual parade of cultures unlike any Elizabeth had seen.

"I am so pleased that we made this trip," Elizabeth said, "and this is only the first day!" Gert harrumphed.

"Me, I prefer being where people know more English so I know more of what's really going on, like why Mohammed calls half the men in this city 'cousin' or why the Arab women meet in the city cemeteries."

Elizabeth couldn't explain the depth of her contentment at being in so foreign a place. It had something to do with claiming something for herself. Or was it reclaiming? Getting involved with Roy somehow had derailed her. She had lost her orientation but now she felt she was righting herself.

CHAPTER 45
THE ROAD OF MYTH

They stood in the horseshoe-shaped arched entrance to the Cathedral of St. Philippe. With the two towers on either side of the entry, the former seventeenth-century mosque, converted by the French into a Christian church, had not lost its mosque-like appearance. Also highlighting their surroundings were two gleaming white marble palaces that exemplified the best of Moorish architecture. One flanked the church, the other was directly across the road.

Mohammed officiously related the history of San Geronimo, entombed within the cathedral.

"In 1596, a young Arab, baptized with the name Geronimo, had been captured by a Moorish corsair and taken to Algiers. The Arabs wanted him to renounce Christianity, but as he steadfastly refused, he was condemned to death. Bound hand and foot, he was thrown alive into concrete from which a block was made. The block containing his body was built into the corner of a former fort.

"A Benedictine monk recorded the incident. In 1853, when the fort was being destroyed, the mold left by the saint's body was discovered in the location described by the monk so many years before. It showed the youth's features, the cords which bound him, and even the texture of his clothing."

"My heavens, what a brave soul!" said Gert, who fanned her florid face continually although she was shaded by the doorway. "I don't think I could ever be that devout and courageous."

Or deluded, thought Elizabeth, finding the story yet another gruesome example of people using religion to legitimize cruelty and violence. Mythology and history were rife with examples. So were the daily headlines. Since Gert found great comfort in her Catholicism, Elizabeth refrained from sharing her increasing antipathy toward organized religion. Maurice Maeterlinck's frank atheism appealed to her, especially his affirmation that although he didn't believe in God, he did believe in godlike virtues such as honesty, compassion, and wisdom.

"You see, mesdames, all the foreign ladies see and learn more when they take me as a guide, except the French, who are indolent and don't care to see much. "The other guides don't know as much," continued Mohammed, bestowing them with a brilliant toothy smile. "Nor are they quick enough for the British and Americans." He led the way into the cool, dimly lit cathedral.

Later Mohammed dropped them off at the hotel for teatime.

"I feel as if I have lived a week, or shall I say a few centuries, in two days," Gert said as they entered the lobby.

Elizabeth had to admit that she, too, was pleasantly tired and satiated, her mind churning with history. As she removed her large, white brimmed hat, Frank stepped out of the shadows cast by the large pillars.

"Ladies, we meet again. I want to invite you for dinner this evening and hope your dance cards aren't already full." He doffed his straw bowler. Elizabeth noticed he was incredibly handsome, a fact she hadn't fully registered on the ship. His build was muscular and trim, his black wavy hair abundant, and his tan face, with its high cheekbones and full lips, perfectly proportioned.

Gert quizzically looked at Elizabeth, deferring to her for an answer.

"Why not?" she said. "Just so we don't have to walk far."

"Absolutely not. I will meet you at the door with a driver and take you to one of the best restaurants in Algiers," Frank offered. "Name the time. I'll make the arrangements."

That night, like a symphony conductor, he queried Gert and Elizabeth about their recent travel experiences and regaled them with his stories while orchestrating their dinner.

"You must try this," he'd say before directing the waiter, dressed in a spotless white uniform with gold trim and the ubiquitous red fez, to bring them yet another mysterious, delicious delicacy.

As they wound up their lengthy, multiple-course dinner, Elizabeth decided Frank was a force unto himself powered by good looks, charm, competence, and determination.

"Now I can leave tomorrow, knowing you have experienced the best food Algiers has to offer," he said.

"You're leaving so soon?" asked Gert.

"Duty calls. I'm off on a train to Morocco tomorrow. Meeting you two brightened what has otherwise been a trip dominated by business."

Elizabeth gathered that he represented a large Chicago bank seeking to branch out internationally, but beyond that, despite his stories, he hadn't revealed much personally. She decided to probe a little.

"You appear quite familiar with this rather exotic part of the world," Elizabeth said.

"North Africa? Not really. This is my first trip here, but I've been traveling since I left England at seventeen with my uncle to come to the States. Before that, I explored Great Britain from Inverness to Wales whenever I could," Frank explained. "Been all over Europe as well but now I need to be stateside more often than naught. Needless to say, I jumped at the chance to come here when the bank proposed the idea."

He beckoned to the waiter to bring the bill.

"My heavens, you seem quite familiar with Algiers for your first time here," Gert remarked.

"I do my homework before I go anywhere; research a place, its highlights, amenities, even learn a little of the language if I don't know it. Once I get there, I wander the streets, talk with the locals, and find out as much as I can," Frank said. "In the past I wasn't on such a tight schedule, so I stayed as long as possible to get familiar with whatever geography I was in."

After settling with the waiter, he stood up.

"I hate to bring this delightful evening to an end," he said, "but we all have places to go in different directions, you two east to Tunis and myself, west to Rabat."

He insisted on escorting them back to their hotel in the taxi. They bumped along under a sky exploding with stars. The night air was a welcome balm after the heat of the day. Elizabeth, feeling entirely contented for the first time in months, leaned her head back on the seat, listening to Frank's intriguing accent as he traded snippets about Ireland with an obviously charmed Gert.

After helping them out of the car, Frank made an announcement.

"I will see you both stateside," he said before bowing to them. He took Elizabeth's hand and kissed it before jumping back in the car and directing the driver elsewhere.

As she readied herself for bed, Elizabeth speculated about how Frank could locate them in New York since she hadn't given him her address. Nor had he been forthcoming with his. For such a voluble man, he remained enigmatic.

CHAPTER 46
THE ROAD OF MYTH, PART 2

Elizabeth's excitement about the pending road trip from Algiers to Tunis eclipsed her first impressions of Frank, which she later regretted ignoring.

"According to our Cook itinerary, our first stop is the ancient Roman city of Timgad," she informed Gert, who was obsessively packing a few last items. "Some refer to it as the African Pompeii, although it was the Sahara's sand, not a volcanic eruption, that buried it."

"I am just happy we've seen the end of the insufferable Mohammed," said Gert, closing the lid of a trunk. "Phew, I didn't think I could get everything in. Good thing we shipped some clothing and purchases home."

"Maybe our new guide will be a sheik," Elizabeth teased.

"One with a harem like in that musical you were in, *The O'Brien Girl*?" quipped Gert. She pinned her hat over her dark curls and surveyed their quarters for anything left behind.

Bantering about the possibilities, they descended to the lobby to alert the bellman and rendezvous with the new guide and driver who would accompany them on their four-day journey.

"It is a forest of columns!" Gert exclaimed as they approached their first stop, Timgad. Its wide stone roads were lined with pillars. The remains of multiple buildings made of large clay like bricks stretched across the sandy plain. Their new guide, Abu, ordered the driver, whose name Elizabeth found unpronounceable, to park and let them out so they could walk.

"Misses, you must follow me. Something special you must see," said Abu, gesticulating to them, then striding out, his white robes billowing, through the ruins along an old road. He moved toward what looked like a hollowed-out hill. With his hawklike profile and taciturn yet imperious demeanor, Abu qualified for Elizabeth's image of a sheik. The thought amused her as they wound through the brick structures until they entered a huge open-air auditorium.

"Three hundred fifty seats, Miss Hines," Abu said as they stood on the stone stage and looked up at the ascending semicircular rows carved into the hillside. "As good as American stage, no? And probably built around 947 AD, according to archaeologists."

"Very impressive indeed," Elizabeth agreed.

"The sound is quite good. Try it out."

"I'll be the audience and sit for a moment, if you two don't mind," said Gert, breathing heavily from the walk in the blazing sun. She seated herself in the front row. Abu stood, arms crossed expectantly, watching Elizabeth.

"Alright, if you insist. Here's a true New York song for you two."

> *Give my regards to Broadway!*
> *Remember me to Herald Square!*
> *Tell all the gang at Forty Second Street*
> *That I will soon be there!*
> *Whisper of how I'm yearning*
> *To mingle with the old-time throng!*
> *Give my regards to Old Broadway.*
> *And say that I'll be there, 'ere long!*

Abu beamed as her soprano voice resounded clearly throughout the amphitheater. When she finished, he put his palms together and bowed appreciatively.

The fact that rehearsals for *June Days* were scheduled to begin in six weeks was difficult to reconcile with these majestic surroundings. The snow-streaked Aurès Mountains rose abruptly to the west above the distant plains, dotted with the red-striped tents of nomad herders. A caravan of camels rode along the fringes of the site. Several Arab women in long blue robes passed under the large Arch of Trajan in the center of the ruined city, which was turning a burnished gold in the mid-afternoon sunlight.

Elizabeth felt lost in time, awed by the span of history and the endless river of those who had come before. For a few moments, she imagined this outdoor theater, every seat taken, the crowd cheering for some performance.

★ ★ ★

Those insights lingered as they traveled eastward along a surprisingly good road that Abu said was mostly built by the French. Wherever they stopped, bands of dark-eyed children gathered to admire the automobile and beg, which their chauffeur discouraged by yelling and shaking his fist at them until they scampered away.

"Another tragic story." said Gert when they stood outside the car studying the eerie cone shaped formations and multicolored cascades of the famous hot springs of Hammam Maskhoutine. Abu had just explained the legend of the cones as the transformed members of a wedding party of a sheik who, insistent on marrying his beautiful sister, brought a curse down upon them turning them all to stone.

"There are ten baths of varying temperatures and full of minerals, particularly iron and calcium carbonate, which are said to be most healing," Abu explained. "Some are so hot, you can boil an egg in them. The Romans built the bath facilities, which are still in use, as you can see."

He pointed to a woman with large silver earrings and clanking anklets walking in magenta robes behind a man in a white burnoose astride a donkey. Obviously, they were headed toward one of the cauldron-like springs bubbling with blue water.

"I can't get over how ancient everything is here," Gert said to no one in particular. Looking at the man on the donkey, she asked Abu a question. "Why doesn't he offer her a ride?"

"Men are privileged here," he said, shrugging his shoulders. "Modern European ways haven't made their way outside the big cities. But you see, he is proud of his wife. You can tell by the amount and quality of jewelry she wears."

Elizabeth thought of Izzy and how vociferously she would have objected to the cultural situation of women here. Even the usually equable Gert was reacting. Yes, European and American women could now vote, get educated, and have careers, but they still had to constantly deal with covert sex discrimination in many forms and venues. Was that really a better situation than that of the gorgeously outfitted woman attending the baths with her husband? The question remained, persistent and unanswerable, as they resumed their travel, passing through fields of what looked like barley swaying in the light breeze. Larks skimmed about as they headed for the seaport of Annaba close to the Tunisian border.

1925–1928

CHAPTER 47

THE SHOW GOES ON

At the first rehearsal the Shubert brothers revealed their decision to open *June Days* in Chicago as a trial. Since the play was a three-act rewrite of the former *Charm School,* with the inclusion of a new score, they wanted to test audience receptivity before they invested more money to produce the play elsewhere. Initially, Elizabeth was dismayed at the news because the run was more uncertain than she expected and she had no potential shows in the offing. In addition, she was enjoying the comforts of being home again and spring was her favorite time of year in New York.

Roy hadn't attended the rehearsal, which both relieved and concerned her. His understudy, someone she had never worked with, was an earnest, quiet man with a wonderful tenor voice but a somewhat stiff dance partner. They had just finished the second act and were taking a midafternoon break when the beefy stage manager called them together.

"Train travel arrangements have been made for all of you. No need to make your own," he said. "You will be fitted for costumes here, but the dress rehearsal will take place in Chicago." He thumbed through his black notebook. "Oh, and Mr. Royston will join us in Chicago."

Stepping outside into the light spring rain, Elizabeth felt the familiar post-performance combination of pleasant tiredness and exhilaration. Though the Chicago news was initially disturbing, it further prolonged her meeting with Flo Ziegfeld. The new plan also gave her a grace period before she saw Roy again. She slipped into the back of the waiting car and rolled her window halfway down to better hear and smell the refreshing rain.

"Here she be, our very own star!" exclaimed Fred, grinning his impish grin and insistently helping her out of the car when the driver parked in front of the apartment building. "Cable came for you, Miss." As they entered the foyer, he rifled through papers on his reception podium and handed her a telegram. She didn't open it until she was back in the library, facing more looming correspondence and awaiting Gert, who was preparing tea.

The telegram, dated the day before, read: "We did it! Married in Paris at the Gallery. Mother in attendance, a few friends, lots of champagne and music. Missed you at the festivities. Love, Izzy and Charles"

"I suppose this is good news," Elizabeth said to Gert as she entered the room carrying a tray laden with two teacups, a pot, and an assortment of Frannie's delicious cookies. "Look at this telegram."

"Her mother must be relieved," Gert said, pouring them tea. In Europe they had made a pact to have tea together every afternoon they could when they returned to America.

"Yes, I'm sure that is the case," agreed Elizabeth. She had reservations about Izzy's marital arrangement but, much like the Roy situation, she considered any discussion of her concerns potentially harmful to the parties involved. The only person she confided in was Joanie, who was still in Saranac Lake but rumored to be doing better. Elizabeth decided she would write a letter to her friend after tea.

Dear Joanie,

I hope my postcards from Africa reached you. I thought pictures were more informative portrayals of the many exotic settings Gert and I found ourselves in. It is somewhat peculiar being back in the regular routines of work and practice after ten weeks in so many foreign places. Despite the disappointing outcome of the Roy situation, I am glad I traveled so far afield. So much immersion into cultural histories, archaeology, and art enhanced my perspective about our human existence and consequently increased appreciation of the life I have been able to lead so far.

Rehearsals for the newest Shubert production, *June Days*, started this week. The opening, however, will be in Chicago. The producers want to see the audience reception for a rewrite of the former play, *Charm School*. (Hopefully, it will be good enough to warrant backing the production elsewhere.) I wanted to spend the spring here, but I will be off to Chicago by the end of May. If all goes well, a New York opening is tentatively planned for August. With no other contractual possibilities in the future, I hope for the best even though it means daily performances with Roy, whom I have yet to see. He apparently is still in England and joins the cast in Chicago a few days before the dress rehearsal.

Speaking of England, I don't know if Izzy informed you—our favorite suffragette is now married. She and Charles, her dear friend and fellow artist, tied the knot in the Grand Palais, where her paintings were displayed. I fear we will not see her on this side of the Atlantic again. She has become the consummate expat and finds the Parisian lifestyle avant-garde and therefore particularly appealing. Her marriage provides her with more material resources and further liberates her from her parents. I do worry about her well-being in the long term, but I suppose you and I have always been concerned about Izzy's choices and that won't change.

Thank you for the two cards that were buried in the pile of mail I returned to. I am happy to hear that you made a few friends up there and can now venture out to the library and town when the weather and your health permit.

I do hope to be here in August because your mother told Momma that if your health continues to improve, you may come home during the summer. Wouldn't that be wonderful?! We have so much to share with each other.

Until then, all my love, Elizabeth

Heartened by writing Joanie and thinking of their possible future reunion, Elizabeth decided to ask Pop if he would provisionally assume the role of her manager and accompany her to a meeting with Ziegfeld. Since she had no work pending after *June Days*, it behooved her to find out what the impresario had to offer. She certainly didn't want to meet with him alone, though, even if Ziegfeld and others regarded it strange for a twenty-five-year-old successful actress to still rely on her father for business transactions. The truth was, she did handle her career-related negotiations but feared that Ziegfeld wouldn't stick to business. Besides, Pop could also mediate with Momma, who would certainly react negatively to any mention of Elizabeth working for Flo Ziegfeld.

The fragrances of another delectable Frannie dinner wafted into the library. Elizabeth pushed back from the desk, stretched, and satisfyingly eyed the steadily decreasing mail pile before pulling the rolltop down.

CHAPTER 48

THE ZIEGFELD FACTOR

Elizabeth debated the best time to approach Pop about Ziegfeld. They had enjoyed weekend walks in Central Park when she was younger, so an invitation for a walk wouldn't be abnormal if the weather cooperated and she could get him to join her without Dorothy or anyone else tagging along. Normally, she enjoyed Dorothy's inquisitive presence, but she needed to speak to Pop alone.

The next day the morning chill quickly gave way to the penetrating sun. A few puffy clouds slowly panned across the blue sky while blooming tulips and daffodils nodded in the breeze.

"What a pleasure!" said Pop as they passed through the park's stone entrance, arm in arm. "The smell of lilacs, a beautiful spring day, and some time with my daughter. I'd like to think that is what we're up to, but I suspect something else is afoot."

"You know me too well. I confess to an ulterior motive. You'll understand my insistence on getting you alone and out of the house once I tell you what's up, Pop." Elizabeth laid out her dilemma.

"You were right to come to me, Elizabeth. You can't ignore a man like Ziegfeld but you must protect your stellar reputation, which you worked so hard to establish and maintain. Men as successful and powerful as he are accustomed to getting what and whomever they want whenever they so desire."

They walked in silence for a time along the walkway and through the spread of lawns, towering sycamores, and oaks sprouting vibrantly green leaves before Elizabeth responded.

"I certainly don't want to come across as needy, but the truth is, Pop, I currently don't have any prospects in the wings after *June Days*, however long the run is."

She omitted revealing how distracted she had been by the Roy situation and that her current return to the stage after her trip felt lackluster.

"The other thing is that, like the news business, the musical theater business is changing rapidly," Pop said. "I am not saying this to upset you, but the talkies are becoming quite popular. Look at all the movie theaters cropping up. Could be as big a spread as commercial radio."

"I know but I don't think film acting is for me. I would miss the energy and interaction with a live audience too much."

"You won't know until you try, and I'd bet Ziegfeld already has his eye on the movie business. All the more reason to see what he wants with you." Pop smiled and squeezed her arm. The resolute look on his craggy face reassured Elizabeth that enlisting his help had been a good decision.

By the time they backtracked and rounded onto Madison on their way home, they had agreed to schedule a meeting with Ziegfeld at his new office. They also had discussed some terms of agreement they wanted if a potential contract was offered. They also decided not to reveal anything to Momma until they found out the details. When they reached their building entrance, Elizabeth, relieved and grateful, threw her arms around her surprised father like she used to when she was a girl.

★ ★ ★

Pop scheduled a meeting with Ziegfeld one week before Elizabeth's departure for Chicago.

"That way you can take your time away to consider whatever he has to offer and what your response will be," he counseled. "He should be in good spirits. His *Rio Rita* is a great success."

The day of the meeting, she and Pop stood on West Fifty-Fourth Street, eyeing the rundown neighborhood of crumbling buildings above which the enormous new Ziegfeld theater rose in all its glory. Just across the street, the luxurious Hotel Warwick beckoned.

"Why, he can roll right out of bed and cross the street to his office!" Pop exclaimed.

Elizabeth grinned half-heartedly, knowing Pop was trying to relax her with a little merriment. Truth was that Ziegfeld's reputation represented everything she found distasteful and lascivious about theatrical life. She had no interest in becoming a Ziegfeld showgirl. She struggled with her aversion as they rode the elevator to the seventh floor and stepped out into a melee of gorgeous women and intense-looking men in three-piece suits, all carrying briefcases or sheaves of papers. Some were seated. Others stood as they smoked cigarettes and chatted.

They found their way through the crowd to a large outer office where an officious young woman introduced herself as Matilda Clough, Mr. Ziegfeld's assistant, and pointed to the waiting room.

"The boss arrived a quarter of an hour ago," she said. "Some of those people have been here since noon. Don't know why they bother showing up so early. He doesn't get in here until midafternoon or later. Oh well, nothing I can do about it except chat them up in between paperwork and flower arranging. Mr. Ziegfeld loves fresh flowers, you see, but he hates anything red. I always tell florists that but sometimes they forget."

"You have to remove any red flowers?" Elizabeth asked in disbelief. Matilda, an attractive brown-haired woman about her age, was sensibly dressed, not dolled up like most of the women in the hall. She smiled and nodded.

"That and dust and organize his elephant collection. There are more in his suite." She gesticulated toward the large ceramic elephants flanking the closed door to her right. "He's a bit of a collector, my boss."

I'll say. Elizabeth recalled gossip she'd heard or an article she'd read about the menagerie of exotic animals he kept at his country estate and the showgirls he squired around the city, despite being married. *But I am not collectible.*

Pop, his bowler hat removed, ran his fingers through his hair, which, Elizabeth noticed in surprise, was graying at the temples. He then stood impassively as Matilda lightly tapped on what looked like a mahogany door.

"Send the Hines's in, Goldy."

"That's what he calls me," Matilda said softly, almost apologetically, as she opened the door.

He was seated in an armchair but agilely rose to his feet and extended his well-manicured hand to shake hands. His impeccably cut, light gray suit highlighted both his strong-looking, fit build and his penetrating eyes. Everything about him was sleek, radiating energy and authority.

The room itself was huge with a vaulted ceiling. A pillared outdoor deck, accessed through French doors, extended the room's full length. On every piece of beautiful antique furniture, including an extensive refectory table, were varying sizes of elephants in jade, silver and gold, Tiffany glass vases filled with flowers, silver cigar boxes, and other treasures.

"Pleasure to meet both a legend in the print business and his extremely talented daughter," said Ziegfeld, bowing slightly to Elizabeth before motioning for them to sit on the richly embroidered brown couch opposite his chair.

In his calm, measured voice, he explained why he had contacted Elizabeth.

"I think today's audiences, in addition to the usual vaudevillian showcase or the merriment of musical comedy, want their entertainment to offer well-developed stories with some social relevance," he said. "To that end, I have been in informal discussions with several collaborators. We are gathering a stable of skilled, well-trained actors and actresses with an operatic vocal range suited for a production musically leaning more toward an operetta than comedy."

Despite her prior resistance, Elizabeth found herself intrigued.

"If I am understanding you correctly," Pop said, "you and your partners have a prospective idea but nothing certain yet and therefore no forthcoming contract for Elizabeth to consider?"

"Yes, that is the case. I'm putting out feelers to a select group of actors whose work we admire—actors who value their craft above all else and don't let personal beliefs get in the way." Ziegfeld uncrossed his long legs and leaned forward. "You see, this show will likely depict aspects of life in the South, so we also don't want to hire anyone who objects to sharing the stage with colored people."

"A serious consideration," agreed Pop. "However, I cannot answer for Elizabeth on that issue."

Caught off guard when their attention centered on her, Elizabeth hesitated. It was a subject that she had never spoken aloud about. Many people were either vehemently or covertly prejudiced. She preferred to avoid conflict. Personally, she found that the stock portrayals of Negroes on stage were heavy-handed and verging on malicious under the guise of humor. Addressing Ziegfeld directly, she chose her words carefully.

"My experience acting with Negroes is quite limited," she said. "The shows that I've had the good fortune to act in didn't call for actors in blackface or Negro actors." The intensity of Ziegfeld's gaze discomforted her. She inhaled deeply.

"My lack of experience might be beneficial," she added, "because I don't have many preconceptions. I do, however, expect my fellow cast members to put their best foot forward, support each other, and strive to deliver as excellent a production as they can. My overriding concern is a good work ethic, not the color of someone's skin."

"I suspected as much. Exactly why you are one of the first I've contacted for a possible lead role. Coffee, anyone?"

Ziegfeld unfurled his muscular body, stood up, and reached over to push a button on his desk. He seemed satisfied although it was difficult to tell because his sculpted face remained impassive.

"Yes, to coffee," Pop interjected, "but let me clarify. Are you saying that you don't want to discuss contract terms today? That this is a sort of preliminary interview?"

"I know it is unconventional and not my usual way of going about organizing a production, but this is an unusual project— potentially groundbreaking. At least that is our hope." He offered both cigarettes, which they declined, and resumed his seat.

"Could you say any more about the play? Can we call it that?" asked Elizabeth, whose curiosity had increased. Ziegfeld's glittering dark eyes fixed on hers. He took his time before responding.

"Yes, it will be a play based on a book," he said. "We are in negotiations with the author regarding the script rights. Because the outcome of those negotiations is yet unknown, we can't gather investors or make any of the other arrangements. I can tell you that Jerome Kern and Oscar Hammerstein laid claim to whatever the music will be and, if everything falls into place, I intend for the opening to be here in my new theater. Other than that, I can't give you any specifics. We don't want the press to get wind of anything yet."

Matilda entered bearing a tray with a silver coffeepot and delicate Limoges coffee cups and saucers. She set it down on the long refectory table and poured them each a cup, which she delivered, along with cream and sugar, before exiting. Elizabeth sampled the delicious coffee.

"So you prefer I say nothing if asked about my possible future engagements?" she asked.

"For right now, that is the case."

"Any idea of timing?" Pop asked. "Elizabeth will be in Chicago until July."

"Yes. I know she's under contract with the Shuberts until then," Ziegfeld said. "I hope to have more concrete details by the time you return, Miss Hines. That is, if you're truly interested in working for me."

Caught off guard again, Elizabeth hesitated. Thankfully, Pop interjected.

"I don't think Elizabeth can or should make a commitment until she knows more," he said. The two men eyed each other guardedly.

"I am interested and open to hearing more," said Elizabeth, hoping to diffuse the rising tension. Furthermore, it was true. She was.

"That's the best we can do right now," Ziegfeld conceded, draining his cup and setting it down definitively, indicating their meeting was ending. "I will be in touch. Expect a telegram, Miss Hines."

CHAPTER 49
JUNE DAYS

During previous performances in Chicago, Elizabeth found that the city, despite its wide, well-lit boulevards and lakeside park and beaches, exuded a roughness that New York lacked. Perhaps it was the harsh climate, brutally cold and windy in winter, oppressively humid in summer. Or perhaps it was the constant construction of commercial and industrial businesses within or alongside the residential areas. Or the burgeoning number of speakeasies and criminal organizations involved with producing and delivering illicit alcohol. Although all this activity was also true of New York, everything seemed more blatant and visible in Chicago where the consequential homicides and intrigue were front-page news daily.

"Won't you be seeing Mr. Roy at rehearsal today?" asked Gert, who had volunteered to be Elizabeth's maid and dresser for the play. Initially she'd thought Gert might want to stay put in New York after their recent lengthy European trip, but Dorothy, a self-sufficient fourteen-year-old busy with her school chums and activities, no longer required a nursemaid. Gert abhorred being idle and Elizabeth was happy to have her along instead of making do with whomever the Shuberts' manager dug up.

"Of course," snapped Elizabeth, instantly regretting her tone. She wasn't looking forward to the reunion, but Gert had little idea about the true cause of her reticence. Gert, thin mouth pursed, dark eyebrows drawn together, looked puzzled.

"I am bit jangled—pre-opening jitters," Elizabeth added. Only two more rehearsals to go and I can't imagine how Roy will learn his part in that time."

"Oh, don't worry, Miss E. That man is a pro. He'll catch on quick. Besides, doesn't everyone expect a few hiccups on opening night?"

Elizabeth standing in front of a large oval mirror to clip on her pearl earrings and smooth her blonde hair with her hand.

"Yes, but there's a lot resting on how well the play is received," she replied. *Like what I am doing for the rest of the year?* Pop and she had agreed that the meeting with Mr. Ziegfeld went well, though nothing substantial was forthcoming yet. She wasn't accustomed to experiencing so much uncertainty about her future. Up to that point in her career, one role had flowed into another with little time in between. Charles Cochran, Ziegfeld's British counterpart, had offered her a part in a musical revue that she might have accepted if things had gone differently with Roy. With no desire to return to England, though, she had turned him down. Besides, she was more interested in roles involving a well-developed story and serious acting.

"Off you go," Gert said. "See you for dinner when you can tell me how it went. I'll be here knitting away." Smiling, Gert held up an incomplete pale yellow and off-white square of wool. "I'm barely keeping up with the births. My nieces and nephews keep producing children!"

Elizabeth left for rehearsal.

★ ★ ★

As she stepped out of elevator, she heard Ethel's husky voice.

"Darling Elizabeth, how are you?" greeted her as she was swept into her musky perfumed embrace before being held at arm's length for a thorough inspection. "Your travels agreed with you. You look wonderful. I am just heading over to the Capitol Theatre now so let's taxi over together. You can tell me all about your journey."

In her inimitable, flirtatious way, Ethel commandeered a ride and peppered Elizabeth with questions. Elizabeth, happy about the distraction, outlined the highlights of her travels.

"Roy chose his mother over you?" Ethel said, her large hazel eyes widening in disbelief.

"That's not exactly what I said, but I suppose that is one way of looking at it."

"That is the bottom line, isn't it?" Ethel sniffed disapprovingly as they pulled up to the curb in front of the theater. "Good heavens, you must have been heartbroken." She hugged Elizabeth again before paying the driver. Prompted by Ethel's magnanimous warmth, Elizabeth struggled to quash her rising tears as well as her desire to reveal the truth.

Ethel changed the topic but continued talking as they entered the Greco-Roman Capitol Theatre with its stylized friezes, mosaic tiled floors, and discreetly robed statues. Though the theater was touted as Chicago's newest example of architectural acumen, Elizabeth found its abundance of mimicry, right down to intertwining fake vines and small temples, gaudy and overdone.

"I was here to preview the place yesterday so let me show you where our dressing rooms are," offered Ethel, leading her backstage. They walked down one of the main aisles and across the proscenium. "Here you are!" She stopped and motioned toward a door with Elizabeth's name on it.

Just then, as if on cue, Roy stepped out from the neighboring room into the hall. Elizabeth froze. Ethel stepped between them, giving him a jocular greeting which he returned in his appealing lilt. Elizabeth quickly glanced at him, nodding hello but instinctively avoiding looking at his face. She feigned interest in seeing her quarters and, leaving Ethel and Roy chatting in the hall, went into the large dressing room and shut the door behind her. Lightheaded, she plunked down in her favorite wooden deck chair, which was shipped ahead to wherever she was on the road. Seeing Roy was more difficult than she had anticipated and the fact his room was right next door increased her discomfort. To regain her composure, she repeatedly inhaled, deeply sighing on the exhale, and visualized a sea of people enthusiastically standing and clapping. She had battled doubts prior to other performances but Roy's presence, after what had transpired between them, added another unsettling aspect.

A loud bass voice called out from the hall.

"Delivery for Miss Hines!"

Ethel exchanged a few words with the man and knocked lightly. Reluctantly, Elizabeth opened the door.

"My dear, it seems you already have an admirer," she said, sweeping into the room with a gorgeous flower arrangement of fragrant freesias, white roses, and irises. She set it down on the dressing table, plucked out an embossed card stuffed between the flowers, and handed it to Elizabeth. "Any ideas as to who it could be?"

"No, I can't imagine," said Elizabeth as she opened the card, which read, "Welcome to Chicago. As promised, we will dine together again. In the meantime, break a leg. Frank Warton."

"Well?"

"Just a man Gert and I met on our trip," Elizabeth replied, deliberately downplaying any mention of Frank while wondering how he knew when she would arrive at the theater. His timing was uncanny. She was certain she hadn't told him about her next engagement when they met in Algiers. Besides, she hadn't known then that the play would open in Chicago.

"I hope he isn't a married man looking for someone on the side."

"I don't know," said Elizabeth, feeling flustered. "Gert was with me and our time with him was brief. We didn't discuss much of anything personal."

"It's time to don our dancing shoes," said Ethel, consulting her wristwatch. "Mind if I put mine on here? That way you can avoid being offstage alone with Roy."

"Absolutely not." Elizabeth said, grateful for her friend's protective yet vigorous presence.

★ ★ ★

The morning after opening night, Gert pointed to the newspaper in her hand as she and Elizabeth consumed a room service breakfast.

"According to this *Daily News* critic, Burns Mantle, you saved the day," Gert said. "Listen to this: '*June Days* is a musical comedy prettily staged and woefully stupid. It is helped by Elizabeth Hines. She is a gracious heroine with enough voice to entitle her to the best songs and of great attraction to the dance. But it is fearfully blasted by a youth named Royston—Roy Royston—imported a year or so back by the Shuberts. I have seen few worse performances in the theater than this self-conscious young man gave on opening night. He was overheated and anxious."

Elizabeth frowned and shook her head.

"Hardly," she said. "I did my best. Besides, no one ever built a statue to a critic, and you know I prefer ignoring reviews."

"These last few days before the show you were so knotted up, I thought you'd appreciate some positive feedback," Gert said.

"Yes, and I am awfully glad that my nerves didn't negatively impact my performance." She felt sorry for Roy, though. He had fumbled more lines and cues than she ever remembered him doing. She actually agreed with Mr. Mantle's critique. Despite the revisions to the former *Charm School* and the addition of new songs and dances, the current rendition of the musical remained fanciful and lacking. Still, she had a lead role, and therefore a good income, for the next three months, if not longer.

"How is Mr. Roy?" Gert asked, folding the paper and putting it down.

"I have no idea. We haven't exchanged anything other than greetings." Although curious about Roy's state, Elizabeth was also relieved that their performance had been the focus of their time together.

"This review suggests he isn't himself, poor man," said Gert, eyeing Elizabeth expectantly.

"Seriously, we haven't talked. Oh, I forgot to tell you. That man, Frank Warton, the one we met in Algiers, sent flowers to my dressing room."

"See, I knew he was sweet on you." Gert triumphantly winked.

"I guess I will lunch with him one of these days. The show runs so late, dinner afterwards is out of the question." Elizabeth yawned. She hadn't readjusted to the nightly performance schedule.

"That's right. He works for a Chicago bank," Gert said. "Is he coming to see the show?"

"I don't know. His note didn't say. I need to write a thank you for the flowers and we will go from there."

"That Frank certainly is handsome and so worldly. Bet he makes a good living."

"Hmm, I suppose, I am going to soak my tired body in a nice hot bath," Elizabeth said, definitively not wanting to talk about Frank or Roy.

CHAPTER 50
FANCY FREE

Not until the second Sunday after the show's opening did Elizabeth have enough energy or desire to accept Frank's invitation for a meal. The weather, steamy hot and humid without a breath of wind, had added to her fatigue. His message, left for her at the hotel desk, advised, "Another informal adventure so dress accordingly."

Sporting a lightweight culotte outfit purchased in Nice that she remembered to throw in her suitcase, Elizabeth grabbed her straw hat and went downstairs to find Frank standing in the lobby's shadows. Dressed in a white linen suit, he looked much as he had in Algiers. When he saw her, he swept off his wide-brimmed hat and bowed.

"My dear Miss Hines, what a pleasure to see you in our native land! Shall we?"

Firmly grasping her elbow, he ushered her outdoors into a gleaming burgundy roadster.

Once Elizabeth was settled in the passenger seat, Frank drove confidently and swiftly north along Lake Shore Drive. The breeze felt lovely in contrast to the stifling city heat. The tawny beaches were crowded with people of all ages, seated under multicolored umbrellas or wading and splashing in the lake. Others swam, their arms arcing out of the blue gray water. The scene reminded Elizabeth of Impressionist paintings at the Grand Palais.

"Where are we going?" She shouted to be heard above the motor's constant thrum.

"A place with privacy and a view," Frank answered, keeping his eyes on the road. The urban landscape dropped away, and tall oaks and elms interspersed with houses lined the road. They drove close to an hour before he turned off the main road and slowly pulled the car through a stone arch and down a narrow driveway. He stopped at an immense, Georgian-style house with white pillars at the entrance and a spacious screened-in porch on its south corner.

"If you need a toilet, I can let us in," said Frank. "Otherwise, we will take our picnic and climb down the stairs behind the house to the beach." He opened the car's trunk to lift out a picnic basket, some towels, and what looked like a sizable navy blanket.

"Let's forge ahead. Can I carry anything?" Elizabeth asked. Frank handed her the blanket before leading the way across an expansive lawn to the edge of a bluff where they descended a long sequence of well-maintained wooden stairs.

"Here we are," he said as they emerged onto a private beach. Elizabeth saw people far to the north of them. Otherwise, they had the place to themselves. Frank spread out the blanket and opened the basket.

"Isn't this your favorite champagne?" he asked, pulling out a cold bottle of Veuve Clicquot and two fluted glasses. She nodded, wondering how he knew that and deciding that the man, though appearing nonchalant, was keenly attentive.

"I hope you don't mind that I spirited you away," said Frank, stretching his long body out on the blanket. He propped himself up on one elbow and gazed at the slight waves lapping at the pebbled shore. "I thought we should get to know each other better before being seen in public together. Besides, it is Sunday, and this is my idea of church."

Relieved that they wouldn't be inadvertently spotted by some gossip columnist, she appreciated his foresight.

"Here, here!" he said. Elizabeth clinked his glass with hers in a mock toast. When he smiled, his gray green eyes flecked with light and the steeliness in his face melted away.

"Whose place is this anyway?" she asked.

"A banker colleague. He and his family have a vacation home in the Upper Peninsula, so his wife and kids summer there and he commutes down here whenever necessary. He likes me to use the beach and keep an eye on the place."

"Lucky for you. It's the perfect getaway, especially on a sweltering day like this," said Elizabeth, wondering if he visited the estate alone or not.

"Just say the word whenever you are hungry and I will serve lunch, my lady."

"Actually, I'm going to test the water." She had already removed her flats to dig her toes into the sand. She took a big gulp of champagne, burrowed her glass in the sand so it wouldn't tip over, and walked to the water's edge. The shallows were breathtakingly cold. She went in up to her shins and stood there, transfixed by the expansive quiet of the seemingly horizonless lake.

"I didn't have a chance to warn you. Lake Michigan doesn't warm up until the end of July," said Frank, coming up behind her. He was bare chested. Breathing in the pleasant peppery scent of his skin, Elizabeth tentatively leaned into his tall, robust body. "Even then, when you swim offshore a little, you'll hit bitterly cold water pockets. It rivals swimming in Britain." He draped one arm around her shoulders and nuzzled her hair.

"I wouldn't mind being shipwrecked with the likes of you," he murmured. She turned her face toward his. Encircling her with his other arm, he brought his lips to hers. After their long kiss, he softly pulled away, leaving Elizabeth, tremulous and warm, wondering if her shakiness was visible.

"Man nor woman can live on kisses alone. Let me prepare our feast," he quipped before striding back to the blanket. With his tousled dark hair, rolled-up pants, and naked muscular chest, he looked at least ten years younger. Elizabeth thought she glimpsed the vibrant young man he must have been when he emigrated from England.

While he unpacked, she splashed lake water on her cheeks and forehead, willing herself to calm down. It wasn't easy. The impression of his lips on hers lingered and she realized that she hungered more for his touch than for food. A blend of both would be perfect and after she joined him on the blanket, that is what transpired. They nestled together, alternately chatting, kissing, or munching on slices of cheddar cheese, spicy sausage on crusty bread, and tart apples. After the champagne was finished and they were satiated with food, they lay on their backs, holding hands and scanning the cascading clouds overhead for animal shapes. Frank interrupted their reverie.

"I assume it won't do for you show up on stage sunburned so regretfully," he said. "I think we should depart."

"I suppose you're right although I am not eager to return to the city heat."

"Neither am I, but I also don't want to incur Gert's disapproval."

"I believe you've already made her list of acceptable men but yes, we should get going," said Elizabeth, consulting her wristwatch. "She has been back from mass for several hours and another six days of performances start tomorrow." She sighed. After almost three months off, she found it difficult to adjust to the rigorous schedule and late nights—and all of it for a mediocre play.

"Someday soon, I hope you tell me more about what's entailed in your career," said Frank, buttoning up his shirt and throwing his jacket over his arm before shouldering the basket containing their lunch remnants. "I've never known a professional actress before."

"Acting is probably like most careers worth pursuing—forty to fifty percent fun and inspiring and the rest is hard work and dedication," said Elizabeth, omitting that currently, the equation was more weighted toward the work component. She didn't want to come across as complaining.

"I guess unless you're a real night owl, you don't go out much after a show."

"Some of my peers do but I am not one of them. I enjoy my daylight time and prefer to feel as rested as possible for a performance."

"This is going to take some planning," Frank said as they began their ascent of the steep stairs up the bluff.

At the time, Elizabeth thought he was referring to their disparate work schedules and his desire to continue seeing her.

★ ★ ★

They settled into a pattern—an early dinner, usually on Wednesdays, prior to Elizabeth's eight o'clock performance and Sundays until late afternoon unless Frank traveled out of town for business. Although Frank ensured that they visited Chicago landmarks, such as the Chicago Art Institute and the Field Museum of Natural History, the private Lake Forest beach remained Elizabeth's favorite place. Frank was more relaxed and playful when they picnicked there, and she was relieved to be secluded from the prying eyes of the press, which they had so far succeeded in doing. However, stopping their petting was becoming increasingly difficult. Their intimate encounters left her tingling and aching for more. Frank also had trouble tearing himself away. After one of those interludes, he broke from their prone embrace and sat up.

"This is not where I want our relationship consummated," he announced. "Nor is it how." Knees drawn up to his chest, he held his head between his hands in frustration. His face was stricken and taut.

"I can't keep doing this endlessly," he went on. "I want to be with you. I want us to be together but—" He stopped abruptly. Minutes went by before he was ready to finish his sentence. He straightened up and gathered himself. "There's something I must explain. I told you I was previously married."

Elizabeth nodded.

"The fact is by law I still am, but we haven't lived together in two years," he continued. "We have two children I see as often as I can. We had three but the youngest died and Florence—that's her name—has been an emotional mess since that happened. I didn't see any reason to add to her upset by officially divorcing her." He reached out, cupping Elizabeth's chin with his hand and determinedly looked in her eyes, declared. "Now there is."

Stunned by his admission and all that it portended, Elizabeth nonsensically stuttered, "But I live and work in New York."

"I know, I know. There are many things we must work out," Frank said. "Changes must be made. For one thing, I need to get the wheels rolling and file for divorce so we can get married."

It was the first time Elizabeth left their sanctuary with her stomach roiling in tension as they ascended the familiar earthen steps through the wooded shadows. Months later, she realized Frank hadn't proposed and then waited to see where she stood on the subject of their future. He had delivered a proclamation and assumed that she wanted the same outcome as him.

CHAPTER 51
ROW THE BOAT

Although the reviews continued to be mixed, the theater sold out for every performance. Roy had recovered from his initial clumsiness and partnered Elizabeth with his usual finesse. They established a cordial repartee but didn't spend time together outside of work hours like they used to. The Shuberts, pleased by the ticket sales, announced to the cast and the press that they would schedule a New York opening for September.

Elizabeth welcomed the news since she longed to return to New York and home, even though it meant not seeing Frank for extended periods of time. He, however, became petulant after she shared the development, his dissatisfaction evident in his voice, which became more clipped and brusquely British in tone when he was agitated.

They were finishing their early dinner one Wednesday when he glumly said, "I don't know when I will be able to get to New York."

"I can come here for a bit after the show closes," said Elizabeth. To reassure him, she touched his strong, square hand with its whorls of soft, dark hair on the knuckles.

"That's well and good," he replied, "but months away."

"Yes, but won't it give you the time to officially end your marriage?"

"I suppose. It's not going to be easy and would be more bearable if some evenings I could come home to you."

Elizabeth wanted to remind him she was rarely home in the evenings if she was in a show but thought better of it. He looked so downcast and morose.

Humid, thick air seemed to press into them as they walked the few blocks to the theater. Roiling clouds overhead presaged late-night thunderstorms and Elizabeth speculated that getting a taxi back to the hotel later might be difficult. She decided to speak with Ethel first thing, before the play began, and see what they could arrange for their transportation later. Frank stopped a block short of the theater to avoid reporters, as he usually did. That night, though, there was no lingering embrace. Instead he quickly kissed her on the cheek, turned, and walked away.

★ ★ ★

"It's a go, Pop," said Elizabeth. She phoned him with the news at his office the next morning. "They've renewed my contract for a New York production."

"You must be relieved, my dear, and this gives you time to see what Ziegfeld comes up with." He sounded odd. Was the phone distorting his voice or it was a particularly demanding day in the newsroom? She knew better than to engage Pop in a long conversation when he was in the office, but she was curious.

"How is everyone at home?" she asked.

"We're all well and planning on ten days in Quogue in a few weeks," he replied. He paused. "I suppose I better tell you now, so you aren't surprised."

"Tell me what?"

"Your brother is home."

Elizabeth's whole body stiffened. "Is he visiting Dorothy? How long does he—?" she asked.

"I don't know the full story. Seems his vaudeville company had a bad winter season in Tampa and some players left. He says he needs to regroup."

"Pop, I don't want to take any more of your time. I'll telegraph you next week when I know what train Gert and I will be on, just so you know. We can make our way home from the station. No need to meet us."

Instinctually, she had tried to counterbalance the undue stress that Palmer's presence put on her father. After asking him to convey good wishes to her mother and Dorothy, Elizabeth plunked the heavy black receiver into its cradle, exited the hotel phone niche, and walked back to the suite, somewhat dispirited. She explained the situation to Gert.

"We're going to be a full house once we get back to New York," Gert said. "I suppose they've set up the library for your brother. Wouldn't do to ask Dorothy to move out of his old room now that she's made it into her own."

"I agree. Between his quick stint in the Army and his road productions, he's been gone for the better part of three years. He can't expect things to revert to the way they were before." *Or can he?* Only one thing could be counted on: Palmer would do whatever was most advantageous for himself.

"Dorothy will be glad to have her father around for longer than a weekend and Frannie enjoys cooking for a crowd," said Gert, putting aside her sewing kit after repairing a small rip in one of Elizabeth's skirts.

Unable to find any benefit to her brother's return, Elizabeth murmured in response. After essentially losing both parents, Dorothy had managed to grow into a thoughtful, curious young lady with multiple interests, a small cadre of close friends, and a lovely relationship with her grandparents. What effect would

Palmer's disruptive presence have on her? And yes, Frannie did enjoy cooking but more mouths to feed meant more supplies and more food and hence more expense for Momma and Pop.

Her mind whirling, Elizabeth rifled through the sheaf of letters the hotel concierge had handed her when she went downstairs to use the phone. The bulk of them, written in unfamiliar scripts, were probably fan mail. However, Elizabeth recognized Joanie's writing on one envelope and immediately opened it.

My Dear Elizabeth,

I know you're hard at work in Chicago and I don't know when you're scheduled to return but I wanted to apprise you of some good news. I wanted to tell you myself before you heard it through the proverbial maternal grapevine.

According to the doctors here, the treatment succeeded. I am mostly back on my feet with minimal scarring of my lungs. Thank goodness! I don't think I could endure another round of sleeping outdoors on a screened porch or remain in bed for days on end, reading and resting, mostly in solitude except for visits from my doctor or the ward nurse. I am gradually building up my physical strength and resilience and it looks as if I might be able to return home in a month if all goes well.

The other wonderful news is that I am informally engaged. Can you believe it? I scarcely believe it myself. Christopher is the brother of another patient, Matilda Horne (we call her Tilly), who has become a close friend here. The family lives in Hartford, Connecticut and Christopher came practically every month to visit Tilly. The two of them have been through a great deal together, losing their older brother to the war and their mother to the Spanish flu. Christopher dropped out of his junior year at Yale to take over his father's insurance business because his father, brokenhearted after his wife's death, could barely function.

We share a love for literature, arts, and music. In fact, he is a skilled pianist and probably would be a great writer if he didn't have to run the business, which, according to Tilly, became quite successful under his leadership. He is a good, caring man with a social conscience and a wry sense of humor. We enjoy each other's company immensely.

I can imagine you are quite surprised to hear this news, especially since neither you nor I prioritized marriage as our goal, but life tends to upturn one's plans and expectations, does it not?! The doctors advise that I do not return to the classroom because the stress and the exposure to viruses is too risky. I will content myself with being a supportive partner to Christopher as it is most likely, after this illness, I won't be able to sustain a pregnancy. However, he accepts this rather huge limitation most graciously.

We intend to hold a small engagement party in New York in September with a December wedding if all goes according to plan. I look forward to introducing you to Christopher. Prior to that, I hope to spend some time alone with you when we both return home. Sandwiches in the garden soon, dear friend!

Much Love, Joanie

As a tumble of emotions surged, Elizabeth set the letter down and absentmindedly scanned the two shabby chairs and matching drapes, the worn carpet in a fleur-de-lis pattern and beige walls hung with nondescript, floral paintings in chipped frames. Gert, knitting quietly on the small couch, put her needles down.

"How is Joanie?" she asked. "That is her longest letter yet, isn't it?"

"It is. She's recovered and if the doctors approve, she'll return home just about the time we get back to New York."

"That's wonderful news. We've all been worried. You'll be so happy to have your best friend back."

"That's not her only news. She met a man there. He's a friend's brother and now," Elizabeth hesitantly added, "they're engaged."

Gert clapped her hands together, her broad face beaming.

"Oh. my heavens, the Lord works in wondrous ways, as they say." *Strange but not wondrous*, Elizabeth thought. *Both my best friends will be married and living elsewhere, probably by year's end. Palmer is back home. I have no idea what my next job will be and then there's Frank.*

"I thought you were an advocate for women's independence and autonomy, not conventional marriage and motherhood," Elizabeth said.

"I am but isn't a mixture the best outcome? Izzy will never be anything but independent but now she has someone who appreciates that and, as for Joanie, to find love and companionship after what she's been through is wonderful."

"But Joanie must give up teaching because of her health. She loved teaching."

"Yes. That is a shame, but it would be worse if she had no alternative path to follow." suggested Gert.

Gert's certainty was annoying. Elizabeth remained ambivalent about Izzy's marriage and Joanie's engagement seemed more of a capitulation to circumstance than an actual choice. Did one really choose a path? Or was life a series of adaptations? She wondered what Maurice Maeterlinck would say and fantasized about being back on the terrace in Nice deep in discussion with him and Renée.

CHAPTER 52
THE WINDS OF CHANGE

With Palmer back in residence, home wasn't the respite Elizabeth had grown accustomed to. True to Gert's prediction, her favorite room, the library, had been converted into his quarters. Since it was adjacent to the main entrance, there was little chance of Elizabeth avoiding Palmer when she entered or exited the apartment. Dorothy was the only person in the household who appeared entirely enthused about Palmer's residency, engaging him in conversation and proposing outings to which he sometimes assented. Unlike his previous visits, he ate every meal with the family, which Elizabeth suspected was due to scarcity of income, not his desire to be with them.

Palmer was on good behavior, refraining from late-night carousing and apparently not indulging in any form of gambling. However, every time he left the house alone, Elizabeth felt like she, Gert, and her parents were suspended in dread, wondering in what state he might return.

On a sultry August day one week after her return from Chicago, Elizabeth walked home from a rigorous voice lesson to Fred waving a yellow telegram envelope. He was obviously hopeful that she would open it in his presence.

"Good news, Miss?"

"We'll see. Right now, before I do another thing, I need Frannie's lemonade and a brisk sit in front of a fan," Elizabeth replied. Thankfully, the house was quiet, and Palmer was out. She poured herself a glass of lemonade, retreated to her bedroom, turned on the fan, and kicked off her shoes before plunking herself down in her favorite armchair to read the first telegram from Ziegfeld: "Author agreed. Script in the works. Read Ferber's novel, Showboat. More to come."

Nothing about dates or a pending contract. Just a request, more like a command, but that was to be expected from what she'd heard about Flo Ziegfeld's modus operandi. His brusque style would take some getting used to. Wistfully, she thought of George Cohan's playful, capricious yet meticulous guidance, which brought the best out of his performers. Since *June Days* was scheduled to open at the Astor Theatre right after Labor Day and, although there hadn't been significant changes in the cast, rehearsals began in a week. Elizabeth found herself uncharacteristically indifferent about the prospect, questioning if it was due to the mediocre script or the lackluster quality of the song and dance numbers.

The rupture with Roy definitely dampened the fun she experienced when performing with him. Now they went about their roles like wind-up dolls with their painted-on smiles and repetitive actions. Furthermore, the main topic of conversation among her fellow actors lately was the flourishing film business, the allures of Hollywood, and making it big in the talkies. Everyone seemed to know someone with a little money who went to California and ended up cast in a movie and living the high life. Listening to these stories, she was surprised by her own apathy. To play to the camera's eye without the vibrant interaction of an audience seemed one dimensional and narcissistic, as if one was looking into a mirror. Yet in Chicago and New York theaters were being converted to movie houses at an exponential rate. Their convenient schedules and relatively affordable admission fees made movies more accessible to mainstream America.

Elizabeth rubbed her tender feet as she contemplated how to proceed in the changing landscape of her chosen career. The afternoon sun shining through the casement windows was beginning to radiate the gilded hue she associated with September.

"Miss E., phone call for you. I think it's your beau, Frank," said Gert, lightly rapping on her closed door. Elizabeth scrambled to her feet, ran to the door, thanked Gert, and hurried downstairs to the hallway nook that Pop designated for the phone that was installed while Elizabeth was in Europe.

"One moment, please," the operator said before connecting the line.

"Darling Elizabeth, are you there?" asked Frank in his unmistakable voice although the crackling line caused some distortion.

"Yes, yes, it's me. This is quite unexpected. It's the middle of a workday for you."

"I know but I had a long lunch hour coming to me. I thought I might get lucky and catch you in between commitments. Just wanted to hear your lovely voice."

Elizabeth flushed at his tender words.

"How sweet of you," she stammered. Elizabeth was unaccustomed to conversing on the phone, having only briefly used Pop's work phone for occasional business-related calls.

"Miss me?" asked Frank.

"Oh yes. I think about our beach picnics a lot." It was the truth. At odd moments daily, she revisited memories of their time together. Still, she also found she was forgetting his habitual gestures as well as the smell and feel of him.

"What if I could arrange a visit?"

"That would be a treat. But the play opens in two weeks, and you know what my schedule will be like then."

"It wouldn't be for a month or so," Frank said. "Once I know my dates, can't you get, what do they call it, an understudy, for a night or two?"

"I suppose," she said. His suggestion made her uncomfortable. Elizabeth prided herself on being reliable. She had only missed two nights of work in her entire career due to a nasty case of flu. "It's possible that this will be a relatively short run, maybe six weeks or so. If that's the case, better to come when the show closes."

"I don't know if I can wait that long."

His fervor was both flattering and disquieting. Her responses felt inadequate. Additionally, talking spontaneously into the black hollow receiver was novel and awkward.

"I want to be with you," Frank continued, "and I want to meet your family."

Elizabeth had said very little to Momma and Pop about Frank because she thought it more prudent to refrain until he was officially divorced. As far as they knew, he was a friend made on her trip to Africa who happened to live and work in Chicago.

"Elizabeth, are you there?" asked Frank.

"Yes, yes. Sorry. I am not used to the telephone."

"Thank God for it! At least I can hear your voice. Anyway, let me know the best time for a visit and I'll see what I can arrange. I need to sign off now."

Excited yet flustered after they hung up, she wondered how to introduce her parents to the idea of a married man with two children. Furthermore, she anticipated Palmer's sarcasm when he found out she was being courted by a British banker. When she returned to her room, Gert, tidying Elizabeth's bed, looked up, her dark eyebrows arched inquisitively. Elizabeth flung herself back down in the armchair. She hadn't even told Gert that Frank was married and a father. Her work demands and concerns, her changed home environment, and Frank's request, all seemed like too much to deal with at once.

"He wants to come for a visit," Elizabeth conceded without going into detail.

"How lovely! It appears the man is quite enamored. When?"

"I suggested that he come after the play closes. We both have important things to address," said Elizabeth, changing the subject by pointing to the telegram. "Mr. Ziegfeld assigned me a book to read."

"I guess that is a good sign," said Gert, although she strongly disapproved of men whose lives were constant fodder for gossip and headlines.

"It would be a good sign, but only if I like the book and a contract follows."

★ ★ ★

Edna Ferber's magnificent, courageous novel, rich in character and plot, dealt with serious issues, including poverty, miscegenation, and racism. As a potential play, it could be both dramatic and musical since the bulk of the story takes place on a riverboat traveling on the Mississippi River, presenting various theatrical pieces in towns along the way. The themes presented required serious acting as well as strong musical and dance skills.

Elizabeth, enthralled, found it difficult to put the book down. She hoped Ziegfeld imagined her in the role of Magnolia, the riverboat captain's daughter who develops from a naïve, protected, and talented girl to a mother, abandoned by her gambler husband, singing in nightclubs and casinos to ensure that she and her daughter could survive. Her intuition told her that this production, if it came to pass, would be an extraordinary addition to musical theater.

She confided in Frank in their next phone conversation.

"The novel is so well written and if I got the role of Magnolia, that would be the best part ever."

"If it is as good as you say, a play of that caliber would have a long run, wouldn't it?" Frank posited.

"With Ziegfeld producing, Jerome Kern writing the music, and Oscar Hammerstein's lyrics, I think so. You can't tell anyone I told you all this. Ziegfeld told Pop and I that he doesn't want the press involved until he secures the financial backing and gets the lead actors on board."

At the time, Frank's lack of enthusiasm didn't register and she continued to rave about the enthralling possibilities. He asked a few more questions about where and when the opening might take place, but she didn't yet have answers.

CHAPTER 53
UNCERTAINTY

It was one of those balmy, clear October days that whispers of the departed summer. Oak and sycamore leaves were burnished gold or shades of red under an azure sky. *Perfect for a Central Park picnic*, Elizabeth thought, as she and Frank sat down on an old blanket she'd brought and opened a picnic basket full of Frannie's goodies.

As promised, Frank had booked a trip to New York to coincide with the end of the *June Days* run. A week before his arrival, Elizabeth mustered up her courage to further explain her relationship with Frank and his situation to her parents. It was never easy facing Momma's disapproving interrogations. Momma currently remained skeptical and formal with Frank, who was thankfully oblivious, though Elizabeth knew what the flat, reserved tone in her mother's voice meant.

"Almost as good as our little hideaway," Elizabeth suggested as she and Frank looked out over the expanse of lawn where small clusters of adults, some with children, sat on benches, walked dogs, and threw balls. The occasional bicycle or horseback rider passed in the distance.

"Not exactly private, but it will do," Frank said as he bit into a thick ham sandwich.

"I don't think any reporters will bother us," said Elizabeth. "I am out of the limelight for a while. I've been offered a role in a Charles White production but that won't open until the new year, and I am unsure whether I'll take it. If Ziegfeld comes up with a contract, I would much prefer that."

Frank put down the sandwich, wiped his mouth, and fervently grabbed her hand.

"What if you didn't have to worry about reporters or when, where, and what the next job would be?"

"I imagine that would be somewhat of a relief, although, even if one likes what one does for work, every job has its drawbacks."

"That's not what I am talking about," Frank said, his gray-green eyes flickering impatiently.

Elizabeth was on alert; aware they were treading in uncomfortable territory. She cleared her throat.

"What are you suggesting?"

"Marriage. That's what I suggest."

Elizabeth scrambled internally, not knowing how to respond. The topic had arisen before but not so directly and seriously. She felt both thrilled and anxious at the prospect of marrying Frank.

"Darling," she began, "it is a wonderful idea and when you are free, I would love to. However, I don't think that would solve my dilemmas with work because even if we do get married, I intend to continue acting." She had not so clearly defined her position to him before and was surprised to see his chiseled face grimace in reaction.

"I can't imagine spending months alone while you're off touring in some show," he said in exasperation. "What kind of marriage would that be?"

"There are work-arounds. For example, I could ask that future contracts stipulate that I won't be available for road productions." Though she suggested the idea, Elizabeth really didn't know how that would go over with most producers. Frank's face suddenly became grave and immobile. Pulling away from her, he grabbed his jacket labels as if to straighten himself up.

"It's not just me I am thinking about," he said. "What if we have children?"

She didn't have an answer. In the past, these were questions she skirted around whenever they came up in her mind or in conversation with others.

"I think I could work and be a wife and mother. Why not?"

"Humph. Don't know how that would be. As it is, we struggle to get time together."

"Yes, but we live far away from each other. Imagine if we were under the same roof," Elizabeth said, hoping to placate him.

"That's what I have been imagining for a while now and, by the way, it wouldn't be in New York," he said, discarding the half-eaten sandwich on his napkin. "I can't leave my job nor my children in Chicago." He briefly looked at her. "You know, if we truly want to be together, we both have to undergo some changes."

After their discussion Elizabeth could not muster an appetite so they packed up the food and walked the few blocks to her home, making carefully constrained conversation about their plans for that evening and the following days of Frank's visit. Frank, who was staying elsewhere with an old friend, left her at her building entrance instead of coming in for tea. *Just as well*, she thought. She watched him walk swiftly away without a backward glance; his hands dug deep into his pockets.

★ ★ ★

"Where's Lover Boy?" Palmer quipped, coming out from the library when she entered the apartment. The effect of home cooking and relative inactivity showed in his bulging vest. His pale blue eyes looked pea-sized in his fleshy face. Palmer was never conventionally good looking, but he used to at least have a fresh-faced, boyish presence. It had vanished altogether.

"He'll be by later," Elizabeth said. She quickly sorted her belongings, hoping to avoid conversation, and headed for the kitchen to drop off the picnic remains. Palmer followed.

"What are you two doing tonight?" he asked. "I could be your tour guide, take you to hear some jazz at the Cotton Club and some other hot spots I bet you haven't been to yet." She knew he was referring to the many speakeasies, proliferating since the 1919 Volstead Act, that were constantly raided and shut down by the authorities only to pop up weeks later somewhere else.

"We already have dinner plans," she answered, placing the basket next to the deep zinc sink. She retraced her way back through the hallway but Palmer's large frame partially blocked the route. He seized Elizabeth's arm as she tried to pass.

"You'd better show that fellow a good time so he will stick around and not leave like your last beau," Palmer said, shaking his forefinger at her.

"What did you just say?" Elizabeth asked. She stood her ground instead of avoiding him, as she usually did.

"Despite all that talk of engagement and marriage, you and lover boy, Roy, didn't last, did you? You must have scared him off, somehow. Besides, you're not getting any younger."

"It was you, wasn't it?" Elizabeth said. "*You* were the one who started it all!" Hot waves of anger rose from her stomach into her throat as she clenched her trembling hands to refrain from slapping his florid, fleshy face. Palmer shrugged.

"Not really. I just added kindling and fanned the proverbial flames."

"Why?" she sputtered.

"Why not? I was offered good compensation for my tips. Also, you've been queen of this castle for too long. It's time for you to set up a kingdom elsewhere. My daughter is here, and I intend to stay. There you have it."

He pulled down on his vest and gave her a mock bow before sauntering down the hallway toward the library.

CHAPTER 54
JUNCTURE

On their weekly phone call Elizabeth told Frank that Ziegfeld had sent another telegram.

"He hopes to begin production early next year and cautioned me to avoid signing any long-term contracts," she explained. "Although I am a bit worried about my income, I suppose that will be good timing because I won't be working during the holidays when Joanie's wedding takes place and hopefully, you'll be visiting as well."

"I don't know yet. I may be able to attend Joanie's wedding with you since it is the weekend before Christmas," Frank said. "However, I need to be with my children over the holiday, especially since this will be our last Christmas as a family."

"I understand, my darling."

"One thing, though," Frank continued. "When I come next, I want to officially ask your father for your hand in marriage." Caught off guard, Elizabeth couldn't help but voice her concern.

"But your divorce isn't final yet."

"That doesn't mean we can't be engaged," he said, "at least in the eyes of your family and close friends."

"If the news got out, though, wouldn't that be potentially harmful for both of us?"

"We need to specify that the news is to be kept among ourselves until we make a formal announcement." Elizabeth didn't want to reveal that Palmer said or did anything that he perceived might work to his advantage, including selling tidbits about her to hungry gossip columnists.

"I suppose. We have many details to work out in the meantime," Elizabeth said, again wondering how she would live with Frank in Chicago and keep actively employed in the theater. Chicago was developing a reputation for fine opera as well as cutting-edge jazz clubs and recording studios, but the heart of musical theater still belonged to New York. To leave family and home behind for good also gave her pause.

Before they hung up, Frank agreed they had a lot to talk over but said he preferred to do so in person. Excited and nervous about Frank's proposition and the forthcoming changes it implied, Elizabeth also noted how he skirted the issue of her future career in their discussions although it remained paramount to her. In almost every phone call he repeated the phrase, "I want to come home to you."

★ ★ ★

"Are you sure this is what you want?" asked Pop. The rest of the family still abed, he and Elizabeth sat eating breakfast and appreciating the lull. There had been constant activity between the Thanksgiving holiday, Joanie's wedding, and Frank's whirlwind visit and formal proposal. Behind the spectacles that he now wore constantly, Pop's brown eyes were strained and his once chestnut-colored hair was streaked with gray.

"I enjoy his company and we do love each other," said Elizabeth, wanting to avoid compounding his worry. She continued paying for her lessons and her personal needs from her savings but in the absence of an ongoing role, she had been unable to contribute to the household expenses, which Pop had carried for the better part of the year. "Besides, Frank is a committed father to his two children, which is quite reassuring should we decide to have children someday."

"All good points and from what he tells me, he has a secure position at a major bank," Pop said, "so I assume it won't be necessary for you to work."

"I don't want to stop working altogether but I don't want necessity to force me into accepting roles that I am not enthused about," Elizabeth said, thinking of George White's recent offer to star in what he called *Manhattan Mary*. She briefly considered the play but turned it down because it looked like it might devolve into another of his notorious vaudevillian *Scandals* productions. Ziegfield's request for her to avoid long commitments and the theatrical possibilities evoked by the captivating *Showboat* novel also influenced her decision.

"I understand. You've worked hard to get to this place in your career. You should be able to pick and choose your options." affirmed Pop, bestowing a tired smile on her. "Hmm. I do love the holidays but with the additional choral concerts, as Saint Bartholomew's choir master, I feel like I've been working two full-time jobs for the past two months."

"You have been," agreed Elizabeth. "By the way, no need to worry about our wedding. Frank and I don't intend to have a large wedding with a lavish reception. Neither of us want the attention that entails. As you know, he's been married once, and we don't know when his divorce will be finalized, and I don't want my wedding to be potential fodder for gossip or intrusion."

"As you so desire. Momma and I want you to have whatever you want if we can make it happen," Pop said, squeezing her hand. For a few moments eating their toast and marmalade, they sat quietly, his warm hand atop hers.

CHAPTER 55

BECOMING A MRS.

"Is it true that New York City is losing you to Chicago?" asked Tom Keogh, his tweed suit as rumpled and threadbare as it was at their last interview. The friendliness in his glance was unmistakable, reassuring Elizabeth that contacting Tom to spread the word was the right choice.

"Yes, I will join my husband, Frank Warton, in Chicago," she said. "However, I expect I will visit New York frequently. As you know, my family lives here. Also, many shows debut here."

Tom scratched his thick hair with his pen and then scribbled in his battered notebook.

"It sounds as if you intend to continue in musical comedy and not forsake the stage for the domestic life, as some have speculated."

"I'd jump at the chance when and if I find a suitable part."

She refrained from mentioning *Showboat* since the word on the street was that Ziegfeld's financial backers had withdrawn their support. Some said it was due to his intention to employ a racially mixed cast. Having read the novel, Elizabeth personally agreed with Ziegfeld's idea. Casting the show any other way jeopardized some core themes in Ferber's masterpiece.

"Didn't you receive a few offers since the start of the year?"

"Several. However, I am interested in the combination of serious themes and acting with the musical genre. I believe this is the direction that modern theater needs to take to stay relevant yet entertaining," said Elizabeth. "What with the increasing popularity of radio broadcasts and movies, musical comedy has a lot more competition for an audience these days." She recrossed her legs and surveyed the stained blue wallpaper and scuffed linoleum floor of the newspaper's meeting room that Pop had offered for this interview.

"Forgive me for asking," said Tom, "but I'm curious and I'm sure our readers will be as well: Do you see yourself working in addition to being a wife and eventually, perhaps, a mother?"

"Why not? Should running a household and raising children be the sole responsibility of women?" Elizabeth asked, grinning and thinking that Izzy would be pleased if this part of the interview made it into print. "Besides, I am happiest working so it will benefit everyone in the family if I continue to do so."

Tom pointed his pen at her. A slight smile traveled across his face.

"There you go again, just like the last time we got together," he said. "I'm the person asking the questions, not the other way around."

"Yes. I know, but it is a question for our times, isn't it? American society is undergoing so many changes in this century so far."

"We could talk at length about that topic." Tom agreed. "However, I need to turn the conversation back to the more personal aspects. Why keep the marriage secret for four months before announcing it?"

"Neither Frank nor I wanted to attract attention," she answered, omitting that they'd kept it secret partially because Frank's divorce proceedings dragged on for several months. When his wife balked at signing the finalized legal agreement, they decided to exchange their vows in front of a justice of the peace in Portchester instead of New York City. They'd figured that would further ensure privacy from the press as they waited for Frank's marriage to dissolve.

"Tell us more about how the two of you met."

"Last year, between shows, I took a fabulous ten-week trip to Europe with my companion, Gertrude Burns. Frank and I first encountered each other while traveling to North Africa. We didn't meet during the entire three-day journey across the Mediterranean, only just as the boat pulled into the harbor in Algiers. We saw more of each other when we were stateside when I was performing in Chicago. Frank, although born in Britain, has a position in banking there."

"I must say, Miss Hines, your exploits continue to astonish. That's an unusual trip for two women to take. Oh, forgive me, what name do you prefer these days?" Tom stopped scribbling, looked up, his deep blue eyes expectant.

"Professionally, I will retain my stage name but in other aspects of my life, I will be Mrs. Frank R. Warton." Saying her new name publicly felt peculiar.

CHAPTER 56
END OF THE LINE

900 N. Michigan Ave, Chicago, Illinois

1928

Outside Frank and Elizabeth's apartment, the waking city hummed. Pigeons perched on the window ledges cooed and clucked. On the street trucks hauled produce from the countryside to the downtown markets. Taxis trawled the avenues for morning commuters. Inside, the elevator down the hall rumbled.

Frank, smartly dressed for work in a light gray wool suit and tie, sipped coffee at their round kitchen table.

"Look at this!" he exclaimed. "Your case made the *Tribune*."

He handed Elizabeth the front page. Generally, she avoided reading news first thing in the morning. Its emphasis on crime, violence, and scandal disturbed her. Reluctantly, she skimmed the column:

Elizabeth Hines, the "Albany printer's daughter who rose to stardom on Broadway," was awarded $12,000 over the legal suit she brought against Florenz Ziegfeld due to the cancellation of a verbal contract and the significantly delayed production of Showboat.

> *Miss Hines, also known as Mrs. Frank R. Warton, originally sought an award of $100,000 but found the settlement amount acceptable. Mr. Ziegfeld was so pleased with the smallness of the award that he said he intends to give his eight-year-old daughter a new roadster.*

Small victory for a distasteful process, Elizabeth thought.

"Aren't you happy you went through with it, dear?" Frank asked.

"I suppose. Couldn't have done it without you." She handed the paper back to Frank, who beamed with satisfaction. Truthfully, she regretted shutting the door on possibly the best role of her career thus far. Having turned down several options, though, she couldn't afford to keep waiting while Ziegfeld struggled and continually failed to secure the financial backing he needed to produce such a costly show.

"You're not going to lend any of the proceeds to your gadabout brother, are you?"

"Heavens, no! I will help Pop address Dorothy's college expenses, but we'll bypass Palmer altogether."

"Good. Some consequences for his flagrant irresponsibility are overdue. Those poor suckers who bankrolled his theater troupe will never get their money back."

"Enough about my ne'er-do-well brother," she said. "Pop and I will convince Dorothy to live at home to keep costs down while she attends Columbia for journalism."

"I see. Another career woman in the Hines family," said Frank, leaning over to plant a kiss on Elizabeth's cheek. "You ladies are something." He slurped the last of his coffee as he rose from the table. "Time for me to get going. What are you up to today?"

"Gert and I are off to explore. She wants to find a good yarn shop and I need to locate a source for fabrics," Elizabeth said, trying to sound cheerful. "I intend to set up my sewing machine one of these days."

Gert's offer to move to Chicago had been a godsend. Her companionship and practical help significantly soothed Elizabeth, who felt homesick living in a new city and overwhelmed with running a household.

"Good thing, that sewing machine, when the time comes. Babies go through many changes of clothes," Frank said, looking over his shoulder as he left the kitchen to prepare for his day.

Frank was eager to be a father again and Gert was enthused about helping raise another child, but Elizabeth was hesitant. She preferred pondering a recent offer for a lead role in a prospective WGN radio drama. It wasn't the stage, but the schedule would be more amenable for eventual child-rearing. Hearing of her arrival in Chicago, the producer had phoned. She'd told him she needed a few months to complete the move and get her bearings before giving him a firm answer.

Sitting quietly in her blue quilted robe, she sipped coffee, munched buttered toast, and watched the sparrows in the courtyard flitting in and out of the large elm tree with bits of hay or straw for nesting. She envied their commitment. How eager they seemed about what was to follow.

Frank looked in the hallway mirror to straighten his tie.

"I don't know why you want to work after doing so almost continuously for fourteen years. Besides, it makes me look bad, as if I can't provide for my beautiful wife."

"I haven't taken the job. In fact, the show isn't even running and won't be for at least another six months," Elizabeth said. "The producer is pulling together a small cast as well hiring a writer. I thought it might be fun and I'd meet some locals."

"You can meet other women volunteering for some good cause." He hesitated. "That's what Florence did."

Of course she did, Elizabeth thought. *Florence never had a career.* She chose not to voice her opinion and to focus on the topic at hand.

"I want to see what they have to offer and tour the studio," she said. "I don't intend to sign any contract."

"I suppose there's no harm in that but remember any decision going forward is to be made by both of us," Frank said, clamping on his homburg hat as he headed out to the bank.

Elizabeth noted that he deliberately had not kissed her. As the door shut behind him, she sighed, knowing the signs of Frank's frustration. It would take him a few days to soften and warm up to her again. In the meantime, curious to see where the popular radio hit, *Amos'n'Andy,* was made, she intended to go through with her afternoon meeting at the WGN studios in the Drake Hotel.

★ ★ ★

"Welcome to WGN. How may I help you?" asked the pert, smartly dressed, blonde receptionist behind a horseshoe-shaped desk that dominated the lobby. Elizabeth gave her name. The woman pointed to several black leather chairs along the wall. "Please, have a seat," she said, "while I announce that you're here."

Elizabeth sat as the receptionist disappeared through huge double doors at the far end of the hall, her high heels clicking like castanets on the parquet floor. In no time a florid-faced, stout man with short cropped brown hair and a pencil behind one ear followed the receptionist back into the lobby.

"Ah, Miss Hines," he said, extending his hand. "Or do you prefer Mrs. Warton? In any case, pleasure to meet you."

"Thank you," she said, shaking his fleshy hand. "I keep my stage name for work."

"After spending all that time cultivating a career under one name, I suppose it makes sense. I'm Albert Smith, production manager. The crew calls me "Smitty" so, you see, I have a work name, too," he said, grinning while absentmindedly scratching one large ear. "Oh dear. Sally, you didn't remind me to take the pencil from behind my ear." The receptionist shrugged her linen-clad shoulders and turned her palms face up in mock irritation before resuming her position behind the desk.

"Please follow me, Miss Hines. Let me show you what we made here out of two handball courts."

They entered a dark, windowless warren strewn with various kinds of equipment, some freestanding, others on long tables interspersed with some desks and chairs.

"Here's where we broadcast dramatic shows," he explained. Several high stools stood behind some microphones on a small stage. Wires snaked from the mics along the floor. A huge round clock on the back wall read, "Standby" and "On Air" in big block letters. "The soundman operates over there."

Smitty pointed to a corner where a large sheet of metal hung like some weird sculpture. A vat of sand and coconut shells lay alongside bags labeled "Cornstarch." In another corner, a man in a fedora sat at a table, thumbing through a sheaf of papers and reading from them into a desktop mic under neon lights.

"The latest news from the Associated Press feed," Smitty explained as they passed through the darkened expanse into a brightly lit, huge space arrayed with desks and chairs. The pervasive acrid smell of burnt coffee and cigarettes reminded Elizabeth of Pop's newspaper office.

"Have a seat, Miss Hines," said Smitty, offering her one of the few blue upholstered chairs. He sat at a desk, perching one leg casually on a desk corner, the other on the floor.

"Let me set the stage, so to speak," he began, laughing at his own joke. "Radio theater differs significantly from what you're used to. Instead of having singing, dancing, and theatrical sets, we create environment with sound effects and characters through vocal qualities and accents as well as their relative placement to the other performers and their distance from the mic. By combining dialogue, sound effects, music, and occasional narration, we invoke and rely on the listener's imagination to flesh out the story. If you want to be a successful radio actor, it helps to be skilled in vocally portraying multiple dialects and age ranges. That way you can play a variety of roles, each of which has a price tag. The more you can play, the better the pay, if you get my drift." Elizabeth nodded. She already had some reservations. The picture he presented radically differed from the performing she was accustomed to.

"Before I go on, any questions?"

"Yes. You mentioned music but seemed to indicate there is no singing."

"That's correct. No singing for the dramatic shows we have in mind. However, we will use some recorded music for transitions between scenes."

"And will there be a live audience?" asked Elizabeth, hoping for an affirmative answer.

"Nope. We reserve that for live broadcasts of opera or symphonies." Smitty paused. "We're aiming to create something to interest housewives, keep them company in that window between completing their morning chores and preparing the family dinner. A woman's genre, if you want to call it that." He smiled, obviously pleased with the idea. Inwardly, Elizabeth recoiled. The image of an isolated housewife with a day full of domestic tasks and only a radio drama for company repulsed her.

"When I was on the stage, I believed musical comedy lifted people's spirits," she said. "That made all the hard work rehearsing worth it." Compensating for her increasing dread, she tried engaging in conversation, but Smitty remained focused on his pitch.

"Speaking of rehearsals, ours would be different from what you're probably used to. The cast sits around a table in that room over there," he said, tilting his head to indicate the general direction. "They read the script aloud several times over a couple of days without sound effects. Musical bridges and sound effects are added at the dress rehearsal. It all comes together much faster than your average Broadway show." Smitty crossed his arms. "Let me see. Did I forget anything? Oh, as I said earlier, initially, payment is role-based. The more frequently you appear, the more the moola. If you become a big radio star like our *Amos 'n' Andy* boys, of course that changes the numbers. Any questions, Miss Hines?"

As he stood, his gaze suddenly became stony and challenging. She shook her head and anxiously smoothed her skirt as she rose.

"Thank you. Not right now. You've given me a lot to consider."

She couldn't wait to get out of the windowless confines of the studio, which felt more oppressive than a dimly lit, empty theater. Smitty requested that Elizabeth give him a firm answer within the month and led her back through the labyrinthine rooms to the sterile, sunlit lobby, where he bid her a curt farewell.

The short walk from the Drake back to the apartment was a respite although the weather was as turbulent as her thoughts. Fast-moving gray clouds masked and unmasked the brilliant spring sun. Tree buds verged on opening but seemed unwilling to release themselves into the cold north wind that intermittently ripped down the sidewalks. *Am I selling out if I take a radio role? Should I hold out for a theater role?* Since the resolution of the Ziegfeld suit, no substantive offer had come her way. Frank thought the outcome was successful but maybe theatrical producers other than Ziegfeld now considered her a potential legal liability. *Is my stage career over?*

She couldn't talk over her career concerns with Frank. Nor could she confide in Gert, who was so singularly focused on helping to raise Elizabeth's offspring. *Men never have to make this compromise*, she thought as she tripped over an uneven seam of pavement. Regaining her balance, she continued up the block to the green awning that spanned the apartment entrance. As she drew near, she spotted the portly doorman in his too-tight uniform. Again, his name escaped her.

"Welcome home, Mrs. Warton," he said.

Elizabeth flashed to coming home to 326 Madison Avenue, to Pop and Momma, years ago when the world was opening to her. She pictured her young self, the realization of her dream lighting her face and her heart. Could any other dream replace it? Could a radio role fulfill her? Could life with Frank fulfill her?

"Your name again?" Elizabeth asked. "Do forgive me."

"Lloyd."

"I promise to remember and please call me Elizabeth."

By the time I was born, my grandmother had been off the stage for twenty-five years. I didn't know of her illustrious identity as Elizabeth Hines, the Broadway ingénue touted as one of America's most beautiful young women of the 1920s. To me, she was a small woman in high heels with ginger-colored hair who walked with regal poise and loved to play show tunes on the upright piano in our living room. Though my legs didn't touch the floor, I sat next to her on the piano bench and sang the lyrics she taught me: "My funny valentine, sweet comic valentine . . ." or "They're writing songs of love but not for me."

My immediate family lived in the northern Chicago suburbs where much of life revolved around the country club and its prescribed rituals of golf, tennis, and swimming. Elizabeth (Nanny to me) was not of this tribe. She was a decidedly urban person to whom literature, languages, and the arts were pursuits. Sports were not on her radar except for horse racing to which her husband was addicted. His habit had endangered their family finances more than once. After her husband, my grandfather, died when I was eight, she often took the train to visit us for overnights or holiday weekends. Even then her past as a musical comedy star was never discussed.

My infrequent overnights in Nanny's Michigan Avenue apartment were magical and made me feel as if I'd been transported to another time and country. I loved the whoosh of the wood-paneled elevator with its gleaming gold trim. The velvet-draped windows and Oriental rugs made me feel like I was entering Ali Baba's lair.

Only much later, when I began to research her life, did I realize her apartment décor was a visual clue to her flamboyant, rich past. Perhaps adolescent narcissism and becoming a boarding school student at age twelve impeded my awareness of other signs of her former career. Or perhaps my father's socially pretentious parents forbade discussion of her background.

When Nanny unexpectedly died at age seventy-two, I was away at college. Her history was relegated to three scrapbooks filled with yellowing press releases interspersed with personal notes from admirers. My mother gave me these books shortly before her own death in 2015.

The silence around my grandmother's history was the ground from which this narrative grew. It is the story of a well-bred young woman trying to differentiate and succeed on her own merit in a male-dominated society. As I read the history of the times more thoroughly, my admiration of Nanny increased. Through excelling as an actor and dancer, she had resisted the prevailing patriarchal and sociocultural beliefs that so limited women's possibilities in the early twentieth century and carved her own path through adolescence and young adulthood.

By all accounts, she maintained her integrity and morality, remaining a considerate, genuine, and kind person despite the vagaries of fame and the theater business. New York City's development into the apex of modernity and an internationally renowned theatrical and musical center form the backdrop of most of this book.

Though much of the story is conjecture, many of the imagined scenes are informed by extensive reading about the sociopolitical history of the Roaring Twenties in the United States and abroad; several biographies, including those of George M. Cohan and Florenz Ziegfeld; an amazing travelogue written by a British couple who drove across Northern Africa in 1921; genealogical research; and old footage of or about musical comedy.

The issues and circumstances Elizabeth faced have uncanny parallels to current events. Racism, misogyny, and women's rights continue to have major sociopolitical impact a hundred years later. The recent COVID-19 pandemic upturned the entire world on multiple levels, much like the Spanish Flu did from 1917 to 1919. The Prohibition era (1920-1933) led to the development of bootlegging, the clandestine production of alcohol, and a consequent rise in crime and mortality. Today, the invention of powerful pharmaceutical drugs such as fentanyl has helped cause a dangerous upsurge in nefarious drug manufacturing and smuggling as well as addiction and drug-related deaths.

My grandmother's story, far too powerful to be relegated to scrapbooks, needed to be told and shared. I hope readers are inspired by this remarkable woman who navigated her way to career success despite discouragement, adversity, and heartbreak.

Author Photo credit:
Leslye Smith, StudioSmith.com

ABOUT THE AUTHOR

LEISHA DOUGLAS recently retired from a lengthy career as a psychotherapist and mental health counselor to pursue her first love, creative writing. Her stories and poems have been published in literary journals, including *The Cortland Review*, *Helix, The Minetta Review, The Midwest Quarterly, Upstreet, The RavensPerch* and *The Big Other*. Her poetry has been nominated for a Pushcart Prize and featured in several anthologies. Over the years, she has also collaborated with several artists to produce some limited-edition publications combining art, photography, and poetry. She co-directed the long-running, renowned Katonah Poetry Series with her friend and colleague, former US Poet Laureate, Billy Collins, and was also Poet Advisor to the Series until 2024.

ACKNOWLEDGMENTS

My sincere gratitude to Lorraine Ash and her passionate editorial midwifery, which guided me through the creation and completion of this book. To her husband, Bill, for stepping in with his technical skills when needed, and to Maureen Wlodarczyk for her thorough genealogical research.

Many thanks to my first readers, Moira Thielking, Nancy Rosanoff, Gail Greenstein, Barry Wiseman, John Roberts, and Robin Brandes.

Arms full of appreciation for my writerly friends who cheered me onward: Marlene Gallagher, Rebecca Rogan, Michael Yusko, Myrna Goodman, Margherita Pagni, Jim Garber, and Mark Irwin.

There aren't enough words to thank Jim Melvin for his unwavering support and the great coffee he has provided during our years together.

Lastly, thanks to the Sibylline team (Vicki DeArmon, Julia Park, Tracey, and Suzy Vitello) for bringing this story to the world.

STUDY GUIDE QUESTIONS

1. What motivates Elizabeth to develop her career?

2. Is Elizabeth a feminist?

3. What are the implications of her relationship with Roy?

4. How is sexism portrayed in this novel? What does it feel and sound like?

5. How does Elizabeth resist oppression and maintain her values?

6. What do the marriages of Elizabeth and her friends, Izzy and Joan, reveal about their respective ideas regarding adulthood and life?

Sibylline Press is proud to publish the brilliant work of women authors over 50. We are a woman-owned publishing company and, like our authors, represent women of a certain age.